Arcana Book One:
Rise of the Moon

JB Caine

Copyright © 2021 JB Caine

All Rights Reserved.

ISBN 978-0-578-81378-3

Dedication

I would like to take a moment to express my deepest gratitude to the folks who have been my helpers, cheerleaders, and support team. Without them, I don't think I could have made this lifelong dream come true. First and foremost, thank you to Buck and Haley, who are not only my biggest supporters, but believed in me so much that they were willing to ignore me as I disappeared into my writing room for hours at a time. Any writer will testify that this is possibly the greatest expression of love a family can show to an aspiring novelist.

I'd also like to send some love to my muses: Jessica, thanks for giving Lia some of your soul; and Shawn, you (just like Treigh) steal any scene you're in. I love you both!

I didn't even realize until after I finished my first draft of *Rise of the Moon* how important having an excellent editor is. Barbara, you were my first and biggest fan, and gave me both a reader's and an editor's pair of eyes. And Kelly, your advice and perspective (and blessed critical eye) has been invaluable to me, and I can't thank you enough.

I've been so blessed to have so many folks in my corner from the jump. Thank you for believing in my dream. I hope I did you proud.

COMING SOON! *Arcana Book Two: Rush to Judgement*

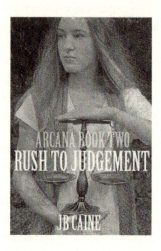

Follow JB CAINE on social media!

@realjbcaine

@authorjbcaine

www.jbcaine.com

Energy of the cosmos
I bind you and release you
Find life eternal
In service to the Universe

The Great Mage chanted in rhythm as he stared intently into the fire that burned within the cauldron. He grabbed a handful of grey powder and tossed it into the air over the flames, which popped and sparked a greenish blue in response.

Energy harnessed and
Blood to blood

Twenty voices joined the song and one by one approached the cauldron, carving small sigils into the skin of their left forearms, letting two drops of blood from each wound drip into the flames, and then one more onto small pieces of paper arranged carefully around the pot.

Blood to blood
For all time
So mote it be

5 | RISE OF THE MOON

Chapter 1

High school is a highly evolved form of torture. Or so my best friend would have me believe.

"I swear on all that is holy, Lia, the devil himself created math and laughs at our daily punishment." My bestie Treigh Allen looked at me squarely and, to drive the point home, threw himself dramatically against the lockers.

"Good Lord, Treigh," I laughed, "it's not THAT bad. I mean, the odds of us ever actually having to use Trig are pretty slim..." He squinted at me hard and shifted from his dramatic pose into a jaded lean. "...okay, the chances are exactly zero. But at least Mr. Nash is pretty cool."

"Please do not rain on my pity parade. I'm pretty sure I scored a negative twelvety-seven on that quiz."

"Oh, come on. I'm sure you passed."

"Says the girl who passes everything. Ev. Ree. Thing."

"You say that like it's a bad thing." I winked at Treigh. "It's not the end of the world. It may not be my favorite subject, but at least we're in the same class. Next period I don't want to deal with anyone. Seriously. I feel like a one-woman leper colony in English." Despite my dread of second period, it was hard to be anything but cheerful around Treigh, even when he was complaining. Maybe especially when he was complaining. No one complained quite as eloquently as he did.

"Say no more, my queen. I will escort you and ease your suffering."

I shoved my carefully-color-coded-to-match-my-textbook red folder into the locker and pulled the blue book and folder out. "You're my hero."

We walked arm-in-arm through the courtyard, dodging the thousand other meandering bodies and the occasional judgmental glance. We were an odd pair, to be sure...Treigh Allen, who looked like he stepped right out of a Nordstrom's ad with his designer everything and flawless grooming. I, Lia Alvarez, on the other hand, looked more like an ad for Hot Topic with my black cut-up tee shirt and red plaid skirt.

As we pulled up to Mrs. West's classroom, Treigh took a bow so deep that his Gucci sunglasses nearly slid off his head and headed for the concrete. He squealed and caught them as they fell.

"That was too close. Gave me a heart attack."

"You are not allowed to die on me. You're my light in the darkness." I eyed the classroom, checking to see who had arrived before me.

"Keep talking like that and you're going to make me unbearably arrogant."

"Impossible. But I AM going to make you late. Go!"

"Girl. You know Haney is never going to hold a tardy against me." He leaned over and kissed my cheek. "Play nice with the other children, darling."

I affectionately rolled my eyes and smiled. "Get."

"And I'm gone. See you at lunch!"

Still smiling, because Treigh always had that effect on me, I turned to face what should have been my favorite class. Literature was my great love, my escape, and yet this group of ultra-suburban juniors made it feel like Purgatory. I sighed, my grin fading slightly, and made my way to my seat. I edged myself into the far right corner of the room, away from as many people as possible. It wasn't that I didn't like my classmates...some of them were actually really nice. TOO nice. I'd been plopped into a class of complete extroverts, and if I didn't put the physical barrier of space between myself and them, they'd likely talk to me all period. About nothing. It didn't matter if I actually participated in the conversation. It just never stopped.

"Hey, Alvarez. Impressive boots." It was Gemma, the fully-crowned high queen of St. Augustine High. She was looking very intently at me with a cryptic half-smile that I couldn't ever quite interpret. Could be that sort of distant approval the high school aristocracy used to grant favor on the huddled masses below them, or it could be sarcasm. It was pretty hard to tell, particularly with Gemma.

"Um, thanks. They were a present."

"I'm pretty sure you could kill someone with them. Are they real?"

I paused for an awkward moment before responding, trying to figure out exactly what "real" meant. Then it dawned on me. "Oh, yes, they're genuine Docs. See the yellow stitches...?" I started to explain, but Gemma just nodded and turned her attention to the newest arrival.

"Hey, Alex! I have been waiting ALL DAY to ask you about that text you sent Lauren…" And off she went.

I heaved another sigh, this one a mix of awkwardness and fangirling as Alex Conroy walked into class. I wasn't sure exactly what had just happened between Gemma and me. Feeling awkward had the side effect of making me feel vaguely hostile, though I knew it wasn't real anger. I just always felt this way around Gemma, and as a result, disliked having to interact with her at all. I threw myself down in my seat and glared over at Gemma and Alex.

I had been in classes with Alex since the seventh grade, and had probably had a crush on him that entire time. Not that he knew anything about it, of course. Oh, no. Instead, I had wallowed in what I viewed as a tragic and unrequited love for the past four years, on and off. I'd dated a couple of guys, but Alex had always been my ideal. He was slender, with chocolatey hair that fell into his green eyes quite a lot, no matter how he tried to gel it. I imagined myself reaching up to brush it to the side for him, and...

RIIIIIIING!! The tardy bell jarred me back into reality. Mrs. West came inside and closed the door.

"Good morning, everybody! We're onto a new unit today; we're going to be reading a play." Groans filled the classroom, but I sat up a little straighter as I remembered the syllabus. "Yeah, yeah, your lives are miserable," Mrs. West teased. "But today we start *The Crucible* by Arthur Miller. Is anyone familiar with it?"

Without thinking, I shot my hand up in the air in an uncharacteristic show of enthusiasm. Mrs. West raised one eyebrow and looked at me with interest. "Lia? What can you tell me?"

"It's about the Salem Witch Trials..." I began.

"That's a common mistake, " Mrs. West interrupted. "Can anyone put the play into its correct historical context?"

Gemma spoke up without raising her hand. "It's actually a commentary about McCarthyism during the 20th century. It uses the Salem Witch Trials as an allegory..."

I slid down in my seat as Mrs. West went on to explain the function of an allegory and Arthur Miller's inspiration and passed out the class copies. If she had let me finish what I was saying, I'd have gotten around to that. I raised my eyes as the books came my way, just in time to make brief eye contact with Gemma, who was giving me a look that could have been sympathy or judgement. It was sort of hard to tell. Again. I groaned inwardly. It was going to be that kind of day.

Biology and History passed without incident, but I was still fuming when I plopped down beside Treigh on our favorite people-watching bench at lunch.

"I hope your morning went better than mine," I began. "In case you've ever wondered, it's not actually possible to die of embarrassment. If it were, I'd have done it in English."

He looked over the tops of his sunglasses. "Do tell."

I relayed the story of my mortification, as Treigh punctuated it with well-timed noises of outrage.

"I don't care what West says. The Witch Trial angle is more interesting anyway," my friend affirmed.

"I know, right? I mean, I understand that the principle of false accusation and stuff is the same, but come ON. Politics is BORING. And besides, if they wanted us to focus on the 20th century aspect, they would have put it at the end of the year, not the beginning of American Lit."

"I couldn't agree more, my dear. And Gemma Harris needs to stop trying to be teacher's pet all the time. She doesn't need ALL the attention on the planet." He sniffed in disgust.

"And besides," I continued, "the Salem Witch Trials have historical value, right? Why can't we study them directly? People might actually pay attention in class if we could read about THAT."

"No doubt you're right. But this is our lot. I must say, though, I passed your man candy on my way out of your class. He was looking mighty tasty today. Speaking of..." Treigh inclined his head toward the lunchline, where Alex stood punching his student number into the cashier's keypad. "Skinny jeans and an untucked dress shirt? Both careless and calculated. So very like an Aries. Well played," he approved.

I stared wistfully across the lunch patio. "I know. He doesn't lower himself to try to fit in. Seriously, look around this lunchroom. Most of the people in here look like they don't know how to find their own clothing sizes. How did this happen in, like, 50 years? Men used to wear tailored suits and fedoras. Now they look like they wear hand-me-downs from three different-sized people and THAT is supposed to be fashionable." I snorted disdainfully. "Our culture has lost all its class."

"I beg your pardon, madam," Treigh protested.

"Not YOU, of course. You are perfect in every way. You actually iron."

"That is because I am a KING of style, not a slave to it. Just so we're clear."

I chuckled, my momentary outrage fading. "I hope he wasn't listening in second period. I felt so dumb."

"YOU are not dumb, my dear. YOU are brilliant. Which is WHY Miss Gemma feels the need to try to look smart in front of you. Never forget that. Especially not since you have to see her again in Drama. Do NOT let yourself look rattled or upset. Do NOT give her the satisfaction."

"Yessir, " I smiled, bumping him with my shoulder affectionately. I began poking vaguely at the cheese congealing on my school pizza and made a face.

"You going to eat that?" Treigh asked.

"No, go ahead," I shrugged, pushing the paper plate toward him. "Have you ever wondered if there were any real witches in Salem during the trials? I mean, actual Pagans who came over with the Puritans searching for religious freedom? They would have really had to keep a low profile, you know?"

"To be honest," he said around his bite of my pizza, "I never really thought about it. But there had to have been a couple, right?"

"It must have been quite a struggle, you know? Trying to be dedicated to their religion, knowing what would happen if they got caught. It would have been terrifying day-to-day. It would make a really good story."

"You should write it, then. You're good at that storytelling stuff. And you can thank me in the dedication for being your most devoted fan."

I smiled, more to myself than to him, as the ideas began to swirl. "Maybe I will."

Chapter 2

Drama class was always scheduled for seventh period, the last class of the day. It was a practical arrangement; when we were rehearsing a play, having class at the end of the day cut an entire hour out of after-school rehearsals. And when we weren't rehearsing, class was either a study hall or decompression period.

I sat on the stage, waiting for the Drama teacher to finish talking to one of the stagecraft kids. As Mr. Adams approached, Gemma called for the class to quiet down and pay attention. Mr. Adams nodded acknowledgement to her for her efforts.

"Okay, folks," he began, "as most of you know, we are hosting the district Thespian competition this year. I'd really like to see us have entries in every category. With that in mind, I've posted a sign-up sheet on the exit door on stage right. Please, for the love of all things holy, don't sign up for a musical event if you can't sing. Don't make me be the one to tell you. Friends don't let friends make fools of themselves.

"We also didn't submit an original play last year or the year before, and I'd like to see one of you writer/director types out there stretch your compositional muscles. We only get to submit one, so if more than one of you wants to fill that spot, you'll have to pitch your ideas to me first...so everyone will need to choose their scripts or prepare their pitches between now and the day after tomorrow, okay?"

My pulse quickened. Write a play? This opportunity had presented itself on the very day I'd had a story idea! Surely this was meant to be! My mind started whirling like a carnival ride, creating the protagonist in an oppressive and cruel New World, struggling to stay true to her inner voice...

People had started to make their way over to the sign-up sheet, eager to get their first choice of competition event. I stood and pushed my way to the door, pen in hand and brain buzzing. I excitedly scribbled my name under the Playwriting subheading and stepped back, feeling breathless and excited.

"Oh, you're thinking of writing, too?" The voice came from behind me, and I cringed. *Gemma.* I ground my teeth together and slowly turned around, narrowing my dark eyes. "I've done pretty much every other category in competition," Gemma continued, "so I really want to try things from the director side, you know?"

"I never...I didn't know you had an interest in writing, Gemma." My answer came out slowly, measured. Carefully hiding the response screaming in my brain that went more like, *Is there any part of my existence you are not going to invade?*

"Oh, well, I like to challenge myself. Don't you?"

"Well, yeah, I guess. Writing is sort of my thing, though. I just have a story idea and this gives me a chance to put it together, so..."

"You do? What are you going to write about?"

I was suddenly wary. What was she up to? "Um, witches, sort of. I got the idea in English class..."

Gemma laughed, and I couldn't tell if she was laughing AT me or NEAR me. "That is just so YOU. Always going for the Gothic angle. Remember that time you got in that argument with that kid in English class about whether or not Edgar Allan Poe was actually an alcoholic and a creep for marrying his cousin? Poe would have just flipped if he knew he'd have a devoted fan like you someday. I bet you know a lot about witches and horror stories and things. I don't know if that's the kind of play Mr. Adams is looking for, though. Sort of shock theatre..."

"It's not shock theatre, and what do you...you know what? Never mind. You write your pitch and I'll write mine, and we'll see which one he chooses."

Gemma blinked back at me, surprised by the sudden change in tone. "Okay, then. I guess we'll see. May the best play win." Gemma's smile was a mask of civility, but I knew we'd both be taking this competition seriously. The proverbial gauntlet had been thrown down.

At the end of the day, I rushed home and fired up my laptop. I cross-checked formats and expectations for script pitches. I wrote a synopsis and character list. I drafted a rough staging plan, including anticipated props, sets, costumes, and lighting ideas. I kept it simple...this was intended to be a short play after all...mustn't try to do too much. Mustn't plan it like one would plan a film...my brain spun and my fingers flew across the keyboard.

There was no way I was going to let Gemma beat me out of this.

The next morning, I ran, wild-eyed, up to Treigh.

"Treigh! You have to come over tonight. I need you to go over my script pitch."

"Whoa, whoa, whoa...slow your roll there, dearest. Are you okay? Did you even sleep?"

"What? No, well, not much anyway. But seriously, can you come over for an hour or so? I really need another set of eyes on this."

"You know I am never going to let you down, Lia, and I will be there, for whatever help I can provide. Is this your Salem story?"

"Yes!" I replied breathlessly. "It's going to be so good! But I have to pitch against Gemma, and I just have to be ready. Adams HAS to choose me."

"Okay, okay, just relax. It's going to be fine. You do realize, though, that the extent of my metaphysical expertise is horoscopes and Harry Potter, right? Are you sure I'm the best person to..."

"Don't even joke about something like that. I'd never trust anyone else to see this before my pitch."

"You don't need to even worry, girl. You've got this. There's no way Adams would choose her over you when you're this passionate about your script. I'll come over right after I drop Ty off at home, okay?" Tyler was Treigh's younger, but much taller, brother.

"Thank you so much! I'm freaking out."

"Breathe, just breathe. It's going to be fine. Just get through the day, and we'll go over all of it tonight. Adams won't know what hit him, and Gemma will be crying in a corner when you're done with her."

Just getting through the day was a task in itself. My classes were a blur, I was distracted and distant, and my play became my sole focus. After school, I drove home as fast as I dared, and waited anxiously for Treigh to arrive.

I pulled into the driveway beside the small yellow and white house that was truly my mother's dream home. When you tell people that you live in Florida, they imagine one of two things: either you live on the beach, or you live at Disney World. The truth is that most of Florida isn't like either of those things. A lot of it is swamp, a lot of it is cookie-cutter suburbs, and a lot of it is cattle ranches. St. Augustine isn't really any of that either. I mean, there is a beach, but that's not where my mom chose to settle. We were nicely situated a little bit north of the historic district in the oldest city in the United States. Our little bungalow-style house was nestled amongst huge ancient oak trees, not a palm to be seen.

I climbed out of my car and, instead of going in the side door to the kitchen, I walked around to the oversized screened porch on the front of the house to watch for Treigh. After an excruciating half hour, his silver Altima cruised around the corner and parked on the street in front of my house. He strolled up the front walk, shaking his head and talking to himself in frustration.

"Have the voices finally gotten to you?" I asked him.

"Girl, this child is going to be the death of me. I'm going to go prematurely gray trying to keep peace between him and my dad. Being a big brother can be a colossal pain in the rear."

"You want to talk about it?"

"No, girl, I live it, and that's bad enough. Suffice to say that if that boy has a bedroom door when I get home, I'll be surprised."

"Ew. Slamming?" Last time Tyler Allen had taken to slamming doors on his father, he'd come home one afternoon to find out that his bedroom door had been removed from its hinges and stored in the garage until his attitude improved.

"So much slamming. But enough about that. Let's hear about your story plan."

I summarized the story I had in mind...a woman against the establishment, a tragic tale of the cost of being one's authentic self, no matter the cost. When I finished, Treigh gushed approval.

"Okay, you've sold me, my love, but Adams is going to be a tougher customer. How are you going to stage this? You have to think business here. Economy of effort...maximum effect with minimum sets and expenses."

He was right, and that's why I needed his input. The story was good, but Gemma's would be good, too. I needed to set myself apart with impressive, yet simple stagecraft. Treigh wasn't in drama, but he hung out with enough of the cast members to know the mechanics of the business. Leave it to him to remind me of the practical aspects of the pitch. He'd make quite a marketing manager someday, I was sure.

After running through the pitch a couple of times and ironing out some staging ideas to make the most of lights as a way of creating different locations instead of building multiple sets, Treigh gave me a big hug and went home to see if his little brother had managed to smooth things over, or was grounded until Judgement Day.

My mom showed up with Chinese take-out, bless her. We plopped down at the kitchen table and I told her all about my play, my pitch, and my competition with Gemma. Unlike a lot of teenagers, I really didn't have a lot of conflict with my mom. Maybe that's because it had always really been just the two of us. She and my dad had never been married, and he really had never been all that involved in my life, other than holiday cards and some money now and then. The truth was that I'd never met the man, and he seemed to have no interest in meeting me either. I wasn't actually bitter about it; I sort of liked feeling like I had her all to myself, and though I had never pressed the subject, because ew gross, I got the impression they hadn't been much more than a fling. According to Mom, he lived in London, and she had no pictures of him.

"So, why do you think this girl decided to enter the playwriting competition all of a sudden?" my mom asked.

"She said she'd already competed in all the other categories." I couldn't keep the saltiness out of my voice, and I didn't really try to.

"Do you think she's feeling as competitive as you are?"

"Honestly, Mom, I don't know. I can't get a good read on her. We've had a class or two together for the last couple of years, and she seems civil enough, but I always feel like there's a whole behind-the-scenes agenda I'm not quite getting, you know?"

"Maybe she doesn't have an agenda." My mom, ever the optimist.

I shrugged. "It's hard to tell. But she's kind of the Queen Bee of the junior class. I don't know. Maybe I'm just jealous."

"You don't need to be jealous of anyone. You're the most interesting teenager I know."

"Not that you have any bias on that subject at all," I smiled, and hugged her over the eggrolls.

"Nope. None at all," she grinned back.

Chapter 3

Wednesday night, I found myself waking up nearly every hour, itching with anxiety about my script pitch, and nervous that I might oversleep. At just after five a.m., I gave up and dragged myself out of bed. I started the shower, turning the water as hot as I could stand it. Even though I'd showered before bed the night before, I felt like I needed the water thrumming against my skin in order to push me into full consciousness.

As I stood under the water, the protagonist in my play pulled at my attention, forming and changing and evolving into the tragic heroine I imagined her to be. Esther. Hebrew for "hidden or secret". A woman alone, a woman standing against society, fighting for her right to be herself by remaining hidden...a poetic irony, I thought. As I turned off the water and stepped out into the steamy bathroom, I imagined that I WAS Esther, and I felt my character's inner strength, fueled by solitude and the judgement of others.

I wiped the steam off the mirror and looked at my face. My dark hair and brown eyes stood out starkly against my fair skin in the steam from the shower. I towel-dried my hair and combed it out deliberately, imagining Esther doing the same, but hundreds of years distant in time. I smiled. I would bring Esther to life and tell her story. She was an unstoppable force, like me.

An hour later, I found myself staring in another mirror, a full-length one this time. I evaluated my outfit, simple but carefully chosen to assert my uniqueness, a silent message to Gemma and anyone else who tried to challenge me. I had selected my Emily the Strange "Lost For Life" tank top and my favorite pair of ripped blue jeans, with red plaid tights underneath. My trademark black Doc Martens with roses embroidered on them not only made me feel invincible, they also boosted my petite frame by over an inch. My black hair and kitten bangs were glossy and straight, and my "war paint" (as I called my makeup) was pin-up perfect. I wore three silver pendants: a pair of angel wings, a dragon claw holding an onyx sphere, and a crescent moon.

I liked how I felt: Strong. Confident. Unapologetically unique.

I headed down the stairs and toward the kitchen, hoping to grab something on my way out the door. Surprisingly, my mother (who was very much not a morning person) was already up and bustling about, and the kitchen was filled with the energizing scent of peppermint tea.

"Good morning, sunshine!" my mother greeted me. "I made a travel cup of tea for you! Take a couple of your Aunt Kitty's biscotti, too. You'll need your energy today!" My powerhouse of a mother, Maddy Alvarez, had paid several visits to my room the night before as I had been repeatedly rehearsing my pitch in front of Treigh. She hadn't said much, but she clearly knew something was up, and that it was something I considered important.

The kindness of the supportive gesture electrified my already buoyant mood, and I grabbed my mother from behind in a fierce hug. "You're the best, Momma!" I cooed. I grabbed the thermal cup and biscotti and swept out the door toward the car.

"Don't you just look like you're feeling yourself today?" Treigh greeted me as he swept into Trig. "I'm loving your whole vibe right now. You must be feeling pretty good about this afternoon, huh?"

"You know, I really am," I replied. "I think I'm really going to make an impression on Adams. Gemma thinks this is a play about witches, and it is, sort of, but it's really about a woman being true to herself. I think Adams will appreciate that."

"Gemma who? No, seriously. You are going to kill this. I just know it."

"Thanks for all your help last night. I feel so much better having gone through it a few times. I'm not usually one to have the stage to myself, you know? I was sort of panicking."

"Hey, that is what I am here for." The bell rang to signal the start of class, and we took our seats. Mr. Nash stood up from his desk with a stack of papers in his hand.

"Well, guys, I've graded Tuesday's quiz, and it's pretty clear that some of you aren't really understanding how to do derivatives..."

Treigh groaned and slumped in his seat as Mr. Nash made his way up and down the rows. He plopped my paper down, and I nodded at the circled 82 on top. Behind me, Treigh had a sharp intake of breath, and as I turned to look, he was beaming, holding up a 64. *I passed*, he mouthed at me, doing a miniature victory dance in his seat. I shook my head and turned around, grinning. Hooray for Thursday.

An hour later, I found myself staring across the room at Gemma, my mouth agape as I eavesdropped shamelessly on the conversation she was having with Alex and Trina, one of her other devoted followers.

"I mean, it's set in a high school and everything, so it's relatable, but the main thing is that it's about female empowerment. About this girl not wanting to follow the crowd's expectations, you know? I think Adams will appreciate that..."

How. Is. This. Possible? My mind froze. What were the odds that Gemma had chosen the same central theme for her own play? Tiny doubts began to creep into my mind. What if Adams agreed that a modern setting was more relatable? What if he thought a play set in Puritanical Salem was too obscure? Or worse yet, too cliché? All my work and preparation...what if somehow the decision came down to some arbitrary whim about settings?

I raised my hand abruptly. "Mrs. West? Can I please go to the restroom?"

Mrs. West looked up from her computer, surprised. "Well, yes, Lia. Make it quick, please."

Without another word, I snagged the lanyard that held the bathroom pass and bolted out the door. The fight or flight response had my pulse pounding in my veins, and I felt the need to walk...somewhere...anywhere. Just out of that room where Queen Gemma was holding court. I wandered past the restrooms, past the vending machines, past the administrative building, and found myself on the sidewalk that led past the back of the art classrooms. There was a small patio where art students brought works of sculpture on which to spray paint or sealant, and I stopped in front of the projects that were drying in the October sun.

As with most high school art classes, the majority of the art was unremarkable, but I stared at it anyway, mostly as a diversion while I tried to calm my nerves. I passed my eyes over the brightly-colored coil and pinch pots which would, no doubt, become gifts for parents or grandparents, lacking any other practical use.

At the edge of my vision, a glint of light drew my attention. I turned toward it and found myself looking at a tall and slender vase that someone had carefully constructed which stood out from the thick and clumsy pottery around it. The glaze swirled in varying shades of blue, from sky blue to a deep indigo, and it had been painstakingly inlaid with a mirrored mosaic pattern. As I looked closer, I could see that the tiny mirror chips formed a silhouette of a crescent moon wrapping around solidly half of the vase. I reached up and fingered the crescent moon pendant hanging around my neck. Coincidence? Probably. And yet, focusing on the pair of moons filled me with a sense of calm, of serenity. My panic slowly abated and, after counting ten deep breaths, I straightened my posture and made my way back to class.

Though the initial burst of confidence I had felt at the beginning of the day had faded, so had the anxiety that had gripped me during English. I went through the motions of my day, as distracted as the day before, mentally preparing for my script pitch. Treigh walked me to drama class, repeatedly reassuring me that my pitch would crush Gemma's and blow Mr. Adams' mind. While I appreciated Treigh's enthusiasm and encouragement, I really just wanted to give my pitch and be done with it.

Mr. Adams started class by making all the musical performers audition to ensure that their singing skills were up to par for competition. Fortunately, the class had taken his warning to heart, and only the skilled singers had chosen to enter in a musical category. At last, the time came for the playwriting pitches.

"Gemma," said Mr. Adams, "let's hear your proposal."

"Certainly." Gemma stood up and took a step forward. She took a deep and, I was just sure, shuddering breath. Could it be that the Queen herself was nervous? "My play is called *Reversal*. It's set at a high school not at all different from this one. Over the course of the 20 minutes, we will follow in the footsteps of Savannah, who appears to be a typical high school girl. Throughout the day, she will face people who will represent the challenges a typical girl faces: body image, gender stereotyping, social expectations, and academic pressure. These people will be archetypes, of course, but each interaction will show the pressure girls are under in today's society. At the end, she will choose to accept some and defy others."

My stomach churned. Gemma's concept was good. Really good. What a cruel twist of fate.

"An interesting concept, Gemma. Cast size?" Mr. Adams scribbled a few notes on his iPad.

"Six specific roles, and an unspecified number of extras."

"Do-able. Props and costumes?"

"Nothing that we wouldn't have just lying around. Classroom stuff, books, that sort of thing."

"So you have several settings, or just one?"

At this, Gemma hesitated. "Well, several, I guess. Classrooms, hallways, the cafeteria, the restroom."

Mr. Adams took off his glasses and chewed on the tip of the frame. "And how would you portray those changes? What kind of set are we talking about here?"

"Umm...maybe we could paint some moveable panels that could flip around to create different backdrops while the stage crew trades out the chairs and things."

My pulse quickened. Gemma hadn't considered the need for simple stagecraft. There was no way Mr. Adams was going to have all those sets built for a 20-minute play.

"Okay, Gemma, thanks. Very solid idea. Lia? Let's hear what you've come up with."

As Gemma slowly returned to her seat, her eyes locked with mine for just a moment. The jubilance that must have been evident in my eyes was in sharp contrast to the defeat in Gemma's, and in that instant, I genuinely felt sorry for my rival.

"That really sounds like a great script," I said to her as we passed each other. Gemma smiled wanly. We both knew how the contest between us was going to end.

Chapter 4

You've heard the saying, be careful what you wish for? Well, there's a lot of wisdom behind it. I had defeated (though narrowly, if I'm honest) my competition, and my idea had won the right for a spot on the stage. Now I had a month to write the script and get the thing staged for Districts. Which means I really had like a week and a half to write a 20-minute play. Suddenly, I was feeling slightly overwhelmed.

People just assumed that because I was into the Goth look that I was also an expert on everything even vaguely supernatural. They weren't totally off base, but I was really more of an expert on vampire lore than witches. Somehow, that didn't seem very helpful at the moment. Even though the story was about a witch, yes, it wasn't about the kind of witch one typically sees in literature. No special schools for magic. No late night cavorting with the devil. None of that. I wanted Esther to be more like a modern-day neo-Pagan: a nature-worshipper who believed in the ancient elemental magic of the earth. The problem was that that meant research. And research would take time I didn't have.

I found myself lying on my bedroom floor, staring at the ceiling and wondering where to start. I had Googled *witchcraft* and *Wicca* and *Pagan* and *ancient rites*, and I was overwhelmed with information, unsure of which direction to follow. It was thus that my mother found me.

"Lia, honey, do you have any dirty laun--good heavens, are you okay?"

"Momma, I've bitten off more than I can chew. I'm writing about a 17th-century witch, and I don't know anything about witches. I don't know how to make my play feel authentic. I'm stuck."

"Witches? Like real ones?"

"Yes, like Wiccans. Or whatever the 17th-century equivalent is."

"Do you know any Wiccans?" my mom asked.

"I know someone who claims to be a witch. But she doesn't really know anything about the religion at all. She just wears a pentagram and watches a lot of *Supernatural*."

"Huh. Good show."

"Yep. But not helpful."

"Well," Mom started slowly, unsure whether she should go on, "I might know someone."

I sat up. "You know a witch?"

"We're related to one. But I don't know that she does much with it anymore. She probably could help, though."

Related to one? I started mentally listing my relatives, then abruptly turned to stare at my mother. "*Aunt Kitty?*" Aunt Kitty was actually my mother's older sister who lived a couple of towns over. She baked a lot and gardened a lot and dressed like a bit of a hippie.

"Aunt Kitty," my mother affirmed. "She doesn't really advertise it, because people have a tendency to be jerks to anyone who stands out from the crowd. Know what I mean?" She winked at me.

"I think I can relate, yeah." I smiled. "Can we maybe visit her this weekend?"

"I bet she'd really like that. She's always been particularly fond of you. Let me give her a call." Mom started out of my room, then suddenly turned on her heel and poked her head back in. "Laundry?"

"I'll bring it down, thanks." Things were looking up.

The drive to Aunt Kitty's house wasn't a long one, maybe an hour, but I could count on my fingers how many times we'd made the trip. She came to see us on holidays, but we didn't go to her house very often. I'd gone to see her a couple of times for trick-or-treating when I was little, and she'd picked me up after school a few times when my mom had had to work late or went on a date. Neither of those things happened all that often, and so I hadn't spent a lot of time at Kitty's. In fact, I probably hadn't been there in three years. Mostly I remembered that the front yard was a wild garden, and the inside was colorful and cluttered and smelled good.

As we neared her cottage-style home, I found myself jittery with excitement. Everything made sense now. I always knew Aunt Kitty was nice, but a bit different from the rest of the family. All her little eccentricities started falling into place now that I knew she was a witch. I wondered vaguely how my mom had introduced the subject when she'd called. But I guess it didn't matter much...her sister had been pleased to have us over, and here we were.

I loved the *crunch-crunch* sound our car made when we pulled into the gravel driveway. The house was a typical single story concrete-block home, but over the years, Aunt Kitty's efforts had made it look more like a stone cottage. A river-rock facade had been added (probably by Kitty herself), and the concrete sides of the house were all but covered with tall hedges which hid its plainness. The wild yard had a flagstone path winding through it to the front step, and as we got out of the car, a rustle of curtains at the window told me our arrival had been noted.

The door opened and out stepped Aunt Kitty. She was tall, about five-foot-seven, which was unusual for our family, where the women typically topped out at five-foot-four. She was slender, with a mousy brown pixie haircut and silver wire-rimmed glasses. She wore a sleeveless turquoise maxi-dress that just brushed the butterfly tattoo peeking out on her right ankle. A huge smile greeted us as she watched us get out of the car.

"Hi, gals!" she called. "Come on in! I've got scones!" And with that, she disappeared inside. We walked up the path in silence, and I noted fat bumblebees buzzing around a large group of Echinacea blooms, giving the garden a hum of energy and life. Despite it being October, it was still plenty hot in northern Florida, and we were grateful to follow her into the air conditioned house. The inside of the house smelled as good as I remembered, the smell of orange scones mixing with something spicier and less familiar. As we entered the living room, she came in from the kitchen with a tray of the baked goods and a brightly-colored tea service.

"It was just so nice to hear from you all yesterday! I was thinking about going out and getting some new plants, but this is so much better! The garden center will be open tomorrow, so that can wait. I'm thinking I should start planting some winter squash and maybe some onions, what do you think, Maddy?" I was amazed she could get all of that out in one breath.

"Um, yes, definitely onions. Soup season will catch up to us sooner or later." Mom accepted one of the proffered scones.

"Exactly my thinking, yes indeed. So, Lia, tell me about this play you're writing! Your mom tells me your idea won some sort of contest?"

I side-eyed my mother, who clearly had built my victory over Gemma into a much larger story. "Not exactly...there was only one other person up for it, but yes, my idea won." I summarized my idea for Esther's story, highlighting the irony of her freedom lying in her ability to stay hidden from the society around her. Aunt Kitty listened with sparkling eyes and sipped her tea.

"Such a wonderful idea, Lia, really. It was such a historically difficult time for women. If they showed any personal power or independence outside of running a family, they were suspected of witchcraft. If they knew any herbal medicine, they couldn't use it to benefit very many people, or they'd get accused and probably killed. Heck, if they had something someone else wanted, even if they'd inherited it from a father or deceased husband, someone could accuse them and strip them of their property. People don't remember how bad it was, now that it's so much better for us."

"Us? You mean witches?"

"No, honey, I mean women. Most of the women accused and executed weren't practitioners at all. Just women who made someone else nervous or jealous."

I wouldn't be deterred from my quest, however. "Do you think there might have been any real witches in Salem at the time of the Trials?"

"It's certainly possible, though the Puritans were a pretty tight lot. Probably any witches back then would have appeared more like quirky, wise, old women. People tend to ignore women like that until they need them for something. Makes a pretty good disguise."

It seemed to me that her last statement had held a little double entendre. I didn't want to offend her. My mom sipped her tea and let me bail myself out. "I think it's a fascinating subject," I said, trying to sound both vague and genuine at the same time.

Aunt Kitty smiled and leaned back in her chair. I looked at her, trying to read her benign expression.

"Are you a witch, Aunt Kitty?" Smooth. That's me.

"Of sorts, I suppose. I've never been in a coven or anything like that, but I believe nature has a spirit that is alive and connects us all. I believe that there is a benevolent energy that guides us and the gift of tiny magicks everywhere. I believe that if we understand the energy of the elements, we can learn to harness and use it. It's not unlike science, really; it just can't be measured in a laboratory."

"Do you cast spells and things?" I felt like an idiot, but I had to ask.

"Not really. I mean, I have done those sorts of things, but now I pretty much stick to herbal magic and wishing blessings and protection on those I love. I try to be a good steward of the Earth. I remain grateful to the Goddess for her blessings."

I didn't want to seem disappointed, but I had built up something a bit more grand in my mind when I discovered I had a witch in the family.

"I'll tell you what, I've pulled out a couple of boxes of things I thought you'd find useful. Why don't you go poke through them while your mom and I catch up, and then you can ask me any specific questions you have. How's that?"

"That sounds terrific," I breathed gratefully. I could feel my awkward showing, and I was afraid I was going to start asking even more ignorant-sounding questions.

"The boxes are on the bed in the guest room. Help yourself."

"Thanks, Aunt Kitty." I set down my teacup and stood, half-hugged her, and then scurried from the room to dig for treasure.

I don't know what I expected, but I'm pretty sure it wasn't a couple of medium-sized plastic tubs. In the movies, there's always some old steamer trunk in the corner of the attic, or a box inlaid with brass symbols in an ancient language. But nope. I was looking at gray-blue plastic Walmart bins. All right then.

I pulled the top off the first one and the spicy scent which hovered under every other scent in this house wafted out at a much higher level. It smelled like peppery earth, like oil from trees, like fragrant leaves burning. I reached into the box and pulled out a velvet dress of the darkest shade of blue. It was beautiful and romantic and glamorous, and something I totally could not picture my aunt wearing...and yet, she had. Probably lots of times.

I had, at this point, sort of this surreal moment of realization that my aunt was someone far deeper than the lady who could bake nearly anything. She wasn't just this sort of funky senior citizen with cool stuff in her house. She had been...she still was...many things I couldn't possibly picture. I shook my head to clear it. I wasn't really ready for this kind of existentialist thinking right now. But I knew that this epiphany would continue to poke at my brain and my perception of not only my aunt, but my mom, too.

The next item in the box was a small shoebox full of candles of various lengths and shapes. Most of them had been used before, and several had symbols carved into them. I didn't understand what any of the symbols meant, but I recognized them as runes. There was also a brass pot, and a small iron cauldron with residue of what looked like ashes in the bottom. One sniff told me that the ashes were the remains of many layers of incense. There were several small baggies of labeled incenses, and a tube of what looked like charcoal discs. I found what looked like a dagger wrapped in silvery-gray silk. I felt a small chill as I touched the silver handle.

The next box contained mainly papers: handwritten notes about the uses of specific herbs, photos of people I would never know, greeting cards and calendars with a variety of mythological images. And then there was the thing I'd been looking for: a book. Not just any book, but my aunt's personal journal with prayers and chants and recipes. I had hit the motherlode! Sort of.

I don't know exactly what I expected...cures for warts or boils? Maybe. But there was nothing like that as far as I could tell. There were prayers for protection, blessings for loved ones far away, meditations to remove toxic people from one's life. None of it was the kind of shocking stuff you'd imagine a witch's book would contain.

But any of it would have been enough to get you killed in 1650. That was a sobering thought.

As I leafed through the book, something slipped out and fluttered to the ground. I reached down and picked it up. A tarot card. It was beautiful. It depicted a dark-haired woman with luminous skin reaching down through the clouds with outstretched arms. She was reflected in the rippling water below. It was card number 18: The Moon. I couldn't stop staring at it. I didn't want to.

Somehow, this one card seemed more important than any of the other paraphernalia that I'd pawed through. It seemed somehow alive, vibrant. The card appeared to be marking the page with an incantation entitled, "Drawing Down the Moon." Seemed fitting, I supposed, but I couldn't bear to put it back into the book. Instead, I slipped the card into my pocket, took a picture of the incantation with my cellphone, set the grimoire aside, and packed my aunt's other belongings carefully back into the tubs.

I'm pretty sure I meant to ask her if I could borrow the card. Yep, I definitely meant to. Yet somehow, I didn't.

Chapter 5

When you tell someone you're going to write something (a novel, a story, a poem, a play), the most common response you get is something like, "Oh, I could never do that...you're so creative!" And what I had come to discover over the ten days following my visit to Aunt Kitty's house was that being creative is actually a pretty small part of writing anything longer than two pages. It's a dogfight against procrastination and self-doubt.

Starting the play was easy...I'd open onto a bare stage with Esther performing a ritual alone in near darkness. The symbolism and visual impact was good. Then I'd introduce conflict in her interactions with other people and highlight the false front of piety she had to wear with her Puritan neighbors. Excellent. That's when it all got muddy. I couldn't figure out how I wanted the play to end. Should she successfully hide her truth, only to be forced into a Puritan lifestyle? Should she be found out and put on trial? Should she "come out" to her community in a big climactic scene? I just couldn't decide. The one thing that seemed certain is that there was no happy ending for Esther.

Ultimately, I decided on a symbolic ending wherein Esther's activities are discovered by none other than her love interest. He would beg her to repent, to follow the Puritan ways, and she would heartbreakingly refuse him, because she had to live her truth, even if that meant losing the man she loved. Despondent, he would leave, probably to report her to local officials, lest his own devotion to his God be called into question. She would flee into the woods before they came and, with a little creative lighting, "explode" into moonlight, then to a black stage. I was truly happy with it...its themes could be broadened to anyone who struggled with "otherness" in an unforgiving society.

So once that was all sorted, I had a whole new set of issues. Casting. Rehearsals. (gulp) Directing. And only three weeks to get it all done.

Once Mr. Adams had green-lighted my script, he gave me a few minutes at the end of class to attempt to recruit a half-decent cast. I stood in front of my drama group gripping my clipboard like a shield and hoping it would somehow work like one. Everyone looked in my direction, but solidly half of them weren't listening. You know who was listening? Gemma. She was listening, with a tight-lipped look on her face and her head tilted just slightly to the right.

"So, um, hi...I know a lot of you have already started preparing individual stuff for the drama festival, but if there's anyone who'd like to take on a second event, or who hasn't really clicked into a category yet, I'm looking for a few people for the cast of my play. I've taken the liberty of creating character summaries, and I'll put this clipboard over on the stage apron for anyone who might like to sign up. I'll probably need you to stay like an hour after school three times a week for the next three weeks. If anyone has questions, I can try to answer them..."

There was a bit of mumbling, but no hands went up. I felt that old anxiety creeping up. What if I couldn't get any good actors to work on my play? Or what if no one signed up at all? I was playing Esther, so at least that was covered, but I couldn't exactly make it a one-woman show. I set my clipboard down on the apron and walked toward the prop room to see if there was anything that might be useful for the play. Maybe I'd get lucky and a half-dozen people would decide to take a chance on me.

Well, not a half-dozen, but four. Four people out of forty. Oh, well, sometimes you have to take what you can get. I could shift a few things and make it work with four. Maybe a couple of other people would just stand in as extras. I examined the names to figure out casting, since with so few, I wouldn't have to audition anyone.

Sienna Price, Grant Parker, Gemma Harris, Docia Hernandez. Wait a minute. Back up. GEMMA HARRIS? Gemma had volunteered to be in my play? What?

I didn't know what to think about this. Gemma was unquestionably one of the best actresses in class, which sort of begged the question: why would she try to be a non-lead in my play instead of doing a monologue or duet? Furthermore, I had just beat her out for the opportunity to have an original play staged, so why would she then lower herself to being in her rival's production? It seemed pretty fishy to me.

I was just trying to figure out how to ask her about it without sounding overly confrontational when the release bell rang and everyone, including Gemma, stampeded out the auditorium doors and headed for the parking lot. I let out a resigned grunt and followed suit, while whipping my phone out and texting Treigh as I walked.

Hey, r u going straight home? U won't believe what just happened.
Ooo tea time?
LOL. Nothing like that but ur going 2 b in shock.

OK meet u in 5 at ur car

Five minutes dragged on. I was downright twitchy by the time Treigh showed up.

"Okay, now tell me what happened. Exaggerate as necessary."

"I don't think it'll be necessary," I replied. "So you know how I had to cast my show today."

"No, I didn't know that, but now I do. Go on."

"Okay, well, I had to cast the show and, you know, most of the class has already committed to other events and stuff, so that makes my job that much harder." I paused for breath. "I was all worried about whether I'd get anyone at all, and then who I might get might be people who won't, um, do my play justice, right?" Treigh nodded, but I plowed ahead without giving him time to comment. "I had four people sign up, which is slightly less than I'd hoped for, but I can work with it. I got Sienna, Grant, and Docia, and...wait for it...GEMMA. Gemma volunteered to be in my freaking play. Why? Why would she do that?" I threw my hands up in the air in exasperation.

"Gemma."

"Yes, Gemma."

"Gemma who you just beat out for the playwriting slot."

"YES, that Gemma."

"Oooh, girl, I do NOT trust that one bit."

"Exactly what I thought! But I can't turn her down! I've only got FOUR PEOPLE plus me! And she's actually good! I mean, the others are fine, I'm not complaining, but Gemma is actually really good. I can't tell her, 'no, you can't be in my play!'"

"You most certainly cannot," Treigh agreed, "but you better keep an eye on her."

"You're not wrong, but how can I know what she's up to?"

"You could ask."

"Yeah, like she'd tell me..."

"No, I mean really. Go ask. Right now." Treigh pointed behind me, and sure enough, in the next row, Gemma, Trina, and Alex were walking together through the parking lot. "And I'm gone..." Treigh patted me on the shoulder and bolted, laughing and leaving me to my own devices.

"Payback, Treigh!" I yelled after him. Still, he had a point. I had wanted to talk to Gemma anyway at the end of drama class, and only seven minutes had passed. No reason not to stay my course. I took a deep breath and pulled myself up to my full five-foot-four (thank you, Docs) and made my way between the parked cars. "Hey, Gemma! Wait up a second!"

It took her a second to spot me, but when she did, all three of them stopped at once, looking at me quizzically. I sped up my pace to almost a jog and caught up. "Hey," I caught my breath when I realized Alex was looking at me REALLY intently, "hey," I said to him separately. Awkward.

His voice was distinctly Keanu-like. "Hey."

"What's up, Lia?" Gemma and Trina greeted me in unison. Then they look at each other and smirked.

"Yeah, hi. I actually wanted to talk to you, Gemma. About my play. I tried to catch you before drama was over, but you were gone too fast."

"Okay," she replied. The three of them were staring at me. More awkward.

"I mean, uh, I don't want to bore your friends...I just had a couple of technical questions for you…" They continued to stare, none of them speaking or making a move. "Is this a bad time?"

"No, I guess, not. Guys, why don't you go ahead. I'll meet you at Smoothie Monger in ten minutes, okay?"

"Yeah, fine," Alex shrugged. "See you, Lia." My heart was pounding so hard, I thought I might crack a rib.

"You, too!" Too happy. Ugh. Awkwardest. Alex half-nodded and he and Trina turned and kept walking toward his blue Mustang.

"So what did you want to talk about?" Gemma asked, her arms crossed and her eyes fixed on mine. She spun a small gold band around and around on her pointer finger.

"I...well...I know this is a strange question, Gemma, but like, why did you sign up to be in my play? I know that sounds bad...I don't mean it that way. I just mean that you're good at all kinds of acting, and you probably could get superiors in any event you picked. What made you pick my play?"

"You mean why did I sign up to work with the girl who got picked over me for Playwriting?"

"Well, I guess, yeah. That's a blunt way to put it. But yeah."

"Because I've already done all of those other events, I told you." Her voice had a tiny edge to it. "I like ensemble acting."

"Oh, okay. That's it?"

"What do you think, I've signed on so I can sabotage you because you beat me?" Her eyes were sparkling, but I wasn't sure if it was with humor or malice.

"No, I didn't think that…" Even I didn't believe my lame protestations.

"Sure you did. And I don't blame you. Some people might be petty enough to do something like that. But not me. I just felt like doing an ensemble. I don't feel like carrying a lead right now. I've got too much going on."

"Okay, well, you really are good. I'm glad to have you in the play. Honestly, it just surprised me."

"Thanks for just asking instead of assuming. Listen, I have to go. Alex and Trina will be waiting for me. Was there anything else?" I shook my head. "Don't worry, Lia. I'll give you my best." She winked and smiled broadly but never uncrossed her arms, leaving me with a confusing mix of body language and a head full of doubts.

Chapter 6

After-school rehearsals were not a new experience for those of us in 7th period drama, but this was the first time I'd ever had to actually run the rehearsal myself. During class time, Mr. Adams was generally out and about, but his time was spread across all of us, and since at least a third of the class had chosen to do solo events for the festival, that meant that everyone got maybe 3 or 4 minutes of his time on average. He was also resolute that I should have the full directorial experience, so when the bell sounded at the end of the day, he went into his office backstage to handle festival preparations, and I was on my own with my cast.

I had taken to carrying the tarot card around with me, in my backpack inside my copy of *The Crucible*. Each day before we started rehearsing, I'd reach into my backpack and run my fingers around the smooth edges of the card. It became sort of a focusing and calming ritual for me.

It's not that things weren't running smoothly; they pretty much were. But it made me feel uncomfortable to criticize and direct people my own age.

"Grant, you're too far to the left. Come a bit farther in."

"Docia, it's pronounced be-troh-thd. Long O."

"Guys, you have to get this timing down. You can't start the answer before I've finished asking my question. You can't answer a phone before it rings!"

"Be careful not to turn your back to the audience. They won't be able to hear your lines."

It was exhausting.

And then there was the additional distraction of the fact that on Wednesdays, Alex (oh, and Trina, too) stayed after school and waited for Gemma to finish rehearsal so they could go for their weekly smoothie. First of all, I couldn't believe that was even a thing. A weekly smoothie? And beyond that, I was already under pressure and brimming with anxiety, and now here was the secret love of my life, sitting in the house and seeing me get more and more frazzled. The Universe was tormenting me. The truth was, I also couldn't bear to throw them out and claim "closed rehearsal". How was I supposed to say something like that to Alex?

On the last Wednesday before the festival, with either my eternal glory or ultimate humiliation just three days away, Gemma approached me at the end of rehearsal. I was packing up my clipboard and notes.

"Hey, Lia...what do you think about me wearing this sort of pirate lady costume my mom has from a few Halloweens ago?" She showed me a photo of a costume with a cream-colored chemise, a blue skirt, and a black bustier. "I know it's not exactly period, but if I don't wear the bustier, it's sort of Puritan-y. What do you think?"

I looked at the picture and zoomed in on the neckline. "Yeah, I think it will be fine. Thanks for finding it."

"I thought you'd feel that way," she nodded. "Hey, you want to come get a smoothie with us?"

I froze in place for a millisecond, not sure I'd heard correctly. "Really? I mean, yeah, okay. Thanks. Are you sure it's okay with Alex and Trina?"

She waved her hand dismissively. "I'm sure it is. I'm going to head out. We'll meet you there."

"Great," I replied a little too quickly. I felt my heart rate rapidly rising. "Is it okay if I invite somebody?"

"Who, Treigh? Sure, that's fine." She turned and headed toward the back of the house. "See you there!"

When the door closed behind her, I fumbled in my backpack for my phone. A smoothie with Alex? I mean, it's not like HE asked me, but he'd be there... I hit Treigh's icon, and the phone rang twice before he picked up.

"Well, well, a voice instead of a text? What HAS happened?" Treigh laughed.

"Treigh, what are you doing right now?" I sounded a little panicked.

"What's wrong?"

"Wrong? Nothing. Well, maybe nothing. I don't know. Gemma just invited me to join the trio at Smoothie Monger. You have to come. I can't handle the awkward. And besides, if she's up to something, I might need backup."

Treigh sniffed in a combination of amusement and annoyance. "Has she done anything these past couple of weeks to try and screw up your show?"

"Well, no, but…"

"Has she said anything nasty, petty, or sarcastic?"

"No, not really, but…"

"Now, I'd like to point out that I've been waiting every single night for updates on any tea that might come out of these rehearsals, and so far, there's been nada. Maybe she just likes you."

"Are you coming to Smoothie Monger or not?"

"Are you paying?"

"Naturally."

"Then I'll be there. I'll see you in 15 minutes."

"You're a hungry angel," I laughed.
"You know that's right."

Smoothie Monger was just like other smoothie shops in that there was no real intent that customers would sit down and consume their frozen concoctions in the store. As a result, there were only two tables, each with three chairs. Because there were five of us, there was no room for any other patrons who might wish to do the same. That didn't seem to bother anyone but me.

As I expected, Gemma, Trina, and Alex were already seated and sipping when Treigh and I arrived. It would have made an interesting snapshot, actually: two Hollister queens, a prince of Urban Outfitters, the lord of Lord and Taylor, and the princess of Hot Topic. Having smoothies together. We were like a mall advertisement.

Treigh was earning his smoothie by being the great ice-breaker. "So, how are rehearsals going from the acting side?" His smile was fixed on Gemma.

"It's coming together," Gemma replied. "I'm actually impressed that everyone seems to be off-book in only two weeks. It helps that it's a short play."

Treigh nodded and looked expectantly at me. I stared back. He shot a quick look in Alex's direction, then back at me. Clearly, he expected me to say something.

"Um, Alex, how does it look from the audience's point of view?"

"I don't know. Pretty good. I was on my phone most of the time. Sorry."

Honestly, I don't think it would have hurt less if he had stabbed me with his straw. It must have shown in my face, because he quickly followed up with, "I'll be in the audience on Saturday night, though."

"Oh, good," I said, trying not to sound too terribly dejected. "I hope you like it."

"I think it looks pretty good," Trina offered. I shot her a grateful smile and went back to focusing on my smoothie.

"Alex, you haven't even watched it once? Seriously?" Gemma gave him a friendly punch on the shoulder. "What kind of friend are you, anyway?"

"One with a new iPhone," he replied with a smirk.

"You are a rotten friend," she pouted. "Anyway, Lia, don't take it personally. If we put it on Instagram, he might actually pay attention to it."

"Hey, now, don't judge." Treigh chuckled.

The other four of us laughed along with him. I smiled and sucked down the last of my frozen goodness. Half an hour later, we got up from the tables and made our way toward the parking lot. Gemma grabbed my arm and pulled me back.

"Hey, listen," she began, and for maybe the first time, I could clearly tell what emotion was on her face. She felt awkward, unsure. I knew that look all too well, only it was usually on my own face. "I know that we've had sort of a tense association. It always seems like we're at odds with each other. But I think you're really cool. That's really why I volunteered to be in your play. You're a really interesting person." She looked at her feet. "I'd rather be friends than rivals, you know?" She started spinning that ring again, and I wondered if maybe it was a nervous tic.

I could feel my mouth hanging open. I'm pretty sure you could have knocked me over with a feather at that moment. "I'd rather be friends, too," was about all I could manage to reply.

She raised her eyes and smiled. "Cool."

"Cool," I smiled back.

When I reported the conversation to Treigh later, he sniffled and fake-sobbed, "They grow up so fast."

"You think she means it?" I asked him.

"You need to relax and have some faith. You Leos are so paranoid about people."

"Coming from the Libra who trusts everybody?" I raised an eyebrow at him.

"Shut up. I hate you." He hugged me and got in his car. "Text me later."

"I will. Hey, thanks for coming."

"Thanks for paying."

"Happy to bribe you." We grinned at each other and he slammed the door. We made the ASL *I love you* sign at each other as he backed out, and then he drove off. I was a little nervous about trusting what was happening here, but it was starting to look like I had actually made three new friends. Oh, and one of them was Alex Conroy.

Chapter 7

Before I knew it, the final day of the drama festival had arrived. The original plays were always the last event on the program. There were four original plays performing this year, each from a different school. Most schools didn't submit originals, because frankly, they were more work than most teenagers were willing to commit to. I felt very lucky that my cast had, for the most part, been very dedicated to putting forth their best effort. Grant still sometimes flubbed a line, and in the back of my mind, I still had the tiniest doubts about Gemma's intentions. But here we were, and it was showtime.

I felt the familiar rush of butterflies as I looked out at the house from backstage right. No matter how many times I'd stood at this spot, that onset of nerves never failed to find me. This anxiety, more than anything else, is what had always kept me from auditioning for larger roles. The thought of carrying a performance by myself, even for a little while, was petrifying. Tonight, though...tonight the stakes were even higher. Not only would the audience be judging my performance, so would a set of ACTUAL JUDGES, and they'd also be judging my WORK...my HEART. Mr. Adams had told me that a self-written play was tantamount to exposing a corner of one's soul, and now I could appreciate what he'd been saying. I shifted nervously, bouncing from foot-to-foot, watching the performance before mine, trying to see the judges' faces beyond the stage lights, a chorus of what-ifs singing arias in my mind.

What if they don't get the point?
What if the dialogue isn't authentic enough?
What if I can't play the part I wrote for myself?
WHAT IF THEY DON'T LIKE IT?

And, perhaps the greatest fear of all, *What if I'm not really a good writer?*

I began to pace, reciting the lines to the opening scene in my mind. It was so important to set the tone with this ritual. The essence of Esther's character had to be revealed here, her struggle against the establishment to be true to her nature. Her struggle for peaceful co-existence in an intolerant world. I looked at the pendant I held in my hand, a good-luck gift from Aunt Kitty and my mom...a silver disk, representing the full moon, framed on either side by an outward-facing crescent....the symbol of the Goddess. It was a beautiful and meaningful gift, as a prop, it felt...unfinished. Suddenly, without thinking, I ran out the stage right doors as the stage manager, Noelle, hissed at me in a whisper, "WHERE ARE YOU FREAKING GOING?"

I didn't have long, but I knew I was missing something. I darted into the girls' dressing room and dove for my backpack. As my hand closed on the card, I felt calmer. Now it was right. Now it was compete. Now I could do the scene. I slipped back into the backstage area while Noelle muttered something under her breath that I was probably glad I couldn't hear.

I began to practice the steps to the circle dance I had choreographed as the final scene of the previous play came to a close. *5-6-7-8, step across, arm sweep, bend...*

The house and stage lights came up as the kids from Grandview High took their bows to mediocre applause. They grabbed the two chairs they had used for their scene, and Noelle ran out, placing a small table and handful of props for my opening, and removing a wooden lamp post.

Dip, arms in an arc, sweep, jump, spin...

"OW!" I hissed as pain stabbed through the ball of my bare foot and up my leg. I stopped dancing and looked down at my foot, catching a glimpse of the injury just as the lights were falling. It was bleeding. Rats.

"And now, let's give a round of applause to Lia Alvarez and her play, 'Salem Moon'!" There was a smattering of applause, a snitch of derisive laughter from some small corner of the house, and then a hush fell over the audience.

I took one more look at my bleeding foot. "Dammit," I swore under my breath. There was nothing to be done for it now. The show must go on, as they say. With a deep breath, I stepped into the chasseé turns that would carry me to my mark at center stage.

I hit my mark flawlessly, and the soft track of Celtic music I had selected filled the darkness. I began my dance, following a circular track around the table and holding the pendant aloft. As I spun past the front of the little table, I dropped The Moon card into the brass bowl in the center.

"Selene, by the one Power
Acting for me and through me
I hereby draw down the moon
And the power that moves the moon
Into myself
According to Free Will and
For the good of all
Selene, enter me now!
I hereby draw down the Moon for
The consecration of this talisman.

Thank you, Selene, light in the darkness.
The Power that moves the Moon
Moves through me always
Through all time and space
And so mote it be!"

    I had rehearsed this scene so many times, and yet this time, something was different. I had the very distinct sense of being watched. I know, that's not surprising, since it was the first time I'd performed for judges and a real audience. But still, there seemed to be more to it than that. As if someone was watching with interest from the wings.

    I didn't have time to focus on the feeling. I had a performance to do.

    As the final scene approached, I couldn't help feeling like I'd been nearly sleepwalking through the play--not the way you'd normally think of sleepwalking; more like this was a dream in which I was Esther. I felt her struggle to stay hidden, her fear of discovery. I felt her love for Robert Black, the only man who could even make her consider adopting the Puritan life. I felt her internal struggle as she tried to conform for his sake, and her ultimate heartbreak and eventual betrayal when she couldn't. I felt her struggle as never had before, even while I was writing the scenes.

    It turns out I needn't have worried about Gemma. She hit every mark, nailed every line. Even though I was the lead, she was the true star of the show. In the final scene where Grant tearfully left my side to report my witchy activities to Gemma, the matriarch of the town elders, she managed to take her character from being a villain to being a woman with complex feelings, but clear loyalties, doing what she thought God would command of her, even if the demands of her faith caused her pain. She was the perfect foil to Esther. Even I found her character sympathetic.

    We built up to the climactic moment where the tech crew would dim the stage, then abruptly pulse an overly-bright tight spotlight, followed by pitch blackness. My intent was to symbolically represent Esther's death, and I felt her hopelessness deep in my soul. Her final cry of outrage was completely authentic as it burst from my lips just as the spotlight bathed and blinded me. And then the lights went out, and I felt as though that inky blackness was flowing through me, like it was alive and part of me.

    The auditorium sat in total darkness for ten full seconds, and when the house lights gradually came up, the audience remained cloaked in silence for solidly another five.

    Those five seconds of shocked silence validated me far more even than the raucous applause that followed.

One more original play had to perform after ours, and then we were able to go out into the audience and visit with our friends and family. My mom and Aunt Kitty greeted me with flowers and hugs, though Aunt Kitty had a distinct aura of tension around her.

"Honey, that was so good!" my mother gushed. "All that work really paid off!"

"Thanks, Momma," I smiled, holding the bunch of sunflowers she'd handed me. "And thanks, Aunt Kitty, for all your help on the background. I hope I did it justice."

"It was very...authentic," she said carefully. "And I think you did a marvelous job with the characters." She was smiling, but there was a hesitation in her voice. "I'm sure you'll get top marks."

"Thanks," I responded. Before I could press her on her cryptic reaction, arms grabbed me from behind and crushed me in a tight embrace.

"I am so proud of you, darling!" Treigh exclaimed. "You were absolutely amazingly unbelievable! That ending! I'm shook!"

"Aww, thank you! I'm glad it had the impact I wanted. I was going for something memorable."

"Believe me, no one is going to forget what they just saw! How in the world did you do that at the end?"

"Oh, it was just the lighting crew. Nothing hard at all."

"Unreal. I had no idea they could do that!"

"They were great," I agreed. "That spotlight was timed perfectly."

"I'm so proud of you," he grinned and hugged me again.

Alex, Trina, and Gemma came walking up as he released my shoulders.

"That looked so different from the rehearsals we saw!" Trina said in amazement.

"The lights and everything make a huge difference," I concurred.

"That was so cool at the end," said Alex. My heart jumped into my throat. If I died now, I died content.

"Thanks," was all I could manage to say.

Gemma spoke up, "Hey, we need to go. They're about to do the oral critiques. We have to get onstage."

"Oh, right!" I hugged my mom and great aunt and Treigh again, then started moving slowly back toward the stage.

"Really cool," Alex repeated. "Especially that glowy thing."

"Thanks," I said again, and then I was caught up in the current of moving bodies and ushered back toward the stage. It was only after I had made it back up onto the apron that it registered to me what he had said. *What glowy thing?*

Chapter 8

"Glowing?" I stared at Treigh in disbelief. He sat on the foot of my bed, absently petting my cat Vincent.

"Glowing!" he confirmed. "Like those glow-in-the-dark stars you used to have on your ceiling. Except not that greenish color. More silver."

"Maybe it was some sort of optical illusion from the bright spot light and then total darkness."

"Yeah, maybe. I thought maybe it was some sort of body paint."

I shook my head. "No, whatever it was, it was totally accidental."

"Well, whatever it was, it wowed the judges. Straight superiors, girl! You go!" He high-fived me. "My girl got skills."

"Your girl is apparently an X-file."

"Like that's new. Apparently, you also wowed Alex. He kept talking about it. You've been officially noticed! Now get ready! I'm taking you to lunch to celebrate."

I grabbed some clothes out of my dresser and trotted into the bathroom. Yes, it was lunchtime, and Treigh had roused me from a dead sleep when he arrived. Don't judge. I hadn't been able to sleep all night, no matter how tired I was after the festival. My brain kept itching, and I didn't lose consciousness until the first rays of dawn had started peeking up on the horizon.

A hasty shower and messy bun later, and I re-appeared in my room in a tee shirt and shorts.

Treigh was lying on my bed, scrolling through social media posts on his phone. "Girl, you a hot mess."

"You're not wrong. I'm wiped out."

"Nothing some sushi can't cure, I'll bet."

"You're sweet to take me. I don't know how much I can eat, though. I feel weird."

He sat up abruptly and looked suspiciously at my pillow. "Do you think you're getting sick?"

"No, not that kind of weird. I didn't sleep well, and I have this strange feeling. Like I'm forgetting something, or I'm supposed to do something and can't remember what. I don't know. I'm sure it's just coming down off all the stress from the play."

"You sure you want to go to lunch?"

The truth is, I really didn't. But Treigh had made such a big deal about celebrating and being proud of me that I didn't want to let him down. "I'm sure I'll be fine. I bet some miso soup would perk me right up."

"That's the spirit!"

Fifteen minutes later, we were sitting in Kamikaze Sushi with a sizable plate of rolls in front of us.

"I'm so proud of you, girl. That play was just too good."

I smiled into my Mexican Roll. "Thanks, Treigh. I gotta admit, I was really nervous. I was so sure something would go wrong. But the audience and judges seemed to like it, and the whole cast came through, even Gemma."

"Darn right. And you worry too much."

"Kinda my thing."

"Look, Lia, you know I love you like family, but the truth is, it's good that you've got a couple of new people. I always worry about you. I mean, you're my best friend, and nothing is ever going to change that. But there's stuff I love that you hate and vice versa. I don't want you to feel like you don't have anyone but me, you know?"

I could tell that he was trying not to upset me or offend me, but it was hard not to feel like something was fundamentally changing. "I hear what you're saying. I do. I'll try not to scare off the friends-in-training." I tried to make it sound light, but there was an undercurrent of something like bitterness in my words.

"That's all I ask. But don't think, even for a minute, that I'm going anywhere. I mean it."

I smiled wanly, and he could tell I wasn't fully convinced. And then he unexpectedly jumped up and slid into my side of the booth. "THIS," he announced to the entire restaurant, "IS MY BEST FRIEND. I VOW TO NEVER LEAVE HER SIDE, METAPHORICALLY SPEAKING." I was dying of embarrassment, but also appreciated his very public declaration of loyalty. "MAY THE UNIVERSE STRIKE ME DOWN IF I EVER DESERT HER!"

"Alright, alright," I laughed, convinced that if I didn't stop him, we'd likely be thrown out of the restaurant or become the next viral video on YouTube.

"Good." He slid back to his side of the booth. "You gonna finish that Cali Roll?"

Perky might be a bit of an exaggeration, but I did feel a bit better after some soup and sushi. Probably it hadn't hurt my spirits much that Treigh was so adamant about our friendship, and also about the impression I'd made on Alex.

I'd tried to talk to him in the past, with no success. I had deliberately sat next to him in eighth grade Biology, with the grand plan of "accidentally" becoming his indispensable lab partner. Then the teacher rearranged all the seats alphabetically, and we were brutally separated by 12 letters.

Then, the next year, I had rearranged my schedule so I'd be in his photography class. Surely, this was an opportunity to be helpful to him, since I had actually learned about photography from an online elective course the prior summer. This plan seemed like a winner...until he got switched into Drivers Ed. Curses. Foiled again.

After four years of hardly being noticed, I was finally starting to make some progress with this beautiful creature. All it took, apparently, was for me to glow in the dark.

Once I got home, I felt like I had a head full of tornadoes. I was filled with anxiety about what Treigh had said about us needing to have friends besides each other. I was also questioning every conversation I'd ever had with Alex, wondering if there was even the remotest possibility that I might actually have a chance with him. After liking him for so long, the notion was actually pretty intimidating. As scary as that was, it was much more fun to think about than becoming friends with Gemma and Trina, so I allowed myself to retreat into fantasy, wondering vaguely if I could get away with wearing black to both Homecoming and Junior Prom.

My reverie was interrupted by the tinny ringing of the phone. I recognized my aunt's number on the caller ID.

"Hi, Aunt Kitty! Thanks again for coming to my play yesterday. I really appreciated you being there."

"Hi, Lia. You're very welcome, dear. Listen, I know this is going to sound strange, but I was calling for a very specific reason. Have you been feeling okay today?"

I was puzzled by the question. "Well, yes. I mean, I'm tired after the Festival and everything, but otherwise I'm fine. Why?"

"I just...well, I wanted to be sure. You're sure nothing odd has happened?"

"Like what?" Now my curiosity was officially piqued.

"I don't know, strange dreams? Funny feelings, like you're being watched? Feeling sort of static-y?"

I laughed. "No, nothing like that. Just wired and tired."

"Okay, honey, I just wanted to check on you. It really was a good job you did."

"That means a lot. Thank you."

"You're welcome, dear. If anything weird happens, call me, okay?"

"Okay, I promise. Do you want to talk to Mom?"

"No, that's okay. I'll call her later this week. Talk to you soon, Lia."

"You bet. Bye, Aunt Kitty."

I hung up feeling even more anxious than I had before. What in the world would prompt her to ask me those kinds of questions? Did she know something I didn't?

The card. She must have figured out that I had taken it. Was this one of those, "do you have anything you want to tell me?" setups that parents sometimes do? I mean, she wasn't actually a parent, so maybe she didn't know how to execute that play properly. I made my way to my room and grabbed my backpack off my desk. I reached inside and pulled out my copy of *The Crucible* and opened it to the page where I'd wedged the card in for safekeeping. I ran my finger around the smooth edges and studied the picture again. I stared into the eyes of the woman in the drawing and felt myself being drawn in. She seemed so powerful, and yet somehow I knew that she was sad...lonely.

I squeaked in surprise and alarm when my mother popped her head into my room, startling me. I snapped the book shut, as if she'd caught me reading something private. I guess, in a way, she had. I looked around my room randomly...for what? A hiding spot? What was wrong with me?

"Good gravy, Lia. Are you alright?"

"Yes. You, uh, startled me. Did you want something?"

"Who was on the phone?" she asked, now eyeing me suspiciously. Because I wasn't acting shady. No, not at all.

"It was Aunt Kitty."

"Oh? What did she want?"

"She, um, wanted to tell me again how much she liked the show."

"Uh-huh." I was getting a genuine Mom-look now. "Well, you did a great job. You sure that's all she wanted?"

"Yep!" I tried to sound perky. Which sounded way too perky. "That was all!"

"Okay, then. Did you have fun with Treigh?"

"Treigh? Yes! We had a great time. Lots of sushi. Thank you for asking." Now I was starting to sound like a complete idiot, and I wasn't even really sure why. Because I'd borrowed something from my aunt without asking? The truth was that if my mom saw the card on my desk, out in the open, she probably wouldn't think anything of it. So why did I feel the need to keep it secret, hidden?

"You're acting really weird," she said candidly. "What's up?"

My mom and I had always been really close. There's no way she wouldn't notice me acting like a felon. But somehow, I couldn't bring myself to tell her that I had pocketed the card. Besides, I had every intention of returning it, didn't I? Yes, of course, I did. Of course.

"I'm just all out of sorts from the Festival yesterday, I think. I'm overtired, and I still couldn't sleep last night, and now I'm all jittery." Technically, all of that was true.

She nodded slowly, unconvinced, sure she wasn't getting the whole story. "Didn't you sleep until 11:30 today?"

"Well, yes, but I didn't fall asleep until like 6. So only a few hours of sleep."

"Alright, if you say so. Take a little nap if you want. But you do have some homework to do by tomorrow, yes?"

"Yeah, some math and some AP Psych. I'll get it done. I promise."

She nodded again. "Okay, I'll check on you in an hour or so."

"Okay," I said, relieved, "thanks, Mom. Everything's okay." I went over and flopped on my bed like, *see? I'm going to take a nap, just like you said!*

"Sleep well," she said, snapping my light off and closing my door partway. If you fall completely asleep, I'll wake you at 4 so you can get all your stuff done."

"Thanks, Mom." As her footfalls faded down the hall, I felt a pang of regret at not telling her what was going on in my head. The back-and-forth in my mind was giving me a headache, and I closed my eyes, willing the thoughts away. It wasn't long before I'd fallen asleep.

Chapter 9

Afternoon nap dreams are probably the weirdest ones I ever have. On the rare occasions when I nap, I'm usually in that shallow half-sleep that lends itself to dreams melding themselves with reality in the strangest ways. This afternoon's dreams were no different.

I am sitting on my bed, reading <u>The Crucible</u>. A flash of light catches my attention, and I look over to the full-length mirror that hangs on the back of my bedroom door. Only it's not a mirror now. It's a watery image of a raven-haired woman looking wistfully toward a slow-moving river that seems to flow beneath her feet. The night sky behind her is dotted with a million stars, far more than I'd ever seen before. She is reaching out with both hands toward something I cannot see, while two wolves flank her and howl, echoing the longing she feels. On either side of the river are fields of golden flowers.

I realize that this is the same image I have tucked into my book's pages, but it is different somehow. The water appears to shimmer and flow. The heads of the flowers seem to sway ever-so-slightly in the wind that I cannot feel. The same breeze stirs her dark hair and her silvery gown.

I raise my eyes to her face, and she is looking at me, her eyes locking onto mine.

And her look of wistful sadness fades into an enigmatic smile. I am glad that she is smiling, but I am also afraid, and I'm not sure why. Her lips are moving, but I can't hear what she is saying. I can't find a voice to ask her what her words mean.

I find myself standing in front of the mirror, but I have no memory of standing up or moving across the room.

My eyes are still locked on hers. And now it is me she is reaching for, her lips still moving silently. I try to reach toward her, to take her hands in mine, but the mirror is between us, and we stand there, fingertips to fingertips, on either side of the glass barrier. From beneath our fingertips, cracks began to spiderweb their way across the surface.

"Lia, it's 4:10. Time to get yourself up, or you won't be able to sleep tonight." My mother, true to her word.

I mumbled something incoherent and struggled into a seated position. It took me a moment to find my bearings. "Thanks. I'm thirsty."

"Alright, Sleeping Beauty. I'll bring you some water. Don't go back to sleep."

"M'kay."

My mom slipped out the door and I stared at the perfect, unblemished surface of the mirror and my own pale reflection. On a whim, I stood and placed my fingertips on the cool glass.

And nothing happened. Obviously. I felt like an idiot.

After another restless night, which I attributed to homework, ill-timed naps with strange dreams, and my nagging discomfort after Aunt Kitty's call, I showed up looking somewhat less than my best on Monday morning. I didn't think anyone would really hold it against me, though, because...well, because Monday.

Imagine my joy when Trina came bouncing up to me as I shuffled in from the parking lot. "Hey, Lia! What are you doing next Friday night? Want to come to my Halloween party?" I blinked at her, confused. With all of my focus of the previous weeks dedicated to the play, I had forgotten about perhaps the most important day of the school year: Halloween. It was only a week and a half away, and I hadn't even planned a costume!

"Uh, yeah, Trina, thanks! I'd love to!" I mustered the most chipper smile I could, all the while kicking myself for this critical oversight. How could I have forgotten about Halloween? ME? The most dedicated lover of all things Gothic in the entire school, and I had FORGOTTEN? This was akin to blasphemy.

What could I properly prepare in only eleven days? I tended to avoid cliché costumes for Goth girls...garden-variety vampires, schoolgirl zombies, Harley Quinn. All too overdone. I leaned more toward the obscure. I had done an impressive steampunk last year, and I hadn't even been invited to a party. I had worn it to school (I was so glad they hadn't outlawed costumes yet), and then I had just answered the door for trick-or-treaters, but it was still well worth it. Now I actually had somewhere to show it off, so I really needed to take it to the next level.

Holy Halloween. I just realized that I'd be at a party on Halloween. A party where Alex would also be. Thereby, I would be at a party with Alex on my favorite holiday. The stakes just got a whole lot higher.

I ran through maybe two dozen ideas, but none of them seemed quite right. Either they would cost too much to purchase (period costume for Mary Shelley), they were overly commercial (Sally from *The Nightmare Before Christmas*), or they were too generic (dark elf)...I just couldn't find something that clicked. I didn't want to take a chance that anyone else would have the same costume as I did. Now that I had a tiny bit of Alex's attention, I couldn't bear to lose it. I needed to really think about this one.

I'd been sitting on the couch, agonizing over my costume (or lack thereof), when the doorbell rang.

"Lia, could you get the door?" my mother called from upstairs.

I groaned and hauled myself to my feet. I tried to shake off my lethargy, but still found myself practically dragging myself to the door. When I opened it, I found myself looking at a very distinguished-looking middle-aged man. I couldn't quite place his age, but he looked vaguely familiar. He had grey eyes and the thick, black hair, and his gaze was almost uncomfortably intense.

"Hi! Can I help you?" I asked.

He smiled, and I found myself feeling suddenly much more awake. "Good afternoon, miss. I'm new in the area, and I'm sorry to bother you, but I found this on your sidewalk, and I thought I'd better bring it to you. It looked like it might be important." I looked down and realized that he was holding my Anatomy and Physiology folder. I couldn't imagine how the bright green folder had made it out of my backpack and onto the sidewalk.

"Oh, wow, thank you. I don't know how it got there! I really appreciate you returning it." I took the folder from his hands and held out my own. "I'm Lia. Welcome to the neighborhood."

He shook my hand gently, and I was surprised that his skin was so cool, considering that Florida October still easily hits 85 degrees. "Nice to meet you, Lia. That's a beautiful pendant." I looked down and realized I was still wearing the tri-moon pendant I'd used in the play. I hadn't taken it off in days.

"Oh, thank you." I felt suddenly self-conscious.

"You are most welcome. I have a million things to do. But I'm sure I'll be seeing you around." He smiled enigmatically and waved as he made his way back down our driveway.

I reluctantly closed the door, tempted to watch and see where he went. I didn't remember seeing any houses for sale in our neighborhood. I figured that watching him would probably be creepy, though, so instead I bounded up the stairs.

"Hey, Mom, there's a new guy in our neighborhood."

"Really?" She looked up from her computer, surprised. "I don't remember seeing any houses for sale."

"I thought the same thing. Maybe he's renting," I shrugged.

"Maybe so. Was he nice?"

"Yeah, I guess. He found my folder outside and brought it up to return it."

"Oh, that was considerate of him." She turned back to the report she was working on.

"I thought so, too. Oh, hey, by the way, I got invited to a Halloween party next Friday night. Is it okay if I go?"

"A party?" She stopped working again, clearly pleased. "That's terrific! Who invited you?"

"Trina. She's Gemma's best friend. You might have seen her at the play."

"Well, I think that's great. Is Treigh going?" Mom always liked it if Treigh was there to look out for me.

"I think so, yes."

"Well, alright then. Home by 1, since it's Halloween. I'm sure there will be some big hullabaloo at midnight. And I'll need Trina's address and phone number."

"You got it. I'll get all the details from her and let you know."

"Sounds good. Hey, listen, I've got a big meeting tomorrow, and I'm having to rework all these slide decks. You okay with a cereal-for-dinner night?"

"As long as there are Lucky Charms, I'm in."

"Ugh...I'm going to jail. I'm a horrible mom."

I laughed and hugged her. "I promise not to tell the cops that you're a slave to your spoiled daughter's whims."

"Thank heavens for that," Mom chuckled. She stood, and we headed to the kitchen for some marshmallow-y goodness.

After a thoroughly sugared-up dinner, I resigned myself to focusing on homework. As much as I'd rather have been combing the internet for costume ideas, that Trig wasn't going to do itself.

I flopped down at my desk and pulled out my book and calculator. I was not exactly sining, cosining, and tangenting like a pro tonight, and before I knew it, the long shadows from the oak outside began to stretch into my room. I knew I should turn the light on, but I just didn't feel like getting up and walking the eight feet to the wall switch. After a few minutes of squinting, I knew I couldn't put it off any longer. I sighed dramatically and looked mournfully across the room at the switch.

And it flipped on.

The room was awash with light, and my jaw was hanging open.

No. Couldn't be. I closed my eyes tightly and looked back at the switch, and with a click, I was sitting in semi-darkness again. Was this real?

On. Off. On. I squeaked and covered my mouth with my hands. What was happening?

I looked around the room in disbelief. A part of me was attempting to remain rational...was I somehow being punked? Who would play a trick like this, and how? I focused my attention on the open bathroom door a few feet away. With a thought, I slammed it shut.

"Everything okay up there?" Mom called from downstairs.

"Uh, yeah, sorry! Didn't mean to close it so hard!" I called back. What was I going to say, *sorry, I slammed the door. I don't know the strength of my own mind?*

I really didn't, though. What was I capable of doing? I focused my attention on random items around the room: shoe, sweater, hairbrush, book, pen. Before I knew it, a dozen items were levitating, orbiting around me. I flipped a switch in my mind and everything clattered to the ground.

"What is going on up there?"

"Sorry, Mom!"

I heard her feet coming up the stairs. Should I tell her? No, definitely not. Not till I was sure what was happening. I wasn't even sure I could do it again. She pushed my door open and poked her head inside.

"Holy moly, what happened in here?"

"What? Nothing! Definitely nothing!" Cool under pressure. That's me.

She looked around at the mess of objects. "What in the world..." She pulled my favorite jacket off of my computer screen. "Just be sure you clean up before bed, okay?"

"I will. Promise." She gave me a long, appraising look, handed me the jacket and walked out.

I let out a whoosh of breath. I needed to get ahold of myself and figure out what was going on. I grabbed my phone and hit speed dial. Treigh's voicemail picked up immediately.

"Treigh, call me asap. Strange things are afoot." I tried not to sound panicky, but in reality, I was pretty close to a grade-A freak out.

Okay, so no Treigh. But I had to talk to somebody... and then I remembered my Aunt's strange warning on the phone the day before. I scrolled through my call log and punched the button next to her number. She answered on the second ring.

Chapter 10

"Hey, Aunt Kitty...so you know how you asked me if anything strange had happened?"

She was suddenly deadly serious. "What happened?"

"I...well, I sort of...became telekinetic."

"You WHAT?"

"Telekinetic. I can move things with my mind."

"I know what telekinetic is, Lia." She paused, processing. "When?"

"It just started like 15 minutes ago. I accidentally switched the light on. And I can pick up small stuff. And close doors from across the room. I don't know what's going on. It's cool, but it's freaking me out."

"I should think so. Have you told your mom?"

"Not yet, I--"

"Don't."

I was startled by her abruptness. "Oh...okay. Is this bad?"

"Not too bad, yet," she hesitated, then went on. "But it could get out of control very quickly. What you can do is exceedingly rare, and probably shouldn't be possible. It's very odd for anything like this to manifest without training. You haven't been training with a witch, have you? Playing with my Book of Shadows?"

"Book of what?"

"Shadows. A grimoire. Spellbook."

"No, nothing like that. I looked through yours and wrote down that one incantation for my play, but that was it."

"When you drew down the moon in your play."

"Well, yes, but I don't know anything about being a witch, not really. Did I do something?" I asked, suddenly afraid.

"I think you may have. It didn't look anything like the ritual we used to do in the Circle, but that doesn't really mean anything."

"Um, this might be a dumb question, but my foot was bleeding when I danced around the table. Could that have done anything?"

"Okay, yikes." She paused, thinking. "Blood is like life energy. So that may have intensified the ritual. Still, without a talisman, the most that should have done is make you open to insights and intuitions."

"A talisman?"

"Yes, a blessed object. Something to draw the moon into that carries its own power. If you had something like that, it could amplify the effect."

I fell silent, a dark truth weighing on me.

"Lia? What? What is it?"

"Could this talisman be anything?"

"Technically, sure… Lia, what did you do? What was on that table?"

"Um…I may have accidentally borrowed something from your house." The words came out in a rush. "I really didn't mean to…I was just kind of holding onto it and forgot to ask you. When I realized I had it, I was going to give it back to you the next time I saw you…"

"What. Did. You. Take?"

"It was a card. A tarot card. I promise I didn't damage it or anything."

Aunt Kitty was silent for a moment. "A tarot card? Was it The Moon?"

"Yes. I'm really sorry. I just found it in your book along with the incantation."

"Oh, no." I heard Aunt Kitty's breathing quicken, and I could picture her pacing back and forth in her kitchen.

"What? What is so bad about that card?" I was becoming genuinely scared.

"Lia, that card is more than blessed. It's enchanted by the goddess Selene herself. I just don't understand how it ended up in your hands."

"I told you…I found it in your book."

"Lia, it wasn't in my book. We buried that card with your grandmother."

The next evening, Aunt Kitty paid us a surprise visit, bearing a basket overflowing with baked goods. My mother's eyes widened as she began pulling things out and laying them on the kitchen counter.

"Kitty, it's wonderful that you came out to see us, but I don't know how the two of us could ever eat this much food."

"Nonsense. Part of it is dinner. Do you have olive oil, salt, and pepper?" My mother nodded. "Marvelous." Aunt Kitty reached for a round loaf of rustic-looking bread that smelled like herbal heaven. She grabbed a shallow dish from the cabinet and poured and seasoned the oil. We sat around the kitchen table and she pulled a chunk of the still-warm bread off, dipped it in the oil, and began munching. Mom and I followed suit, reveling in the makeshift meal.

I was twitchy as we ate, not sure how much trouble I was in. Aunt Kitty had reiterated the importance of not talking to people about my newfound skillset or the card, and I had obeyed. I knew that that was the real reason for her visit, not the baking marathon she was using as a cover story.

When dinner was over, she turned her attention on me. "Lia, dear, how about if you take me for a walk so I can burn off some of these carbs?"

"Sure, you bet. Mom, do you need help with the kitchen?"

"Certainly not," she smiled. "There's hardly anything to do. You two have a nice walk."

We stepped out into the cooling night air. For half a block, we walked in silence.

"I'll be sure to give you the card back when you leave," I offered. It was an awkward ice-breaker, but it was all I could think of to say.

She shook her head. "It wouldn't matter if you did. It would just show up somewhere in your room or your backpack. The card chose you, found its way to you. It chooses someone in our family each generation. I didn't have any children, so it passes to you."

"So you knew this would happen?" I asked in disbelief.

"No, honestly, I thought we'd broken the circle. It passed from your grandmother to me, and when she died, I passed the card back to her the day she was buried. I hadn't seen it since, so I thought perhaps that was the end of it. A foolish hope, I suppose."

"Am I cursed?" There was the slightest tremor of panic in my voice.

"No, dear, no. But there will be challenges, to be sure. The magic is hard to control because it comes from the moon goddess Selene herself. She's not evil, but she's also not human, and doesn't feel bound by our society or its rules. It's only a matter of time before she makes herself known to you directly. You'll have to decide how you're going to relate to her."

"I don't understand what that means." My head was beginning to hurt from the magnitude of what Aunt Kitty was discussing so casually.

"It means that you will have to decide what you will be to her. You can worship her, you can serve her, you can deny her. It's in some ways like any relationship. But as in any relationship, your choices have consequences. What I can tell you is this: you cannot control her; she is a goddess. You cannot trick her; she is the mistress of illusion. You also cannot avoid her. She is coming."

"You chose to deny her?"

"Oh, no, not at all. I worshipped her. In some ways, I still do. I just didn't want the temptation of her power anymore. That's why I buried the card." She looked wistful, and looked up at the cloudy sky. Somewhere behind those clouds, the moon was rising.

"What about Grandmother?"

"I don't really know too much about their relationship. Your grandmother wouldn't talk about it. But I know that, for a time at least, she had great power. And it put her in great danger."

This just kept getting worse. "Danger?"

"Yes, not from Selene, if that's what you were thinking. From...others. People who wished to increase their own power by taking Grandmother's."

A realization was nagging at the corners of my mind. "Others? Who already had power?"

My aunt nodded. "Their own was not enough to satisfy them."

I had a moment of clarity. "There are other cards."

"There are indeed. Twenty-one others, if the stories are to be believed. I have seen three others, but we kept them--and their owners--separate. We thought that was safer."

"We?"

"Other practitioners of various forms of magic. Good people do good things with magic, just as they would with their other gifts. Bad people...well, it's better if we don't put too much power in one place as a temptation."

"What happens if the cards are together?" I prodded.

"It's not so much the cards, it's the deities they represent. Each card has been blessed by a different deity. The truth is, I don't know what would happen if more than a couple of cards were in the same place at the same time. We were never brave enough to try to bring deities together like that. It didn't always go well in ancient times, you know."

I nodded. "If the myths I studied are any indication. What about Grandmother? You said she was powerful and in danger. Did she try bringing cards together?"

"I believe that she did, yes, but I don't have much to go on there. She wouldn't discuss it, as I told you."

We walked quietly for awhile. This was all too overwhelming, and it seemed unreal, impossible. Yet somehow it seemed right and true, part of the natural order.

"What do I do, Aunt Kitty? How am I supposed to know what's the right way to handle this? There are no books on how to cope with this kind of thing."

She smiled, and linked her arm in mine. "You are a good person, Lia. Selene has much to offer, and it's best that you think about who you want to be before she starts tempting you. If you follow the goodness in your heart, I believe you will make good decisions. And I will be here for you."

We came around the block and my house came back into sight.

"I have one more thing for you, but I wanted to talk to you first." She approached her car and popped the hatchback. She gingerly picked up a package wrapped in tissue paper. I didn't need to open the wrapping to know what was inside. I could smell the now-familiar aroma.

"The dress," I breathed.

She nodded, smiling at some distant memory and ran her hand across the top of the paper. "This is yours now. Your grandmother gave it to me when she passed the card into my keeping."

"Is it magical?" I breathed, taking the package from her as if it were made of glass.

"Magical?" she laughed. "No, honey, it's just a dress. But Selene likes it. So now it's yours."

After Aunt Kitty left, I found myself sitting on the window seat by my open window, staring at the midnight-blue velvet frock laid out on my bed. Finally, I lifted it up and stood in front of my mirror, holding the dress in front of me, wondering how it had looked on my free-spirited aunt. Wondering how it would look on me. I decided to find out the answer to the latter question.

I pulled off my school clothes and tossed them aside, and slid the fragrant velvet over my head. It was stretchy and slid on easily, and the dress fit surprisingly well, though it was maybe an inch too long and pooled around my feet. The sleeves were form-fitting and reached just below my elbow, and I was pleased to find that they didn't hamper my movement at all. The neckline was a dramatically wide V, but plunged tastefully only as far as the line between my armpits.

I swirled in front of the mirror, and the skirt billowed slightly, sending the strong aroma of incense in a breeze throughout my room.

Looks very becoming on you, said a voice.

I squealed and spun around, but there was no one there.

"Who are you? WHERE are you?"

I thought you and I should get to know each other better. There was clearly no one in the room with me, but it seemed as though the voice was very close. I turned back to the mirror and there was a mist covering my reflection, a face hovering above my own.

I knew I should be creeped out, but somehow I wasn't. Somehow, I had been expecting her, though maybe not exactly in this way.

"Selene."

She smiled. *I've had many names. Selene will do. It was nice of Katherine to give that to you. I've always been fond of the color.*

It took me a moment to realize who she was talking about, and then I remembered that Aunt Kitty's full name was Katherine. "I have so many questions about what's happening," I told her.

The mist in the mirror swirled and flowed, but approximated a human form.

I have no doubt, she began, *and your answers will come in time. I have much to show you, and you have much to learn. Change your clothes. We're going to the beach.*

"What?"

You can't wear that to the beach. You'll ruin it. She stared at me expectantly, offering no further information.

"Why?" While I had some trepidation about questioning a goddess, I also had a well-instilled sense of Stranger Danger.

I would never harm you, Lia. We are bonded, you and I. I have known generations of women in your family, and never harmed one of them. Quite the contrary, actually. Do not fear.

"Uh, yeah, okay…" I stammered, pulling off the gown and throwing my regular clothes back on.

Excellent. I'll meet you at the car. I couldn't help but wonder why a goddess would need to travel in a car.

Because your human body can't travel by moonlight, dear. I started, realizing that I hadn't asked that question out loud. *If you don't want me to hear your thoughts,* she continued, *you might not want to think quite so loudly.*

I stepped quietly out of my room and, quickly noting that my mother had fallen asleep with the TV on in her bedroom, I slipped out of the house and over to my car.

Don't worry, your mother won't realize you're gone, she assured me. *Take us to the sea. I need to show you something.*

Chapter 11

The full moon was glowing above us, alive and pulsing, as I walked from the parking lot toward the sea. I could no longer see Selene, but her voice still spoke in my head. It was nearly as bright as daylight, and the wind whipped at my hair.

Do you feel it? she sighed. *The power? Strong enough to move the ocean, and that same power flows through you now.*

"I feel it," I replied. I felt myself being pulled toward the sea, felt the magic prickling along my skin, ebbing and flowing with the crashing waves, like a million tiny sparks crackling along my surface. I flexed my hands and stretched out my fingers. They felt heavy, thick, engorged with something that was not quite physical.

I will teach you to use it. That much power cannot be contained. It must be let loose into the world. How you direct it will be up to you. There was something in her voice that sounded like both a lesson and a test, all in one.

Two short sets of stairs led to the beach, and I walked in silence until I reached the shoreline. Waves crashed against the hard-packed white sand, which seemed iridescent in the pale light coming from above.

I raised my hands and looked at them, half-expecting to see tiny forks of lightning coming from the tips of my fingers. "What do I do with it?"

Let us start simply, she said, like a teacher beginning a lesson. I kicked off my shoes and tossed them back toward the car. *Reach out to the waves.*

"Do what?"

Reach out to them. Bend them to your will.

"I can control the ocean?" I asked, dumbfounded. I stood thirty feet or so from the waterline, where low waves swirled gently against the beach.

She smiled, as one might smile at a baby who found her toes for the first time. *Not the ocean, no. That is not where your power lies. But you can commune with the tides.*

I stared at the rolling surf. Slowly, I lowered my hands and faced my palms to the ocean. I closed my eyes and focused on the crashing all around me, and a funny thing happened. Not only could I hear the waves, I could feel them pushing and pulling against every molecule in my body. *More*, I thought, and pushed the crackling energy out toward the tide, giving it strength, giving it my power and having it bring that power back to me. I opened my eyes and stared at the ocean, filling my senses with nothing but the thought of more. A small wave rose above the others and crashed onto the beach.

Good, yes, well done, Selene whispered.

The power was surging around me and through me, and the small rolling waves began to foam and rise. They grew taller and crashed harder against the sand, and I felt the sea coming closer and closer, reaching out to me, seeking to engulf me. Indeed, as the intensity of the water increased, the edge of its reach crept closer and closer. The surf began to churn the way it does when a thunderstorm lingers just off the coastline, and the tide surged and crashed against the sand. I continued to pull it closer, my head thrumming with the power that swirled all around me.

The grey-black water clawed toward me, fighting to find me, pull me in, embrace me. I watched as a tall wave began to form, sucking the waterline back as it built strength. It peaked and raced toward me like a battering ram, curving and foaming as it came. With a final roar, it curled along the edge and submitted to the gravity and my power that pulled it toward me. It hovered for a moment, then slammed violently against the beach in front of me. The ground seemed to tremble at the impact, and the seafoam rushed all around my bare feet.

At the touch of cold water, I felt as though a dam had broken inside me, and I felt the power rushing out with the tide as it pulled back, back, back to where it had been when we first set foot on the shore. I fell to my knees in the wet sand.

Quickly, Selene hissed. *Make a wish before the power is gone! What is your heart's desire? Manifest your will!*

I trembled with exhaustion and fell onto all fours, closing my eyes and digging my fingernails into the sand. I couldn't form coherent thoughts, much less make a wish. Since my brain wasn't working, my heart stepped in and Alex's face swam behind my eyelids. I collapsed and rolled onto my back, panting.

So mote it be! Selene cried exultantly.

I slowed my breathing and forced my eyes open. The halo around the full moon pulsated as if with joyous laughter. I closed my eyes again and the now-distant waves now sounded like a lullaby. I gave in and fell into unconscious darkness.

I woke up to the sound of the alarm on my phone. I was lying on the floor of my bedroom with no memory of how I'd gotten there. My clothes were covered in sand, and my head was pounding. I forced myself up and lurched into the bathroom for a shower and some Tylenol.

Revived somewhat, I dressed and got ready for school. What had happened on the beach? Should I even be playing with forces this powerful? And how did I get from St. Augustine Beach to the floor of my bedroom?

All through math, I couldn't concentrate on anything Mr. Nash was saying. All I could think about was the accidental wish that I had made the night before. I knew I'd be seeing Alex next period, and my mind raced, wondering if the wish would somehow manifest itself in English class. When the bell finally rang, I grabbed my things. I wasn't sure if I should rush to class or the parking lot.

"What in the world has gotten into you today, woman?" Treigh asked, falling into step beside me. "Don't tell me you still aren't sleeping. Girl, I'm going to have to…"

"No, no," I interrupted. "I definitely slept. I just…well, I…" How exactly was I going to explain my jumpiness without telling Treigh all about last night? "I made a wish on the moon last night that Alex would ask me to Homecoming."

Treigh stopped walking and stared at me flatly. "Are you serious?"

"Well, yeah…"

"Girl, if you don't…" he blustered, unsure of how to kindly say to me that I was acting like a seven-year-old with a Disney-fied sense of destiny. "If you want to go with him, YOU ask HIM. If he says no, at least you'll know. Wishing on the moon?" He shook his head and started walking again.

I couldn't really blame him. He'd been hearing me gush over Alex for years, and seeing as he wasn't really aware that I'd actually been befriended by the moon goddess, the idea of wishing on the moon probably sounded ridiculous.

"You're probably right. Call it a moment of romantic weakness." I smiled wanly, trying to convince him I wasn't actually losing my mind.

"Pssh." He dropped me at the door of my English class, leaving me to fend for myself. I crawled into my seat, making a mental note not to say anything like that to anyone other than Selene herself.

I waited on proverbial pins and needles for Alex to arrive. When he finally walked in, I whipped my backpack onto my desk and began rifling through it, trying to look busy while watching him out of the corner of my eye. He walked in and made a beeline for Gemma and Trina. I couldn't hear what they were saying, but as I focused on his presence, I felt tiny prickles of power against my skin.

I shook my hands as if I were trying to dry them, hoping to dissipate the building power. I felt like the most visible person in the whole world, even though I knew no one besides me was aware of the minor power surge I'd just had.

The bell rang, and I slid my backpack onto the floor as Mrs. West called for the class' attention. I raised my eyes toward her, only to lock eyes with Alex, who was staring at me as if I'd just grown a second head.

Class was a blur, and at the end, he waited for me by the door. He told Trina and Gemma he'd see them later, and they looked from him to me and back to him, clearly confused by this unexpected development in the social order.

"Uh, hey," Alex said not-so-eloquently.

"Hey," I replied. "Everything okay?" I looked after Gemma and Trina, as they walked away, shaking their heads and talking animatedly to each other.

"Huh? Oh, yeah. Where's your next class?"

"AP Bio...Ms. Fletcher."

"Can I walk with you?"

My heart was pounding so hard, I thought I might crack a rib. "Sure, of course! What's up?" We started walking, and I clutched my backpack to my chest in a vain attempt to keep my pulse under control.

"Nothing, I guess. I just felt like walking with you. Is that okay?" He seemed genuinely confused about his motivations.

"Absolutely," I replied, trying to think of something to say without sounding lame. "I...uh...I really like your shirt."

The truth was that there wasn't much remarkable about the shirt except that he was in it. It was a blue and black plaid lumberjack-turned-hipster type of thing. It was all I could think of to say in that nanosecond, though, and it had the desired effect. He turned his head toward me slightly and grinned, and I thought I might die on the spot. I smiled back, hoping I didn't look like an insane stalker fangirl.

"Thanks. It...it was clean." He smiled again, this time sheepishly. "So, um, listen...I was wondering if you were going to the football game Friday night?"

I hadn't been to a single high school football game in my entire high school career. "I'm not sure...I mean, I hadn't really thought about it yet. Why?"

"Well, I was wondering, like if you were going, if you might want to hang out or something afterwards. Like maybe go for pancakes."

Pancakes?

"Well, sure, who doesn't like pancakes?" I tried to give him my best flirtatious smile, but I'm pretty sure I looked like a crazed Chihuahua.

"Cool. Is this your class?"

"Yeah, thanks for walking me."

"Totally. I'll catch you later." And with that, he turned around and walked off in the direction from which we'd come.

Oh, sweet sunshine.

I had a date. With Alex. On Friday.

Chapter 12

I dropped my books on my desk and whipped out my phone, desperately trying to text Treigh. The result was something that looked remotely Russian. Hard to text when your hand is shaking like you're sitting on a jackhammer.

Class started, and I reluctantly slid my phone into my backpack. It's fair to say that I absorbed absolutely no AP-Bio-related information that day. When the release bell for 4th period rang, I stood up to find Treigh already waiting at the door, looking testy and holding up his phone.

"What, may I ask, is this shenanigans?" he asked in his best accusatory tone. "I'll tell you what it's not: it's not English. Sis, I thought you'd been kidnapped and you were signaling for a rescue."

I laughed. "That, sir, is me attempting to text you while freaking completely out."

He made an impatient gesture with his hand as we began to walk. "About...?"

"Alex asked me out. For Friday."

Treigh stopped walking. "Say what now?" I grinned like a lunatic, and his eyes got huge. "GIRL. Finally! After all this time, he finally got smart!"

"I know, I can't believe it worked."

"What worked?"

"My wish! I can't believe it worked."

"Are you serious right now? You think he asked you out because you wished on a star?"

"The moon," I corrected.

He stared at me. "You done lost your mind."

I realized how crazy I sounded. But if he had only known about the abilities I'd been developing, all the things Selene was promising to teach me, and had taught my aunt and grandmother before me...

"Look, Treigh, I know it sounds nuts," I began as he nodded vigorously, "but there's a lot you don't know. A lot I have to tell you."

"So tell me."

"I can't. Not here. Too many people." It was lunchtime, but I wasn't sure this was a conversation I could have on our bench. I wasn't supposed to tell people, according to Aunt Kitty, but I couldn't go on without Treigh knowing.

"You are freaking me out, Lia. Is everything okay?"

"Yes, I promise, I'm more than okay. I just...it's not a public conversation." We started walking again, and despite my assurances, Treigh was eyeing me with concern.

"Alright. Privacy. Come on." He grabbed my hand and dragged me around to the small seating area outside the guidance office. At this time of day, most of the administration area was deserted. "Now talk." He plopped onto a bench and pulled me down beside him.

"Okay, soooo…" I took a deep breath and spilled all of the top-secret-crypto information I'd been holding onto for the past week. I deliberately didn't look at him as I was talking, because I was afraid I'd see him dialing the authorities to come and get me. After several minutes, I finished my tale and slowly raised my eyes. He was staring at me. Like really staring. Then he burst out laughing.

"Oh, girl...you had me going…aaaahhh…" And then he realized I wasn't laughing. "Wait. Are you serious?" I nodded slowly. "If I didn't know better, I'd swear you were on some kind of crazy designer drug. You're seriously serious?"

I took a deep breath and pointed at an empty chip bag that had been carelessly tossed into the grass. I concentrated hard on it, and it trembled, then rolled about six inches. Treigh raised an eyebrow and looked at me doubtfully.

I took a deep breath and thought about how much I hated litter. Magic was intent plus energy. I focused on how much I wanted that bag not to be in the grass. After a moment's intense effort, I picked it up, floated it rather awkwardly over to the trash bin, and deposited it. When I looked back at Treigh, his eyes were the size of dinner plates.

"Uh, no. Uh-uh. Listen, Lia love, I know my ancestors are island people, but this is a bit out of my area of expertise. I'ma have to take a minute to process this." He stood and walked back toward the main courtyard, looking as serious as I'd ever seen him.

I didn't know what to say to him. This was Treigh, my BFF, my partner in crime, and he was frightened...of me. My eyes stung with tears, and I couldn't find words as I watched him walk away from me. He thought I was a freak. This was the biggest thing that had ever happened to me, and it was going to cost me my best friend. I felt myself beginning to tremble.

He had gone maybe 30 feet when he abruptly stopped.

"Aaargh!" He spun around and walked back to where I was sitting. I almost couldn't see him through the tears filling my eyes. "I want you to know that I am extremely heebie-jeebied by this. You're lucky I love you, dammit!" He looked down at me, trying to appear tough, but I leapt up and threw my arms around his waist, sobbing. He put his arms around me and rested his chin on top of my head. "Now you just cut that out. You knew I wasn't going to abandon my best friend just because she's gone all *Sabrina* or whatever." He hugged me tightly, and I snuffled into his chest. "C'mon, sis. It's all good. Well, not good, but it'll be okay. Don't get mucus on my Gucci. It's okay."

And just like that, all was right in my universe again.

Chapter 13

I wasn't sure what the proper etiquette was for attending a high school sporting event, but Treigh's official advice was "like school, but amped up", whatever that meant. For me, it meant more sparkles with my black. I settled on a strappy black tank top that was embellished with tiny jet beads. It rather reminded me of the bodice of a black wedding dress, and I decided that that was at least putting positive energy into the date. I found my favorite ripped jeans and rolled up the cuffs enough to show off my Docs. I added a red blazer with black lapels, since I didn't want to get cold or mosquito-bitten. Ah, Florida.

I gave my hair a quick brush and pulled my hair into a high and glossy ponytail, painstakingly applied my eyeliner (four times) and red lipstick, and stood back to take in the overall effect. I came to two conclusions: one, that I looked really good, and two, that I looked more like I was going to a concert than a football game. I decided that, given my wardrobe choices, that was inevitable. Still, something was missing.

I started digging through my jewelry drawer when I heard a tapping sound. At first I couldn't find the source, but then I spotted Selene's misty face reflected in my full-length mirror.

I wanted to wish you well tonight.

I caught my breath. I hadn't seen her or heard her voice since the night at the beach, though I had looked for her every evening. "Thank you...for all of this. I can't thank you enough for all you've taught me."

She smiled softly. *Your strength gives me strength*, she said, as if that explained everything. *I am glad to see you making the most of your wish.*

"I'm pretty nervous. I've liked him for a long time."

I should think so. He walks close to the veil. It makes sense that you'd be drawn to him.

I looked at her in alarm. "What does that mean?"

He is close to the spirit world, as are you. It's natural you should sense that in him.

"I still don't understand."

You will, in time. Have fun tonight. She winked. *Oh, and I thought I'd share one more little tidbit with you...as we near the full moon, your power grows. It will wax and wane with the lunar cycle. You might like to try one of your other skills as you get stronger.*

My interest was piqued. "There's more?"

Oh, so much more, she laughed, and the sound was like the tinkling of silver bells. *Look up into the moon and tell me what you see.*

"It's really bright tonight," I began. "I can see the craters and..."

Ah, and there it is. One of your greatest powers. The light you see is not that of the moon. The light you see is that of the sun...it only appears to be the moon. There is really no such thing as moonlight, but everyone knows what moonlight is. The moon holds the power of illusion, and so do you.

I had known that about the moon's light, of course, but I had never really thought about it. "I have the power of illusion?"

Yes, Lia, you do, and you will learn to use it with increasing skill. To begin, though, you might want to start with something simple. Do you know what a glamour is?

"Making something look more beautiful than it is?"

Not exactly, just making it look different than it truly is. It's easiest to begin with something you know well, like your own appearance. Why don't you go give it a try before your date? Start small, then keep practicing when you have more time. Like this. She crossed her hands in front of her face in opposing circles. When her hands parted, her black hair and grey eyes had been replaced by red hair and green eyes. She repeated the movement, and her familiar coloring returned.

"Whoa..." I sputtered.

Now, go play, she chuckled. I blinked, and found myself suddenly alone.

I looked at my reflection and imitated the hand movement Selene had made.

Nothing happened. I tried again, with the same non-result.

I blew at my bangs in frustration. *Concentrate*, I thought. *Start small.* I thought about what she said about the moon, picturing it reflecting the sun's rays. I felt that non-familiar prickle across the surface of my skin and closed my eyes, focusing on the feeling. I kept my eyes closed and repeated the casting gesture slowly. When I pulled my hand away and opened my eyes, my bangs had gone from a glossy black to a glossy wine red. I yipped in delight.

Somewhere in the echoes of my mind, I heard Selene's musical laughter.

I watched out the window until Alex's Jeep pulled into my driveway, then went through a quick check of the contents of my purse. I didn't usually carry one, so I was pretty sure I'd forget something. Wallet, check. Comb, check. Cellphone, check. I heard the doorbell ring and started for the stairs. My mom answered the door, and I could hear her talking to Alex, introducing herself. I got about halfway down the stairs, then ran back up, grabbed my copy of *The Crucible* with the tarot card in it (for luck?), and headed down to meet my date. Alex. My date. I shivered with excitement.

He looked up as I hit the bottom three steps. He looked a little confused, and I make a note to ask my mother what she'd been telling him when I arrived on the scene.

"Hey," I smiled.

"Hey yourself," he replied, and a warm smile spread across his face. I was somewhere between wanting to scream and faint. I couldn't believe he was looking at me like that.

We stood in semi-awkward silence for a moment.

"Well," my mother broke in, "you two have fun. Be back by 11:30. Be safe."

"You bet," Alex said, and stepped past my mother to open the door for me. As soon as his back was to her, she silently pointed at him and shot me a grin and a thumbs up sign.

My eyes widened, and I stepped between them, desperate that he not see her cheerleading me on a date I'd been dreaming of for years. I wrapped her in a quick hug. "See you later, Mom!" I said a little too cheerfully, and then we were out the door.

As Alex drove inland toward the school, an awkward silence fell over us. I guess first dates are always awkward, but somehow, as much time as I had spent thinking about Alex over the past four years, I felt woefully unprepared for this moment. I realized I didn't really know that much about him outside of what classes he took and who his friends were.

"So," I began, attempting to break the ice, "tell me a little about yourself outside of school. Do you have a job or anything?"

"Yeah," Alex responded. He seemed grateful for something to talk about. "I mean, I kind of just work when I want to, but my folks own one of those ghost tour companies in the historic district. Sometimes I guide the tours, and sometimes I work in the office selling tour tickets."

Close to the spirit world, that's what Selene had said. "Oh, that's a great job!" I exclaimed. "Have you ever seen any ghosts on your tours?"

"Nah, not really," he replied. "I mean, I've had some creepy feelings sometimes, but I don't want to jump to conclusions. Most of the time, people see what they want to see, you know?"

"So you don't believe in ghosts?" I felt a glimmer of disappointment.

"Ghosts are good for business," he said matter-of-factly. "I'm open to believing in them, I guess, but I've never actually seen one. I know some of the good stories about St. Augustine's ghosts, though."

"Oooh, tell me a story!" My disappointment faded as he told me stories about the light on the widow's walk of the Casablanca, and the lady in white at Harry's Seafood and Grille. By the time he finished those two stories with tour-like flair, we had arrived at the school's parking lot. Frankly, I was much more interested in his ghost stories than football, but I wasn't going to complain.

I honestly didn't pay much attention to the game. We'd watch for a few minutes and then I'd catch him staring at me as if he were hypnotized, and I'd grin and blush, and we'd go back to watching the game. Several people walked by and said hi, either to Alex or to me, and then raised their eyebrows in surprise when they realized we were there together. I wasn't sure if I should be proud or offended by that.

It was about halfway through the third quarter when I realized he had scooted just a little bit closer to me, and our pinkies were touching. Call me sentimental, but that tiny touch sent my heart fluttering much more so than if he had presumptuously walked into the stadium with his arm around me. That would have been a possessive move, perhaps endearing in its own way, but this was unsure, sweet, vulnerable. I felt like I was living in a dream.

I absently slid my pinky over his and left it there. I tried to make it seem nonchalant, and after a moment, I turned to look at him, only to find him staring at me with an unexpected intensity. I couldn't stop myself...this should have been a tender moment, but I felt an enormous grin spread across my face. I tried to look away, but he bumped me with his shoulder so that I'd look back. He was grinning just as ridiculously as I was. As we looked at each other, he re-positioned his hand and interlaced his fingers with mine. Neither of us seemed to know what to say, so we turned back toward the game. I don't remember a single play from the 4th quarter. All I remember is that his hand never let go of mine.

We left the stadium hand-in-hand when the game was over. We sat on the same side of the booth at IHOP. We shared a pancake stack. I swear, throughout it all, I expected to wake up at any second. At 11:27, he escorted me up the walkway in front of my house, and my face hurt from smiling.

"I had a great time tonight, Alex, thank you."

"Me too," He looked down at me, holding my hands lightly in his. "Are you going to Trina's Halloween party next week?"

"I'm planning to, yes," I replied.

"So, do you want to, you know, go together?" He actually sounded nervous, like there was some condition in the Universe under which I might say no.

"I'd like that."

And then he reached up and laid one hand against my cheek. My heart was thudding so loud, I was surprised that my mother couldn't hear it from inside the house.

Slowly, as if giving me the opportunity to change my mind, he leaned down and, just like that, his lips were on mine, soft and warm. I slid my arms around his waist, partly to be closer to him, and partly to hide how much I was trembling. He pulled his head back reluctantly and looked at me, almost like he was searching for something in my face. He must have seen what he was hoping to, because a smile spread across his face. That troublesome lock of hair fell forward into his eyes the way it so often did.

And I reached up and brushed it back, because now I could.

Chapter 14

I had one goal for the remainder of the weekend: figure out an earth-shaking Halloween costume. It wasn't like me to be a week out with no plan, but at least I had a little time to prepare. I called Treigh and begged him to come over and help. Plus, I couldn't wait to tell him about the date I'd been waiting for since 7th grade. He showed up as Mom and I were finishing lunch, and banged into the kitchen without knocking, kissing my mom on the cheek and snagging a clean spoon out of the dishwasher she was unloading as he slid into a seat at the table.

"Hi, Treigh," Mom greeted him over her shoulder. "Here for the romantic update?"

He took a scoop of mac and cheese out of my bowl. "Definitely. Spill it, sister."

I had just shoved a bite of mac into my mouth, but I gave a closed-mouth grin and blushed.

"Oh, that's promising," Treigh noted.

I swallowed and then smiled for real. "It. Was. Amazing," I breathed. "He was so sweet, and a total gentleman. We watched the game, we actually talked about stuff, we held hands, he even walked me to the front door! Did you know his family owned a ghost tour company? He's totally perfect."

"Well, well. I guess it was worth the wait, then," Treigh smiled and continued helping himself to my lunch.

"Absolutely."

"When are y'all going out again?" he asked.

"Um, Trina's party, I guess. I don't want to jinx it, but I think he had as good a time as I did."

Treigh raised his eyebrows. "Well, of course he did. You're awesome. Has he texted you yet today?"

"Well, no," I began, "but he might be sleeping in or working or something. Or maybe he doesn't want to seem too eager. I don't know. You know how boys are. No offense."

"None taken. But if he's into you, he won't wait too long." He reached over and patted my hand. "Don't worry. You'll probably hear from him while we're out today."

"Where are you off to?" Mom asked as she scooped the last of the mac into my bowl to compensate for the bits Treigh had consumed.

"I know this will come as a shock, but I have no idea what I'm wearing to Trina's costume party. I'm really at a loss. So we're going to hit the party stores and maybe even consignment shops for inspiration."

"Sounds like fun! Have a great time! Do you need any money?"

"No, I'm good. I still have some of my birthday money. Besides, you know me, I'm more likely to buy the actual costume parts at the consignment shop, so they won't cost that much."

"Alright, then, be safe! I'm driving out to a client site this afternoon, but I'll be back by six or so. Text me if you won't be back by then, okay?"

"Will do," I said as I spoon-battled Treigh for the last bite. "I should be back."

"Yes, well, just in case you hear from Romeo."

I grinned and blushed again as I got up and put my bowl and both spoons in the sink. "I'm sure he won't ask me out again for tonight," I tried to sound cool, like my emotions were under control. But they weren't, not even close. My heart was racing at the thought of it, but I didn't want to get my own hopes up. I hugged my mother and grabbed my purse. Let the hunt for the perfect costume begin.

On the drive to the party store, I gave Treigh more details about how the date had gone, and to his credit, he listened and commented on the whole thing. I think it was almost cathartic for him, since he'd heard me coo on about Alex for years. Treigh was genuinely happy for me, but his question about the text haunted me, and I kept checking my phone repeatedly, and every time I checked, there was no notification.

We wandered down the costume aisle, which had very little inventory left, to be honest. It didn't really matter, though; I was looking for an idea, not a store-bought costume. I went through every costume from Aphrodite to Zombies, but nothing was striking a chord. Nothing seemed quite right.

"Seriously, Lia? Nothing? There are, like, a hundred ideas here."

"No, nothing. None of these FEEL right, and this Halloween is important! I'm going to be at a party with Alex! I have to make a good impression!"

"Girlfriend, he's already kissed you. Impression made."

"I know," I conceded, "but I want to look awesome. Unforgettable. What are you going as?"

"The Bachelor. I'm wearing my good suit and bringing roses for all the hotties."

"That's not even a costume. You really are that smooth."

"You know it. Look, this place is a bust. Where to next?"

"Let's try St. Vincent de Paul, and if there's nothing there, we'll go to Goodwill."

"It's a plan. Let's go."

We made our way to the tidy little thrift store and I greeted the nice lady at the counter. I recognized her from prior shopping trips and she acknowledged me with a smile and a nod. Treigh and I wandered around for a few minutes, and I found my way over to a small section with previously-owned formal dresses. Most of them seemed to hail from the 80's, and didn't really inspire me, but as my hands brushed over the satins and velvets, an idea began to form in my mind.

I abandoned the dresses and began perusing the jewelry cabinet. Mostly, it was large cocktail rings and colorful pierced earrings. And then, amongst a section of truly bling-y rhinestone chandelier earrings, a pair that stood out from the rest: a pair of two-inch dangle earrings, a single vertical line of tiny clear crystals with a larger round pseudo-sapphire and the end. There was nothing about them that was my style, but for what was taking shape in my mind, they were perfect. I gave the nice lady my $7, and we were out the door.

"So, is that it, then?" Treigh asked as he looked at my tiny shopping bag.

"Yep. I already have everything else I need."

"Do I get to know what this brilliant idea is? I know every item of clothing you own. What are you planning to wear?"

"It's nothing you've seen before. My aunt gave it to me. I'm going to keep it a surprise, but I'll tell you this much: it's velvet."

"Ooooh, velvet. Alex will like that."

Alex. I hadn't checked my phone in nearly an hour. My heart rate quickened as I pulled my phone out of my pocket. Maybe I hadn't heard the ping while we'd been driving? Maybe there was no signal in the consignment shop? Or maybe I'd missed it while I was paying for the earrings? But no. The reason I hadn't heard the ping alerting me to Alex's message was that there hadn't been one.

"Maybe he had to work?" Treigh offered.

"Yeah, maybe." I smiled wanly. Or maybe he just wasn't thinking about me.

I didn't hear from him Sunday, either. Friday's elation turned to misery and doubt. My mom suggested that I should just text him, but I rejected that idea. He knew I was crazy about him. I wanted HIM to text ME. That's the only way I'd know it was mutual.

I sat by my open bedroom window, staring out at the waning moon. It would be nearly invisible by Friday's party. My eyes began to droop.

I am sitting on the beach, looking out at the ocean.

"Why the long face?" I jump, startled to find Selene sitting beside me, studying me intently.

"Oh, hi! It's nothing, really. I just didn't hear from Alex all weekend, and I don't get it. I really thought our date went well." I sigh and wrap my arms around my knees.

"I'm sure he'll be very pleased to see you tomorrow."

"Do you think so? Because I would've thought I'd have heard something this weekend, even if it was just 'hi, I'm busy, but I'm thinking of you,' you know? Just a token contact?"

She shrugs. "I wouldn't worry. He is yours." She seems so certain.

"Really? I'm glad you're so confident. It makes me feel better. I don't know how I'd handle it if I wanted him for so long only to lose him after just one date."

"You don't have to lose him. Not ever."

I turn my head slowly to look at her. She lays back and stares at the clouds moving across the night sky. I feel like there is something going on of which I am unaware.

"I don't understand," I tell her.

"We don't really ever have to lose anyone. Don't worry," she smiles, and then in a blink, she is gone.

The next morning, despite Treigh's assurances that boys were generally just inconsiderate, and that Alex's lack of communication hadn't necessarily meant anything, I approached my English class with trepidation. I wasn't sure if I should be mad at Alex, or just play it cool. As I walked into class, I scanned the room, somewhat relieved that he hadn't arrived yet. I dropped my bag on my desk, and plopped down, running several scripts in my head so I'd be prepared for anything he might say.

When he finally did walk in, he made his way to his seat, then turned his eyes my way. When he saw me, his whole face lit up into a joyful smile, as if we'd been parted for weeks instead of days. He tossed his books down and rushed toward me to get a few words in before the tardy bell.

"Hey! Wow, you look great!" He grabbed my clenched hands in his and bent to kiss my knuckles.

"Uh, hi. You too." My eloquence knows no bounds.

"Listen, what are you doing after school? Want to go for a drive?" He seemed so eager, so happy to see me. So why no text all weekend? This made no sense.

"I, uh, I don't know if I can, I mean maybe."

"Okay, well, I have to get to my seat. We'll talk about it after class, okay?" He grinned, and I was glad I was sitting, because a look like that would have crippled my knees in a second. I nodded and gave what I thought was a confused smile, but may have looked more like a grimace. He kissed my fingers again and got back to his seat just in time for the tardy bell.

WHAT. WAS. HAPPENING?

Rather than focusing on English, I spent the entire period thinking and overthinking about how I would broach the subject of why I hadn't heard from him. I was far less angry now, and far less insecure about his feelings after our date. But I was thoroughly confused, and I had to understand his actions.

I decided the direct approach was best, so when he met me after class, I punched him in the arm. "How come I didn't hear from you all weekend?"

He looked confused. "What? I...um...I don't know…"

"You don't know? Were you super busy or something?"

"Well, no, I mean, I worked and stuff but not till noon. Was I supposed to call you?"

I hadn't expected that. "I, uh, I guess you didn't say you would or anything, but I just thought you'd have texted me at some point."

He looked at me and seemed genuinely regretful. "I'm sorry I upset you. I honestly just didn't think to do it. I'm a jerk. Can you forgive me?" His eyes took on a mischievous sparkle as he asked the last part.

I sighed. "Yes, of course. But you are a jerk. I thought maybe you decided you didn't like me or something." I looked up at him with a playful pout.

"Impossible," he assured me. He slipped his arm around me as we walked toward my next class. "In fact, I spent all of last period thinking about us going to Trina's party together. As a couple. That kind of together."

And just like that, I forgot my entire weekend full of angst.

I stared at myself in the full-length mirror, pleased with the result. The deep blue velvet was form-fitting in all the right places, and flowing everywhere else. The rich tone against my fair skin made me glow like moonlight against the night sky--exactly the intended effect. The earrings from the consignment store glittered against my jawline and the crescent moon pendant, simple and silver, against my chest. Using the glamour Selene had taught me, I deepened the blackness of my hair and darkened my irises to the color of dark chocolate. I had become the Moon herself. I felt the power of the night flowing through me.

But most people would probably assume I was Morticia Addams.

I was okay with that, too.

It was a little hard to maintain that powerful feeling as I was sitting in my room waiting for Alex to come pick me up. Nerves took over as the minutes ticked by. He was late. Fifteen minutes, twenty… the post-first-date emotional roller coaster threatened to swallow me up again.

And then, from my bedroom window, I watched his car pull up in front of the house. Twenty-seven minutes late. He stepped out of his car casually, looking around my neighborhood as if he weren't entirely sure what to do next. He made his way up the front walk, and then I lost sight of him. It seemed like an eternity later when I finally heard the bell and my mom opening the door to let him in.

A short conversation that sounded quite a lot like the adults in a Charlie Brown cartoon ensued, and then Mom called up the stairs. "Lia! Alex is here!" I shook off my irritation at his tardiness and prepared for my grand entrance.

I stood at the top of the stairs and spotted him as he waited at the base of the steps. Well, sort of waited. Actually, he was staring out the etched-glass sidelight, looking back toward his car. Again I was flooded with disappointment. Why wasn't he looking sheepishly up the stairs, sorry for being late and anxiously awaiting my appearance? I had run this scene through my head a hundred times in the last 28 and a half minutes, and in no version of my fantasy was he looking out the sidelight window. Not one.

I cleared my throat meaningfully and he turned to face me as I descended. His semi-blank expression slowly turned to awe as I came into full view, his eyes widening and his mouth dropping open just a little. The look on his face at that moment erased the negativity of the moments that had led up to it.

Plus, I finally got a good look at his costume, and my heart skipped a beat. The dark slacks and white shirt were part of his normal wardrobe, I was pretty sure, but he had topped it off with a thin black cape (I had seen that exact cape as part of the vampire collection at the party store earlier) and a white mask that covered the right side of his face.

The Phantom of the Opera. Good gravy. I could barely contain my compulsion to swoon.

"I really like your costume. I love Phantom," I blurted out.

His eyes were still as big as dinner plates. "You look…like…whoa."

I grinned. "Thanks."

After an awkward moment, my mother swooped in to break the silence. "Alright, you two! Picture time!" After a few shots on both her phone and mine, my mother wished us a happy and safe party, with a directive to be home by 1:00 a.m. I hugged and air-kissed her, and then Alex ushered me to the car.

Trina's party was somewhat standard fare as high school parties went. There were maybe 30 or so guests, and the crepe paper decor was festive, but forgettable. There was a food table with the usual chips and cookies and cupcakes with spiders drawn on them with purple icing, still sitting snugly in their plastic grocery store box. There were canned sodas and a punchbowl with a gooey green drink thick with bobbing scoops of lime sherbet. I was pretty sure someone would have added an extra ingredient or two to that by now. I didn't trust it.

The costumes ranged from cartoony to gory and everything in between. Scary clowns and superheroes danced to a weird mix of hip hop, pop, rap, and country music. Peals of laughter and yelling echoed through the neighborhood. Trina's parents had set out a tent in the front yard where the adults congregated with their own stash of snacks and greeted trick-or-treaters.

We had been there maybe a half hour when Gemma swept in, a swirl of bangles and skirts, followed mutely by a grouchy-looking Scott Montgomery sporting a green tee shirt with a pillow wedged in across his shoulder blades, the Quasimodo to her sparkling Esmerelda.

"Oh, look at you two! The Phantom and Christine? Did you plan this? Alex, I thought you said yesterday that you weren't sure what you were going to be?"

Alex looked uncomfortable. "Um, yeah...it just sort of came together. But I must have been vibing off of Lia! I mean, how perfect is it that we just HAPPENED to coordinate? Must've been meant to be!" He brightened at this realization, and it was only then that I realized he hadn't actually asked me what my costume was. I loved that I blended with his costume, but he hadn't thought of me as Christine until just this moment. It was just enough that I looked pretty. I felt like I should be vaguely offended. He had also asked me out a week ago, and yet hadn't given his costume a moment's thought until today.

The imbalance in Alex's feelings nagged at the back of my mind. Every time we were together, he was focused, attentive, charming, even affectionate. But in between, I always felt like a footnote. As if reading my doubts, he stepped closer and slid his arm around me. Gemma raised a well-manicured eyebrow and fidgeted with her ring. Scott just stood there looking miserable.

"Huh. Well, that's really sweet." Her voice betrayed her. The tone was somewhere between confusion and irritation.

"OMIGOD, GEMMMAAA!" Trina came bouncing out of the kitchen in a short-skirted Cinderella costume. "You guys are so cuuuute!" Gemma turned her attention to the hostess/princess and rewarded her with a dazzling smile.

"Oh, look at you! What happens to that outfit at midnight?"

Trina giggled. "At midnight, my gown transforms into a fuzzy, footed penguin onesie and all the guests go home."

That elicited a laugh out of the group of us, and Trina grabbed Gemma's arm and dragged her back toward the kitchen. "You have to see this cake my mom baked…" Poor put-upon Scott sighed and shrugged his padded shoulders and followed after her.

"Hang in there, man," Alex called after him. "It's just one night!"

"That poor guy. I wonder how she roped him into that. He looks like he'd rather have dental surgery."

Alex chuckled. "Gemma has a way of convincing people that they should do what she wants." He paused in thought. "I guess it's probably a good thing she's a basically nice person."

"Agreed."

A commotion at the door commanded our attention. It flew open, revealing Treigh in all his glory with a designer suit and an armful of roses. A cry of greeting rose up from around the room, and he stood in the doorframe surveying the group of us.

"The party may now begin," he quipped, and began working his way through the crowd, bestowing roses on cooing girls and stoic boys. I noticed he lingered a little over the rose presentation to Michael Catellan, who smiled shyly at the attention. I made a mental note to get the scoop on that later. By the time Treigh made his way around to us, he had three roses left, two of which he handed directly to me.

"I'd give you one, Alex dear, but if you are half a man, you'd be giving it to this glorious vision of a woman anyway, so I'm just saving you a step. Lia, my queen, you take my breath away." He wiggled his finger, willing me to spin for him so he could see the full effect of my outfit. I did so, and his appreciative nod reflected genuine approval.

"You wear that suit like Ralph Lauren had you in mind all along," I said, and meant it. He really did look impressive.

"Who's to say he didn't? Thank you, darling. How's the party?"

"Better now that you're here. But it's fine. Alex and I have just sort of been making the social rounds. You should see Gemma and her date. Scott Montgomery looks like he wants to flee."

"Poor bastard. She really has him wrapped around her finger." We all laughed, and Treigh excused himself to head for the food table.

"He really is the smoothest guy in history, isn't he?" Alex observed.

"None better," I agreed, as I watched Treigh sniff at the unimpressive spread and head for the kitchen to see what other goodies Trina might be keeping hidden.

"So listen," Alex began, "I mean, the party's cool and everything, but I just had an idea. Would you maybe want to bug out of here in a few minutes and go join one of my family's ghost tours? It's bound to be quite a show tonight, and I think you'd really like it."

My heart thudded against my chest. "Are you kidding me? I'd LOVE it!"

He looked genuinely pleased. "Okay, so let's hang around another 20 minutes so we don't look like we're just ditching the party, and then we'll go catch the 10:00 tour. Is that cool?"

"Ridiculously cool. I'm so excited!"

Chapter 15

I was literally hopping with excitement as we stood outside Alex's family's ghost tour office. Living in St. Augustine, there was no way not to know the lore of various establishments in town, and Alex had regaled me with a few of the stories he knew on our very first date. I had always been fascinated by the stories, and my mom had taken me on a trolley ghost adventure tour when I turned 13, but somehow this seemed like a very different opportunity.

It was a walking tour, so I was pretty glad I had opted for ballet flats instead of the stilettos I had considered wearing. I thought I was wearing them for dancing purposes, but this was infinitely better.

We strolled down St. George's Street, and the guide talked to us about the Colombia restaurant. We turned left down Cuna, a beautiful street lined with quaint pubs and bed and breakfasts. Even though there were maybe twenty people in the tour group, I felt as though Alex and I were walking alone through the dark and tree-lined streets. There was nothing ghostly about it, really, but it was romantic.

As we made our way down Cordova and past the Tolamato Cemetery, the stories ran to murder, mayhem, and mischief, and they were really more entertaining in a macabre way than scary. We turned onto Orange and the tour guide stopped outside the St. George Inn, regaling us with stories about a body-part burial mound from an 18th century British hospital. This particular story was new to me, but I couldn't seem to focus. My attention kept wandering across the street to the Huguenot Cemetery. I couldn't stop staring at a segment of the wall near a pair of oak trees.

The trees themselves were dripping with Spanish moss, and as cemeteries went, this one looked relatively unremarkable. Still, there was something…

From behind one of the trees, I caught a flicker of movement in the moonlight…someone was behind the tree…watching. Just watching.

I couldn't explain it, but I began to have a sense of desperation. I had to know who it was that was watching us. Curiosity was the wrong word…I felt compelled. I let go of Alex's hand and bolted across Orange toward the trees. I could hear Alex calling me, but I couldn't stop, couldn't turn back.

I skidded to a stop next to the oak tree and was staring into the pale face of a girl a few years younger than I was. She stared at me with a mix of shock and fear, but she didn't move.

"Who are you?" I demanded.

She didn't answer, she just pointed at the City Gate down the street.

"Are you lost? Do you need help?"

She shook her head and began to weep silently into her hands. She raised her tear-streaked face to look at me, and pointed at the Gate again. I heard Alex's voice behind me, calling my name, and his footsteps jogging toward me. I couldn't look away from the crying girl, so clearly heartbroken and afraid.

"Let's get you somewhere safe," I said. "This city can get kind of weird at night." I reached out for her arm to guide her back to the inn, or maybe to the tour office. Alex stepped up behind me.

"Lia, what the heck...why did you run away like that?"

"Alex, this girl clearly needs help!" I glared over my shoulder at his apparent callousness in the presence of the traumatized child.

"What girl?"

"What do you mean 'what girl'? This--" I stopped mid-sentence. I was reaching out for thin air, and there was no girl to be seen. I thought to look for her, but I knew somehow that I would not find her, not even a glimpse of her white gown.

We sat on the tiny beach attached to Lighthouse Park and stared out at the Salt Run, a small inlet between St. Augustine and Conch Island. The moon was very bright and the air was thick with magic. I wasn't sure what kind of magic...moon magic or just your run-of-the-mill romantic magic. Maybe a little of both.

"That was really something tonight," Alex said, testing the waters. "You really didn't know the story about the unnamed girl buried in Huguenot Cemetery?"

"No...look, I'm really sorry if I freaked you out. Can we write it off to it being Halloween?"

"If you want. But you don't have anything to apologize for. People react to those tours differently. Most just sort of see it as simple entertainment, but to some people, it's a lot more than that. Seems you're one of those people."

"I guess. But I don't want you to think I'm some kind of weirdo." Self-consciousness was not something I often suffered from, but I wasn't sure if I was ready for Alex to know about what had been happening with me for the last few weeks.

"You can be a weirdo, as long as you're MY weirdo." He pulled me close, and I wasn't sure if the shiver I felt was the autumn cool or something much deeper. I wanted to believe this moment was real, but his hot-and-cold behavior was still pulling at the edges of my mind, filling me with doubt.

"I love that you're saying that, Alex, but what about tomorrow?"

"What do you mean? What about tomorrow?"

"I just mean that, if tomorrow runs true to form, this beautiful moment, this incredible night...well, tomorrow I won't know what it all means. Whenever we're together, you make me feel like I'm the most important person in the world. But as soon as I'm out of your sight, I'm out of your mind."

"I have no idea what you're talking about. Why would you say that?"

"Because, Alex, when we aren't together, I never hear from you. No calls, no texts, nothing."

He stiffened a little and his arm around me loosened. "Funny. I don't remember getting any calls or texts from you either." His voice was hurt, defensive.

"Well, but..." I realized I didn't have a good answer. He was right. I'd been sitting around waiting for him to reach out, not wanting to make the first move. "I guess that's fair. I can still hardly believe all of this. I guess I'm afraid I'll wake up and it won't be real."

A cool wind full of whispers blew across the beach, giving me goosebumps all over my arms. He squeezed me tight again.

"So you're scared."

"Yes, Alex, I'm scared. I've liked you for a long time, and you didn't seem to even notice me until a few weeks ago. I'm afraid I'm reading too much into things."

"I noticed you. I just didn't say anything."

This took me by surprise. "Why not?"

"I'm not sure," he shrugged. "I guess it wasn't the right time then. Now it is."

I turned to look up at him, and his eyes stared intently down at me with an expression, an intensity, that I'd never seen there before. He pulled me so close that I had to grip onto his shirt for balance, and then he kissed me with such ferocity and desperation that I struggled a little to breathe. The chilling, whispering wind whipped around us again, and Alex began to shiver violently. I pulled back, alarmed, and as I did, his eyes rolled skyward, and he fell back onto the sand. His shivering stopped and his eyes closed.

"Alex? Alex!" Panic rose up inside of me and I knelt over him, shaking his shoulders. "Alex, wake up!" I looked around me desperately, seeking help from someone...anyone...I couldn't just leave him here, but our cell phones were in the car, and I didn't know what to do. Had he had some sort of seizure? If I yelled for help, would someone hear me? I knew it wasn't likely. Fear overtook me and I began to cry. "Help! Someone help us!"

The strange breeze blew through again, warm this time, making a *sssshhhh* sound as it lifted my hair in a dark halo around my head. I felt an awareness, a familiar presence.

"Selene! Help me! Help us!"

I have, answered the wind.

"What are you talking about?" I stood, defiant and also afraid, and faced the moon. I dug my toes into the sand. "What have you DONE?"

The small lapping waves before me shuddered with the anger coursing through me. I could feel myself pulling on the power of the sea, though it was several miles distant. All at once, a powerful gust of wind sucked in water from the Salt Run and shot at me like a cannonball, knocking me flat. My head hit the sand a few inches away from Alex's, and everything went black.

I am floating above the gently lapping waves. Every thirty seconds, a powerful beam of light from the striped lighthouse passes through me, undimmed and unimpeded by my body. The pale light of the moon glows cold and distant above me.

Selene, *I plead,* what's happening? Why are you punishing me? What have I done wrong?

Clouds pass before the moon, darkening its aura for a few seconds. Foolish child, do you not see the gift I have given you?

What do you mean? What's wrong with Alex?

I feel the moon sigh. Have I not delivered to you your heart's desire? He is yours, now and forever. No other can touch him. Was this not your wish?

I don't understand. I never wanted harm to come to Alex!

No harm has come to him. He carries a moment's passion into an everlasting dream of you. There is no other in his thoughts, and never will be. He is yours forever.

I begin to weep. My fault, my fault. This is wrong! He didn't choose this. *I gesture at Alex's prone body on the beach, surprised to find that mine is still beside him. A deep-seeded fear bubbles up in me.* Oh, Selene, did he never choose me at all? Is this your doing?

No, child, *she chides me.* This is YOUR doing. It is your power and your aura that draws him into your presence. I have simply held him in that state for you. Now he will never reject you, never leave you, never forget you, never betray you.

My weeping turns to wailing. My heart shatters. It was never real. His feelings were never his own. They were nothing but moon magic. Selene, help me. Help me undo this. He doesn't deserve this! He should be...free... *I know this means my living dream is over. That lock of hair, those eyes, his lips on mine...over, all over.*

Selene does not understand my agony. She does not understand why I am not grateful. I can almost feel her shake her head at my naiveté and foolishness. I can release him from sleep, but the spell over his heart is not mine to break. It is yours, child.

I feel myself being pulled into the orb above me. Higher and higher I rise, until the light blinds me, consumes and absorbs me. I explode outward, becoming tiny raindrops of light.

I lay on the sand, eyes closed, as I felt the first icy drops hit my skin. I sat bolt upright in alarm. "Alex!" I turned toward him, half in fear, half in pain. He groaned and rolled on his side before pushing himself up into a sitting position.

"What the actual hell..." He looked around as if he had no idea where he was or how he got here. "Lia? Did I fall asleep?"

I choked back tears of relief and regret. "Yeah, yeah, I think we both did. We... should probably head back home. I have no idea what time it is."

"Home...yeah..." He shook his head as though trying to clear the cobwebs in his mind, and slowly stood up. "Aw, man, it's starting to rain..."

I nodded mutely, hoping the raindrops would provide good camouflage.

He reached down to where I still sat, offering me a hand up. "Dang...we'd better get to the car before your dress is totally ruined. It's already covered in sand."

I accepted his outstretched hand and stood, brushing what particles I could out of the velvet. "Are you...okay?" I asked.

"Huh? Yeah, I guess so. I don't even remember being tired. I can't believe I fell asleep. I'm okay, I just feel...weird. Like when you wake up from a really long nap, you know? And then you're kind of screwed up afterwards?"

I nodded and snatched my shoes up out of the sand. We walked back to the car in silence, the beam from the lighthouse mocking me as it passed above our heads.

Thankfully, the next day was Saturday. I had no desire to get out of bed for the entire weekend, honestly. The ride home the night before had consisted of small talk about the party and another apology for falling asleep on the beach. There was no mention of the kiss, no mention of what had happened during the ghost tour, no mention of "us". I was broken-hearted to think that any romance that had existed between Alex and me was the result of some hinky accidental magic. It explained a lot, really, especially the difference in how he had been in my presence versus when we were apart.

My phone had buzzed half a dozen times by 11 a.m., but I couldn't bring myself to check it, couldn't bear to look, knowing there would be nothing from him. I didn't even want to look at my phone to play music, because then I would feel responsible to respond to any messages that had come in. At least this way, I could honestly say I hadn't gotten them.

At 11:15, my mother came and tapped at my door, cracking it open. I mumbled something barely coherent and sunk deeper into my comforter.

"Honey, are you okay?" Mom asked. "It's not like you to lay in bed so late."

"I...just don't feel too good, Mom. I'll be okay."

"Are you hung over?" She was careful with her tone, wanting me to be honest, but also potentially disappointed in me.

"No, Mom...I just...I don't really want to talk about it, but I think Alex and I might have broken up last night. Like I'm pretty sure we did. I just want to lie here and be miserable."

"Oh, baby, I'm sorry," She came over and kissed my forehead, which was the only part of my body actually visible amidst the covers. I'm going to the grocery store and some other errands. I'll bring you some cookie dough on the way home, and tonight we'll watch a stupid movie and eat a variety of bad-for-us crap for dinner.

"Thanks, Mom, you're the best."

"I know. Boys suck."

"Boys suck."

"Can I bring you up something to eat or drink before I go?"

"Just a drink, please; I don't feel like eating."

She kissed me again, delivered not one drink, but three, and then she was gone.

Around 12:30, I finally steeled myself and reached for my phone. As I'd expected (but hoped I was wrong), I had no messages from Alex. Three of the six messages were from Treigh, and the other three were social media alerts.

Hey girl what happened 2u last nite?

Did u and alex run off 2 somewhere romantic?
Text me when u wake up.
I groaned and texted back.
Sorry I didn't say bye. We went on ghost tour. Started out great...went all wrong. I think we broke up. I don't really want to talk about it yet. I'll text later I promise. Xoxo

I knew full well that Treigh wouldn't be able to survive without the full story for long, but I hoped this would buy me an hour or two. I was going to need a lot of strength for that conversation.

I dragged myself across the room and looked out the window. It didn't seem fair for it to be such a nice day when I felt so incredibly sad and bereft. Pulling on some ratty sweatpants and a clean tee shirt, I resolved to try and "walk it off" before talking to Treigh. I trudged downstairs and out the front door, locking it behind me. This was definitely an expensive coffee day.

I shuffled down the residential street and toward San Marco Avenue and my favorite hole-in-the-wall coffee shop. There were a few people outside, and a few cars parked along the road. I felt oddly uneasy, a strange prickling at the back of my neck, and I quickened my shuffle to a brisk walk. I turned out of the neighborhood and cut through a hotel parking lot, heading to the familiar red door of Dotz, home of caffeinated goodness. I got myself a latte and thanked the trainee manning the register. The place was surprisingly empty for early afternoon, and I was able to snag a seat in the retro-style chairs in the back.

As I sipped my coffee, an unusually well-dressed couple walked into the place. It was clear they'd never been here before, because they seemed at a loss about how to order. Dotz is run as an occupational training site for the visually impaired, and so it works a little differently than your major coffee chain. The couple looked genuinely confused as they stared at the Keurig machine on the shelf across from the door. The girl who had helped me at the register approached them and assisted them with their order. After a couple of minutes, they were situated with coffees and pastries at a table by the entrance. I had watched the entire scene unfold with somewhat detached interest, and now I observed the couple from my dark and oversized seat.

Even though they were only a few feet away from me (Dotz isn't very big), they leaned over their drinks and spoke in such hushed tones that I couldn't make out anything they were saying. They seemed to be aware that I was watching them, too, because they kept casting furtive glances in my direction. I was suddenly self conscious and a little embarrassed, so I got up and made my way toward the door, exchanging goodbyes with the cashier on my way out. As I passed them, the couple fell into complete silence. The door clicked shut behind me, and I could feel their eyes on me through the large shop window as I made my way back across the parking lot and toward home.

Still a little unnerved by the attention of the strangers, I thought it might be a good idea to call Treigh on my walk home.

"Oh, my Jesus, girl. How could you drop a bomb like that and then wait this long to call me? I have absolutely dying for the tea. First of all, whatever happened, I'm on your side, and I am prepared to go nuclear-level petty on this man."

"And I love you for that," I began, "but it's not necessary. It turns out that the reason he couldn't ever seem to be bothered to call or text me was that I may have unintentionally put him under a spell."

A pause. "Say what now?"

"Um, yeah…" I told him the whole story from the beginning, starting from our departure from the party to the ghost tour, to the passionate kiss on the beach which led to a near-coma and a close encounter with the goddess.

"I didn't think it was possible for me to be at a loss for words, but here I am," he said when I finished the whole roller coaster-y tale.

"And now I'm all weird and paranoid, apparently. I walked to Dotz for coffee, and managed to convince myself that this couple was stalking me. I'm a hot mess." I arrived back home and let myself in.

"Do you want me to come over?" he offered.

"If I'm totally honest, Treigh, I really just want to crawl into bed and blast H.I.M. through my earbuds and pretend this world doesn't exist. I'm walking a line between being mortified and being miserable, and I'm crappy company."

"You never need to put on a face for me, Lia. But if you really just want to be by yourself, just remember that I'm one text away. I'll drop whatever I'm doing and come eat all the junk food your mom is bringing home."

That pulled a smile out of me. "You're a real pal."

"Aren't I, though?"

"All right, I'm gonna go be morose now. I love you."

"Love you too, my gothic goddess. Text me later so I know you're doing okay."

"I will. Bye, Treigh."

I made my way back upstairs, and forced myself to take a quick shower before burrowing back under the covers with my vampire music. My mom got home a couple of hours later, heavily laden with Cheetos, Ben & Jerry's, and an unreasonably large tub of Nutella. Two thousand calories and an Adam Sandler movie later, I was still sad, but I had reached a level of acceptance about the entire situation involving Alex.

What I wasn't at peace about was how my new abilities had manifested themselves without any intention on my part. I had to learn to control it better, and the only one who could really help me with that was Aunt Kitty. I needed to talk to her and find out what she could tell me about Selene and all the side effects that came with ownership of the Moon card.

Chapter 16

I used the excuse of having to return the grimoire as a way of justifying my sudden trip to visit my great aunt. Mom hastily agreed; I think she really wanted it out of the house. She seemed confused as to why I wanted to go alone, but agreed, making me promise to call when I arrived and when I was leaving to head home.

I pulled into the gravel driveway to find Aunt Kitty singing to her herb garden as she pruned the bushes. She greeted me effusively.

"I'm thrilled to see you, dear, but I hope this doesn't mean that your newfound powers have caused any harm?"

I hugged her. "I guess it depends on what you mean by harm," I replied. "I feel like there's so much I don't know, and I'm afraid of what I may be doing accidentally."

"Come on in, honey. I'm glad you came to talk to me about it." We went inside and sat in the front room with all the random tchotchkes. "Now, what's been happening?"

Even summarizing the last couple of weeks took me nearly ten minutes. When I finished, her face was calm, but stern.

"It's really dangerous to let you go on without proper training, I think. But it would strike your mother as incredibly odd if suddenly I was showing up at your house every week."

"Did you have all this same stuff happen to you? How did you deal?"

"Well, I was older, for one, so it was a little different. And I also had some training, so I was better prepared. It's time you had the same. Let's start at the beginning. Let's list every phenomenon you've experienced so far."

"Well, it started with telekinesis…"

"Wrong. It started with channeling moon energy."

"What?"

"The night of the play. I tried to tell myself it was some special effect that you rigged up, but when you drew down the moon, I think you actually drew it into yourself. That's why you glowed."

"Wait, what? Shouldn't it have been drawn into the card?"

"No, Lia, the card doesn't draw IN moon energy, it RADIATES it. The card is tied to Selene herself. When you cast that spell, the combination of life energy from your blood and moon energy from the card drew power from Selene directly into YOU."

"So what's the consequence of that?"

"I can't say. I never did that. But binding yourself directly to the goddess likely amplified whatever natural power our bloodline already carries. So everything you do will be stronger, and since you are bound to her, the stronger you are, the stronger she becomes. Theoretically."

I stared at my aunt. I didn't know what to say to that.

"So the next power you manifested, then, was the ability to communicate directly with Selene. That makes sense, and she will probably want to keep that bond, so that's why you've heard from her regularly. Then came the telekinesis, the glamour, and the ability to influence the feelings of others. These abilities are filled with temptations as well as dangers."

"So tell me what to do? How do I start learning to control it?" The desperation in my voice was growing.

"You're going to need to learn to meditate and visualize, I think. I agree that control is priority one; but then you'll need to learn how to deal with these powers emotionally, and most importantly, ethically."

Aunt Kitty gathered a few items from the house; a cup of water, a bowl of salt, incense, and a candle, and led us through the sliding glass doors and into the private garden in the back of the house. I hadn't been out here much, not at all in the last few years, but now I was looking at it with fresh eyes.

Neatly swept earthen paths were arranged like eight spokes off of a central point. The paths were dotted with white and gray gravel, labeling the cardinal directions. The center was an elaborately decorated birdbath filled with hand-painted stones. The stones themselves were colorful and exotic: mandalas and celestial symbols and runes. Aunt Kitty arranged the items carefully and deliberately amongst the colorful rocks. An altar. This was an altar. The revelation shocked me for some reason. She sat on one side of the spoke representing the direction of east, and indicated that I should sit beside her on the other side of the line.

"Close your eyes and breathe deeply, Lia. Smell the sandalwood? Focus on that scent. I want you to imagine the tendrils of air rising up from the earth, up through your feet and legs, up through your torso, spreading out through your arms, and finally filling your lungs and head. Then, when you exhale, I want you to imagine that air moving in the opposite direction, all the way from the top of your head, back down into the earth. Repeat that slowly for five breaths."

I followed her directions as well as I could, but even for this short period of time, I found it hard not to be distracted. I thought of Alex, of Treigh, even of Gemma. I wondered what Selene expected of me, and what her endgame was. I wondered what abilities would show themselves next, and who would suffer for my lack of control.

"Just breathe, Lia," my aunt instructed. "I can feel your tension, your worry. Push those thoughts away as you exhale. Watch them float away like smoke. Five more breaths; calm yourself."

I tried to focus on the air, just like she told me, and at first, I was frustrated. But as I slowed my breathing to really picture the air moving in and out, I found that I felt each part of my body more acutely, and yet in a detached way. I was aware of my feet, my knees, but with each breath, I actually felt them less. Occasionally, a breeze would caress my skin, but then that sensation would be gone and there was only the air moving in and out of my body.

"Good girl. Now listen to the sound of my voice. I want you to imagine yourself standing in your bedroom. Can you do that?"

"Yes."

"Good. On your bed are several boxes. Each one of them is labeled with one of the gifts Selene has awakened in you. What is the first box you see?"

In my mind, I picked up a white shoebox off my bed. "It's labeled ghosts."

"Excellent," Aunt Kitty continued. "Do you need the contents of this box right now? Do you need to perceive those on the other side?"

"No, not right now."

"Good then. I want you to take a good look at the box lid. Make sure it's closed."

"It's closed."

"There's a padlock on the front. Lock it up for now."

"It's locked now."

"Well done. Now let's look at the others."

We followed that same routine for several other boxes in my mind. Boxes labeled telekinesis, ghosts, and influence were securely locked, while glamour, dreams, and perception had lids on them, but did not need to be locked.

"You can lock and unlock these boxes and move them around at your will. They are yours to use as you see fit," she said. "But what you do with them is now a conscious choice. You will also need to check them several times a day to make sure the locks and lids are not popping open on accident. Last thing, I want you to imagine yourself putting all these boxes, one by one, on a shelf in your closet."

When I finished my mental task of putting away my ability boxes, my aunt instructed me to open my eyes. I was surprised to find that nearly an hour had passed.

"Now, Lia," my aunt said, taking my hand, "this exercise in mental discipline is basic but effective. It does, though, require maintenance. You will not only need to check the locks and lids of the boxes, you will need to, in moments of quiet meditation, take them down one at a time and study them. You will need to consider the contents of each, and how you want to arrange them. Imagine yourself writing a card of rules for each and placing it inside to remind you that just because you CAN do something doesn't always mean you SHOULD."

I nodded, feeling overwhelmed, but more in control.

Chapter 17

Monday was an emotional stew. I seriously considered skipping English so I wouldn't have to face Alex. What would he have told people about us? He smiled and said hello to me in English, but he sat across the room and didn't wait for me when class was over. I took that as a pretty negative sign overall.

Not that I could blame him, really. He probably couldn't even figure out how he felt about me, now that I wasn't influencing him. The memories of those feelings would still be there, though, and if I were him, I'd be very confused about how I could be full of feelings for someone one minute, kissing her like she was going off to war, and then feel almost entirely neutral suddenly and without warning. Who would want that?

Gemma and Trina seemed pretty much oblivious to the entire thing. There was no discernible difference in their behavior toward me, and believe me, I was looking. I had to conclude that Alex hadn't shared any of our drama with them. Yet another point in his favor. Somehow that made me feel even worse.

Treigh kept tiptoeing around me, offering words of validation and support, but I really just wanted to forget the whole thing. If I couldn't recapture the magic between Alex and me without using...well...magic, then I had to learn to let it go. If he didn't feel anything for me without my influence, then it wasn't meant to be. That didn't make it suck any less, though.

At the end of the school day, it started raining. I made my way to my car at the far end of the parking lot. By the time I got there, I was absolutely drenched. Even with the distracting effect of the rain, though, something felt...off. I had that prickling feeling again...the one I had felt Saturday afternoon at the coffee shop. I let myself into my car quickly and locked the doors, looking around the parking lot for anything out of the ordinary. I didn't really see anything that struck me as unusual, other than a couple dozen teenagers dodging raindrops as they ran to their vehicles, so I carefully backed out of my spot and headed out the gate.

I sat at a stop sign, preparing to turn onto Lewis Speedway, and stared across the street at the houses. One of the funny things you'll see in coastal towns are these houses that have downstairs carports with an exterior stairway leading to the residence on the second floor. I'd always thought that was a weird design, because why wouldn't you just make an interior stairway so that you wouldn't have to climb the stairs in torrential rain? I mean, what if you had groceries? It really was stupid to build a house that way.

I inched slowly up the line as I prepared to hang a right, and I noticed that one of the houses had a very nice black Range Rover parked in one of the carports. Two people sat in the front seat. I couldn't see their faces, but I imagined them sitting there, cursing the rain and the idiocy of the architect who thought exterior stairs were a good idea. The thought amused me, and I smiled in spite of my crappy mood.

I finally made the turn, and internally grumbled at the traffic all the way home. Granted, it wasn't a far drive, 15 minutes in good traffic. But early afternoon traffic generally meant I could nearly double that. My phone buzzed repeatedly in the cup holder, but I decided that with the combination of the rain and the traffic, I'd better wait until I got home to check who was trying to reach me. I was pretty sure who it WASN'T, and that made me care a little bit less about who it actually WAS.

When I finally pulled into the driveway, I checked my phone and found texts from Trina asking if I had brought the English handout home, and could I please send her a photo of it? With a rather melodramatic sigh, I reached into the back seat where I had tossed my bag. From this twisted vantage point, I spotted a car driving slowly down my street. That in itself wasn't all that unusual, but none of my neighbors owned a black Range Rover.

The prickling on my neck made sense now, and I felt a rush of adrenaline. There was no way it was a coincidence. I jerked my bag out of the back seat and bolted into the house as quickly as I could manage. Usually, I loved being alone in the house in the couple of hours before my mom got home, but today, I really didn't want to be alone. There was no question in my mind that the couple from the coffee shop owned the silhouettes I'd spotted in the fancy SUV, and that meant I was being watched. Stalked, even.

I checked every lock on every door, set the alarm, and then parked myself by my window to watch the street. I tried calling my mother to see if she could come home early, but I got her voicemail. I didn't leave a message, because I didn't know what to say. The next number I called was my aunt. She picked up on the third ring.

"Aunt Kitty, remember when you asked me if anyone had followed me, or approached me about the card?"

"Lia, what's happened? Are you safe?"

"Yes, I mean, I think so. I think there is a couple following me. There were these two people maybe watching me at Dotz the other day, and now there's this black SUV that I've spotted a couple of times today. I'm pretty sure it's them. But I'm locked in the house and the alarm is on."

"Is there someone who can come over and sit with you until your mother gets home? It would take me over an hour to get to you."

"Yeah, I can call my friend to come over, I think."

"Do it," she said. "And I want you to call me back right after."

"Okay." I was unnerved at the seriousness of her tone. I hung up and called Treigh, and but got his voicemail.

I called my aunt back. "Treigh didn't answer."

"Okay, listen, I think you should go someplace very public. Someplace where you can sit for a little while, someplace that will probably be busy. They probably won't approach you if you aren't alone."

"Who are THEY?"

"I can't be sure, but I would bet they are associated with at least one of the other Tarot cards. No doubt they want to see what kind of person you are, and if you'd be likely to align with whichever faction they represent. I don't think you're in any danger, but I don't like that they are being so sneaky about talking to you. It doesn't bode well for their intentions."

"Like maybe bringing the cards together?"

"Maybe. I've been out of circulation for a long time, so I don't really know their game anymore. I just know that several of the families had ambitions that ran counter to the beliefs I held, and they didn't really take kindly to my refusal to support them."

"Is that why you buried the card?"

"Like I told you, part of it was that, and part of it was that I didn't want the temptation of the power. It not only made me a target to the factions, but power like that makes shortcuts to getting what you want awfully attractive. And sometimes shortcuts have a price. Sometimes people get hurt."

I felt like I shouldn't press the point, but it sounded like there was some deep history of which I was not aware. Something pretty bad must have happened if she had felt the need to turn away from the deep connection with her goddess that the card offered.

"Lia, is there someplace you could go? Maybe where there would be tourists or something that would be crowded?"

"Well, I could go to Dunkin. It's really close to the Fountain of Youth and stuff, and with the rain, there are probably a lot of people looking for coffee or doughnuts."

"Good. Go there. Don't come home until your Mom is done with work. I'll head over that way as well, but it will take me a little while. Check in with me every twenty minutes, okay?"

'Okay, Aunt Kitty. Thanks. I'll go now."

Fifteen minutes later, I was nibbling on a chocolate cake doughnut in a tourist-filled Dunkin Donuts. I had taken a table in the middle, facing the door.

I heard a tinkling sound behind me and realized that I had forgotten about the side door near the bathrooms. The prickling feeling that had been plaguing me on-and-off for days fired up again. I swiveled my head toward the sound and spotted two now-familiar faces coming toward me. My heart thudded in my chest.

"Hello, Lia. I think it's about time we introduced ourselves. I'm Claudia, and this is my brother John. John, be a dear and get me some coffee, will you?" John nodded mutely and walked to the counter.

"Why are you following me?" I demanded.

"You're very direct," Claudia said, studying me. "I like that. I shall return the courtesy. By now, I'm sure you have discovered certain...changes...in your life. Specifically since coming into possession of a certain card. A depiction of the Moon, I believe."

I didn't respond; I didn't trust myself to avoid saying something stupid.

"This must all be very new to you," she offered.

"Well, yes..."

"And we would like to offer to assist in your training. I take it you did not have evident abilities prior to the Awakening of the card?"

"I'm not really sure I should be discussing this with you. I don't even know you."

She raised a perfectly-shaped eyebrow and smiled. I couldn't imagine what was so amusing, but it rather annoyed me.

"I'm pleased to see that you have so much sense, Lia," she said, covering my hand with her own. "I do hope that we can build some sort of trust between us. It is an exciting and important time for you, and proper training is so important, don't you agree?"

She seemed to be making so much sense. "Yes, very important. But why all the cloak and dagger stuff?"

"Oh, I do apologize about that." Her voice was soothing, calming, like hot chocolate. "We weren't sure if it was safe to approach you. You see, my brother and I felt the power building in this area and set out to find its source, which led us to you. Surely your family has told you that you are not the only person who has a card of power?"

"I know there are others, yes," I responded carefully.

"Ah, good then. The Moon has been off the grid for quite some time, it seems. It's nice to know that is has not been lost somehow. At any rate, John and I have come to offer our assistance and guidance, as it appears this is all very new to you. With great power comes great responsibility and all that." Her brother arrived at the table with her coffee, and they both sat down.

"How kind of you," I responded. Why was I feeling so calm? Just minutes ago, I was terrified. And now, here we were, talking like we were old friends. "But I have someone who can train me."

"I'm sure you think so, dear, but I assume you are referring to your aunt? Lovely woman, but she is quite out of practice, I should think. The card has been inactive for what, two decades? No, I doubt she is prepared to properly train you for the deep magic that is to come."

"Deep magic? What?" I was so enthralled by her voice. She seemed so very wise. She might be right...Aunt Kitty herself had told me that she hadn't practiced any major magic in years.

"The time has come for those of us in possession of the Cards of Power to unite and help undo some of the messes the ordinary humans have made."

That sounded like it was important. Alarming, even, but I couldn't bring myself to feel much of anything. I looked down at where her hand still held mine. Why would I allow a stranger to hold my hand? Blinking hard, I pulled my hand back and reached up to tuck my hair behind my ear. Instantly, my heart rate started climbing. She had been doing something to me! Trying to influence me the way I had accidentally influenced Alex. Fear melted away and was replaced by anger, but I also knew it was important to tread carefully.

"You're talking about uniting the cards. I'm not really sure that's a good idea," I said, trying not to reveal how little I actually knew about the different factions arguing about how the cards and their powers should be used.

"I don't think you understand what's at stake here," Claudia pulled her hand back with poorly-concealed disappointment. She stirred cream into her coffee slowly. "We aren't talking about you and your little life, my girl. We are talking about changing the world. This world is a disaster, wouldn't you agree?"

"Well, generally, yes, but..."

"Exactly. And that is precisely because people like us, people who truly understand the connectedness of all things and the true elemental powers of the Universe, we're powerless to use what we know on a large scale. Less evolved creatures like these," she waved at the news report on television mounted in the corner of the room, "are the ones with the power to make policy and decisions. It's a tragedy."

I didn't really know what to say to that. She wasn't wrong. I probably wouldn't have used the term *less evolved*, but I got her point. Even without her trying to use her magic on me, there was a certain amount of logic to her argument.

"Imagine," she continued, "what we could all do together as a united force! We could right the ship of this world's foolishness. We could help the environment, we could make people see reason and behave better. We could be the politicians making decisions and policies instead of these egomaniacs who don't understand how things really work. We could CHANGE things."

"So if we can find all of the cards, reunite the Major Arcana, that would do what, exactly?" She was very persuasive, but she was leaving things out, I could tell.

"Ah, that's the question, isn't it? Bringing all the forces those cards and the families who hold them represent together would change the fabric of reality. It's our belief that magic would be released into the world on a massive scale, and those descendants of the Major families would be awakened to their rightful place in history. Change, glorious change. Creating a better world for everyone, not just ourselves."

"But...what if all those families don't share the same vision?" If things seem too good to be true, they probably are. This definitely fit into that category.

"That's why there are so many families. Diversity. Those individuals, magical or otherwise, who don't share the vision can either be persuaded, brought into line, or removed from power and contained as long as necessary. We wouldn't want anyone using the power with ill intent, of course."

"You said we could change how people act. What about free will?"

"Free will is a luxury not everyone deserves. There are people out there who stubbornly cling to ideas which are not good for the world as a whole. We can bring harmony. Peace. A world where people take care of each other and the earth instead of being ruled by material greed. If we unite, they won't even be aware that changing their minds wasn't their own idea."

The end result sounded good, but I had learned a little something about messing with free will. "I just am not sure if taking away people's free will is right. It doesn't seem right."

"What if we could have taken away Hitler's free will? How many people would be alive now?"

"Yeah, but…"

"Listen to me, Lia," she said quietly. She sipped her coffee and licked her lips. "You are a reasonable and rational person. You can see the good in the future I'm describing, I know you can."

"I do. I really do. But I'm not sure the ends justify the means."

"You'll come around. In time." She was still smiling as her eyes met mine, and though her voice was still pleasant and friendly, her eyes were cold and determined. She stood, squeezing my shoulder with alarming strength as she walked past me, followed by her silent brother.

    I didn't turn around until I heard the jingle bell on the door handle tinkling.

Chapter 18

It took me another 15 minutes before I felt calm enough to make the relatively short drive home. There was so much I didn't know, and I felt completely out of my depth. These factions seemed to have a long history, maybe even a rivalry, maybe worse. And I felt like it was only a matter of time before the magical sharks started circling.

I was disturbed at how easy it had been for Claudia to manipulate me, just by touching my hand. I was enraged that she would even try. And I was afraid of what else she could do if she felt like I was in opposition to her point of view. And what if she was only the first? What if other people came to find me, too? How could I ever trust what any of these people said? I was desperately hoping Aunt Kitty would have answers to some of my questions.

I texted her as soon as I pulled into the driveway to tell her I was safe, and to come to the house instead of the cafe. I imagined she was less than twenty minutes away by this time, so hopefully she'd come to a stop light and check the message.

I went upstairs, put on my softest pajamas, and wrapped myself in the fluffiest afghan I could find in the linen closet. For some reason, surrounding myself with softness seemed awfully important. Mom got home before Aunt Kitty arrived, and came in to find me on the couch, a fluffy burrito.

"Bad day?"

I nodded.

She set down her purse and came to sit beside me. "What do you need?"

"I don't even know, Mom. It's been a heck of a day. Oh, and Aunt Kitty will be here any minute."

"Aunt Kitty? Did she call?"

"Well, I kind of called her."

I felt my mother stiffen in alarm. "Lia, is there something going on that I should know about?"

"Probably. Can we wait till she gets here to talk about it? I'm feeling a little overwhelmed right now."

"I was afraid this would happen. It's starting all over again. I knew I shouldn't have told you about her being a witch, but I wanted to help you with your play…" I couldn't tell if she felt guilty or angry. Maybe both. I wasn't sure how to respond, but I was saved from the necessity by a knock at the door.

My mother got up and whipped the door open. She stared at Aunt Kitty, and I could tell she wasn't sure how she should feel.

"Before you get too upset with me," my aunt began, "you should know that this came completely out of the blue. Lia didn't go looking for it, and I didn't encourage her. The magic found her, not the other way around."

Mom was too emotional to find words, so she just opened the door wider and waved in my direction. My aunt came in and was visibly relieved to find me safe and sound. We all hung there in an uncomfortable silence.

"Well," my mother said at last, "I guess I'd better get the ice cream. I think it's going to be a long night."

About an hour into the conversation, I felt like my head was going to explode. I had heard of tarot cards, of course. But here I was in a crash course about the Major Arcana, their meanings, their reverse meanings, their positions on the Tree of Life... my brain was seriously turning to tapioca.

"Okay, so, I get what the meanings of all the cards are, but how does that align with this specific set of cards?" I asked.

Aunt Kitty had spread a colorful set of cards out on the coffee table, with the 21 Major Arcana cards lying in numerical order. "Let's start with the one we know," she began, "the Moon. Each card, as we've discussed, is bound to a specific deity energy. This one is bound to the energy known as Selene."

"What do you mean, 'the energy known as Selene?' Is that like 'the artist formerly known as Prince?'" Mom was trying to be funny, but the anachronistic joke elicited little more than groans.

"Deities are thought of as separate entities, but truly they are something beyond our understanding. They are manifestations of a very specific combination of energies, which each represent a different facet of the divine in the Universe. Humans have only a limited understanding of other planes of existence, and so deities are one way of relating to the Universe as a whole in convenient snippets, if you will."

"Uhhhh..." I groaned, rubbing my temples.

"I know, it's a lot to try and wrap your head around. But Selene represents one interpretation of divine energy."

"So why does she seem to have her own personality, with sort of human-like qualities?"

"Because our energy, those of us who perceive and believe in Selene, adds to hers, making her aspect stronger. Because our belief, our attention, feeds her strength, she also takes on some human characteristics and often appears to us in human form. It's a symbiotic relationship, really, because she gives us energy in the form of abilities and powers, and we give her energy in the form of faith."

"Okay, so it is beneficial to everyone, right?"

"Ideally, yes. As long as it stays in balance. And Selene represents, as I said, a very specific facet of divine energy, so the abilities and powers she can share are closely tied to what she herself represents. The card and its meaning are a depiction of that.

"The Moon as a tarot card communicates the balance between illusion and faith. If you got the card in a reading, it would be warning you about something being false or misleading. It would be a reminder to trust your intuition rather than what appears to be true. The Moon is also tied to the tides and the Earth's pull on us. Those are the powers Selene can share."

"So that's why Alex was influenced by what I wanted, even though I didn't mean to?"

"Exactly. Your force of will can influence, though not fully control, others' opinions, particularly if they are already inclined to be in agreement or if they are neutral. Selene is mistress of illusion as well, and as such, her strongest skill is that of glamour. She can give you the ability to make yourself, or other parts of reality, to be different than they really are. You've already learned some simple applications of that, I think, but the possibilities for someone skilled at illusion creation are quite complex indeed. That skill, in the wrong hands, could be unbelievably dangerous."

"If someone got really good at it," Mom wondered aloud, "she could literally make people believe almost anything was real. Cause them to do things or make decisions based on a false reality." The implications began to sink in, and I was having trouble processing the kind of responsibility that kind of power would carry with it.

"No wonder those two people wanted to try and snatch me up and 'help' with my training!"

"Just so. I don't know who the players are anymore, because it all got too much for me years ago. I just wanted a simple life."

"How many of the others have you met?" I asked.

"Four in total. I had a brief meeting with the holder of The Fool card about thirty years ago, I knew the couple who held The Lovers card and a man who held the Hermit, and for a time, I was good friends with the woman who held The Empress. She was quite a bit older than I was, and looked out for me while I learned to navigate my way through an understanding of my abilities. Usually the card holders refer to each other by the name of the card rather than given names. I think it's a way of trying to create some sense of anonymity."

"Are you still in touch with any of them?"

"No, I'm afraid not. When I buried that card years ago, I cut off all contact with the other holders."

"Even the Empress?"

Aunt Kitty's eyes were far away with regret. "That one was hard. She was a very dear friend, and I owed her quite a lot. But it was actually her suggestion, to keep me safe. If I wanted to distance myself from some of what the Arcana were doing, I had to distance myself from all of it. There was no in-between."

"What was so bad that you had to cut it all off like that?" My mother asked, her eyes filled with concern, and maybe also a little guilt, because it appeared that her sister had been through something pretty traumatic, and had had to go it alone.

"It's not so much that it was bad," my aunt replied, giving my mother's hand a comforting pat. "It's just that it was constant. There was no day off. And that's not the life I wanted to live."

"Is that what I should do?" I asked.

"I can't tell you what you should do, Lia. No one can, when it comes to this. Not only does it have to be your decision, it has to be one you believe in with your whole heart. If you made a decision because you thought it was what someone else wanted you to do, the card would just keep finding its way back to you. I'm pretty sure of that."

"I feel like I have very little actual information about what these people want. I don't know how I feel about what they were saying...I mean, my gut tells me I shouldn't interfere with other people's decisions, but I can also see situations in which it might be good to push someone to make the right choice. I don't know if their goals were really noble or not; I only know that I didn't like the way they made me feel."

"Sometimes that's the very best guide, Lia. You have always had good instincts about right and wrong, but Selene's presence in your life enhances that skill. Still, you're right about needing more information about what is going on. I am quite sure that Claudia and her brother are only the first people to find you. We need to find out what card they represent. And maybe I can reach out through my old connections to see if I can find out what their true agenda is."

"Do you think Lia is in any danger?"

"No, I suspect not, Maddy. The house is pretty well warded, and even if one of the other Arcana came looking for her, they would be far more interested in recruiting her allegiance than they would in hurting her."

"What do you mean, the house is warded?" Mom asked.

"Oh, I've been casting protection spells on this house since the day you moved in," my aunt said casually, winking. "I've got to take care of my family."

Chapter 19

I debated with myself about whether I should tell Treigh about everything I'd been learning about the Arcana factions and their potential designs on me, and the temptation to share everything was really strong. It occurred to me, though, that I'd probably be putting him in danger. He might be tempted to confront people who seemed to be threatening or watching me, and I also didn't want him worrying about something he couldn't prevent or protect me from. So against my inclinations, I kept my mouth shut about the whole thing.

But I had to do something. I couldn't just sit around waiting for the next card to drop, so to speak. So I got a library pass from Mrs. West and decided to" kick it old school" and check out a book or two. Surprisingly, our library did have a couple of books on my subject of choice: the tarot. I found that the interpretations of various cards seemed to vary a little bit, depending on which deck you were using, and it was clear that the tarot which most concerned me wasn't going to be found in any high school library. While there was some variation in both the card names and their meanings, there were always certain elements of each card that were the same. I scribbled notes in my journal:

0. The Fool (innocence, vulnerability, openness, recklessness)
I. The Magician (power, strength of will, control)
II. The High Priestess (intuition, wisdom, creativity, independence)
III. The Empress (abundance, nature, compassion, creation)
IV. The Emperor (authority, structure, reason, discipline)
V. The Hierophant (wisdom, tradition, rules)
VI. The Lovers (relationships, values, choices, harmony)
VII. The Chariot (determination, victory, honor, control)
VIII. Strength (courage, fortitude, persuasion)
IX. The Hermit (introspection, solitude, independence, enlightenment)
X. The Wheel of Fortune (luck, karma, destiny, chance)
XI. Justice (fairness, truth, karma, judgement)
XII. The Hanged Man (limbo, letting go, change)
XIII. Death (transition, transformation, endings, renewal)
XIV. Temperance (balance, patience, moderation, self-control)
XV. The Devil (temptation, loss of control, feelings of hopelessness, greed)
XVI. The Tower (upheaval, inevitable change, chaos)
XVII. The Star (faith, healing, hope, inspiration)

XVIII.	The Moon (illusion, intuition, emotion, subconscious)
XIX.	The Sun (joy, vitality, freedom, optimism)
XX.	Judgement (accountability, absolution, realism, correctness)
XXI.	The World (accomplishment, fulfillment, completion, liberation)

If the abilities and attitudes of the card-holders mirrored the cards themselves, this might give me some idea of what each of the people involved believed in and stood for. Knowing which card someone held might give me an idea of their agenda.

I was stirred from my concentration by a *thunk* of a bag hitting the table next to the stack of books I'd been poring through.

"Hey, girl, you inspired me. I couldn't stand sitting in that class today. Usually West is cool, but today, all I wanted to do was escape!" Gemma slid into the seat across from me. "Whatcha reading?" She started rifling through the tarot books and then looked at me with a mix of confusion and amusement.

"Well, um, I don't know, you know how I like sort of witchy stuff...I was thinking I might learn to read cards. That probably seems pretty weird." Truthfully, I'd never been more grateful for my stereotype than I was right at this moment. Goth chick and tarot cards wasn't a combination that was terribly hard to explain.

"Oooh, do you have any? Will you read mine?"

"I, uh, I don't have a deck yet." Well, that was true, for what it was worth. "I just wanted to read about it. There are lots of different decks, and I don't know which one I want." Again, not actually a lie. More like a misdirection.

"That is just so YOU! I love it! You have to do a reading for me when you get some. You can, like, practice on me. That would be awesome!" She picked up the newest-looking book on the pile (a relative term, because I'm pretty sure our library hadn't gotten any new print books in at least a decade). "Which card is your favorite so far?"

I couldn't help but appreciate her exuberance. Even though I couldn't talk to her about why I was really studying the cards, it felt good to at least talk about tarot cards generally. It made me feel less secretive, less alone.

"I don't know, I like several of them, I guess. Mostly, I like the ones that represent celestial bodies, I guess. The Star, The Moon, The Sun..."

"Mmhmm..." she agreed, looking at the artwork in the book she held. "I kind of like this one." She held up a picture of The Magician from the New Age deck. "He can cast a spell on me anytime." I laughed.

"I don't think you'd be quite as attracted to The Magician in this book." I pointed to one of the books displaying the Rider Waite deck on the cover. She picked up the book and studied the picture.

"Oh, I don't know, he's still kinda cute."

"Yeah, okay," I chuckled. There was no way I was getting any work done with Gemma sitting here, so I grabbed up the two books I found most useful. "Hold on a sec; I want to check these out before the bell rings." I carried them up to the circulation desk and had the student assistant boop them before returning to the table.

"So…" she began, "what's going on with you and Alex? Are y'all broken up?"

"I don't know, I think so. I think he's not really all that interested. Maybe he got bored." I wasn't really sure I wanted to talk about this, but there was no avoiding it forever.

"Really? I just can't believe that! He was so obsessed with you just a week ago!"

I sighed. "Don't remind me."

"Aw, I'm sorry. You never know with boys. Give him a few days; I bet he'll come around."

Except I knew he wouldn't. I'd have gone my whole life without any meaningful attention from him had it not been for my stupid magical interference.

The bell rang, and Gemma and I stood up to go. I was headed for Spanish, and she was off to Law Studies, but we walked part of the way together.

"So you're really into this witchy stuff, huh?" she asked. "All the tarot cards and ghosts and all that?"

"Well," I wasn't quite sure how to respond to that. "I guess. I find it interesting. This," I shook my bookbag filled with all the library books I'd checked out. "is research for a project I'm working on."

"Ooh, are you writing something new?"

"No, well, maybe. It's just research and ideas right now. I don't really know what direction I'm going to go with it yet."

"Oh, well, I think it's really interesting. Maybe we can talk about it more sometime?"

"Um, yeah, anytime. Have fun in Law."

"Yeah, right, thanks," she laughed. "I'm going to go impale myself on a quiz."

In my neighborhood, there's a median at the end of my street, and on that small, grassy median, there's a random stone bench. That bench had been home to many of my deep thoughts over the years. Treigh and I sat on the bench indulging in Drumstick ice cream cones that I had discovered deep in my freezer. The early-November chill had finally arrived in northern Florida, but that wasn't enough to keep us from bundling up in hoodies and eating ice cream.

"This has been a crazy week. I can't believe I've hardly talked to you outside of class. I feel like I have no idea what's going on in your life," I lamented. I felt particularly guilty because, not only was I totally wrapped up with my own personal drama, but I couldn't even tell him what half of that drama was.

"Oh, girl, don't I know it. I have so many updates..."

"Okay," I said, biting through the top rim of the cone, "start by telling me what's up with you and Michael. Because I saw you giving him googly eyes at the Halloween party, and no one resists your charms for long."

He laughed, and even though it was hard to distinguish under his mahogany skin, I was pretty sure he blushed. "Yeah, that's going pretty good right now, I think. We hung out a lot at Trina's party, and then he let me take him home. We're sort of just talking at this point, but I really like him, but I'm not sure if I want to be so deep in the feels, you know?"

"Boy, you better ask him out. I don't want to hear the whole story a month from now about how you wish you hadn't let this one go."

"I know, I know. But I'm trying to focus on ME right now."

"You always say that, but you're not focusing on YOU. You aren't out there building a business or taking up a new hobby or learning to play the marimba or whatever. You're just trying to keep your heart safe." I shot him a knowing look.

"Girl, you reading me for filth right now. You're not wrong, though." He put his arm around me and bit into his cone. "He is really sweet. Texts me funny memes all the time."

"Aw, see, he's thinking of you, too! I mean, you should do what you want to do, but I think you should give the guy a shot. Seems like he'd be good to you, and you could use some of that."

Treigh sighed. "Ah, but why do I need anyone else when I have you, my queen?"

"Because I'm not going to make out with you, no matter how much I love you." We both laughed, and for a moment, the world seemed perfectly normal. Perfectly in balance.

"So what about you and Alex, then?" Ugh. Moment ruined.

"I don't really have any idea. He didn't really have much to say to me this week, so I'm assuming that whatever we were before, we're not that now."

"I'm sorry, love. I know you liked him for a really long time."

I shrugged, but I began to feel the weight of my disappointment and sadness creep back into the front of my mind. I wanted to tell Treigh why things had gone south with Alex, but I held back. Treigh looked at me, and I could tell he knew there was more to the story.

"Lia, did something happen? That face is more than just your bummed-out face. Talk to me. Did he do something to hurt you?"

"No, no, not at all." My voice trembled as the emotions I'd been avoiding rose inside of me. "I...he...I don't know, he just decided he wasn't that into me, I guess. Maybe he never really was…" Tears slid down my cheeks, quickly turning cold in the chilly air. A wave of self-doubt washed over me as I considered, for maybe the hundredth time this week, the possibility that he had never felt anything real for me at all. Until I drew down the moon during the play, he had not even noticed me. I felt my heart breaking all over again with the knowledge that every tender look, every touch, every kiss, was fake...each precious moment a lie born of illusion. Every one of his feelings had been a product of accidental mind control, projecting my own desires into his subconscious and compelling him to act on them. The very thought of it made me nauseous, filled with a desperate desire to scream and let out the agony I felt. *My own fault...all a lie...none of it was real...* The thoughts wouldn't stop coming.

Treigh pulled me closer, letting me sob against his shoulder. After a couple of minutes, I sniffled and pulled myself together. "Sorry," I mumbled, sniffling.

"Don't you dare apologize," he said. "I'm your best friend. You aren't supposed to keep all that ugly crying to yourself. That's what I'm here for. So I can let you be ugly and then fix your makeup after."

"You're the best."

"You are correct."

I really wanted to tell Treigh about what I had accidentally done. I wanted to tell him about what had happened on the beach after the party. I felt like a horrible person for keeping secrets, but I also felt like it would be wrong to drag Treigh into magical drama and bring that kind of difficulty into his life. As I watched him back out of the driveway and head back home, I tried turning my attention toward how I could make my life safer for the Muggles I cared about.

I knew I wasn't a powerful witch, not yet anyway, and some of the other Arcana members definitely were. As much as Kitty was good for advice, she might not be the best person to supervise magical training if my goal was to learn how to defend myself and even fight back against members of the group who felt the need to harm me if I couldn't be "brought into line", as Claudia had said. I needed powerful allies, and that meant finding other members of the Arcana. And then I needed to figure out if any of them could be trusted to be mentors to me, as The Empress had been for my aunt so many years ago. The problem was that I didn't know how to find any of them, not even Claudia and John.

I didn't, but my aunt might. I got the feeling, though, that she didn't really want to help me find my way farther into that world. Still, there was no avoiding it for me now; surely she would acknowledge that. I pulled out my phone and texted her because, frankly, I was too much of a coward to ask her directly. I rationalized that if I sent a text, she would have an opportunity to think about it rather than just rejecting the notion out of hand.

Hey Aunt Kitty...I was thinking that it might be a good idea if I met one of the other card holders who was actually trustworthy. Do you think the Empress card is still connected with the family you remember?

It was nearly a half an hour before she responded.

I'm not sure if I could get in touch with her, even if I wanted to. Let me see what I can find out.

Thanks, I texted back.

That was probably as much progress as I was going to make on that front for the moment, so perhaps I could turn my attention to other things. Like homework. Normal teenager things. As surreal as my life was these days, I still had Trig and U.S. History to worry about.

Nearly a week passed in some semblance of normalcy. I didn't see Claudia or her brother again, and I didn't hear from my aunt or Selene. Alex had said hi to me in class twice, but I wasn't really sure how I should feel about that. Treigh was becoming more and more interested in Michael, though he tried to claim otherwise (even to himself).

On Friday afternoon, I came home to find my aunt's car in the driveway. Not sure if that was a good sign or a bad one, I took a deep breath before hopping out of the car and up the steps into the kitchen door.

I found her in the living room with my mother and a woman who looked to be about 80. Though she was quite elderly, her eyes were bright and alert, and she had an air of wisdom moreso than age. She turned to smile at me as I entered the room, and I had to fight the urge to kneel at her feet.

"The Empress, I presume," I breathed, in awe that so tiny a woman should fill a room so completely with her presence.

"Ah, my dear," she smiled.

Aunt Kitty stood and took my hand. "Lia, may I present to you Mary Steward, the Empress." She led me over to where Mary was sitting.

"I'm honored." I extended my other hand in greeting.

"I'm very pleased to meet you, Lia," Mary said, taking my hand in hers gently. "Not only have you awakened the Moon, but you have brought my dear Katherine back to me. I am most grateful on both counts." Her eyes looked affectionately at my aunt, and then back at me. I was filled with a sense of comfort as she studied me. "We have a great deal to talk about, I think."

"Absolutely. Thank you so much for agreeing to meet with me." I took a seat on the end of the couch closest to the wing chair where she sat like a queen on her throne. Aunt Kitty sat beside me.

"It was wise of you to suggest that Katherine seek me out. There is much you need to know about the Arcana and the different factions and their agendas. It would be difficult to navigate it all alone, even with Katherine's help." It was strange to hear anyone call my aunt by her full name. I had never heard anyone use it until I met Selene.

"I don't even know what to ask you."

"Well, my dear, why don't I begin by telling you what knowledge I have to share, and we can go from there. Although I don't associate with the couple who contacted you, I do know who they are and who they represent. Claudia represents The Tower and the god Janus."

"Is that good or bad?"

"Like all the cards and their deities, Lia, there are good and bad aspects to the Tower and Janus. They represent change, essentially. Change can be beneficial or harmful, depending on the personalities and politics behind it. The same is true of both the card and the god."

"Claudia did talk about changing things. She said they wanted to make the world better by influencing policy, so that the world wasn't about greed."

The Empress inclined her head slightly. "I don't doubt that she is telling you at least part of the truth. Despite a reputation for causing chaos, the family who holds the Tower is remarkably organized when it comes to their goals."

"Which are what, exactly?"

"Change, as I said. The constant upheaval in this country is probably what brought them here from Europe long ago. Exactly what they seek tends to change with the generations. They are quite involved in politics at the moment, and have been for the better part of a century. As long as I've been alive, at least. They are uncomfortable with the status quo. They are visionary and they are powerful. There are few things in the Universe more elemental than change, and so they never seem to lose steam. They always have some new motivation, some new cause."

"What is their agenda now?"

"They see the political division in this country as a great opportunity for change. I suspect that the dominant members of the family have lobbyists pushing a number of issues. The social justice movement in the past fifty or so years has been very exciting for them."

"Oh, well, that doesn't sound so bad. They want changes that benefit people who have been oppressed?"

"I suspect so. But remember that their goal is upheaval itself, and the consequences or benefits of it are secondary."

"But there could be benefits to the changes they want."

"There could indeed."

I considered this and reflected on my brief conversation with Claudia. "My instinct is not to trust them."

"The Moon is the card of Intuition, Lia. If you feel you should not trust them, you are probably right."

"But they aren't going to leave me alone, are they?"

She considered for a moment. "Well, not right away, no. You are a raw source of power to them, and the Moon has talents that they would find very helpful. They would consider you quite an asset."

"Is she in danger?" Aunt Kitty interjected. "Some of the families are willing to be fairly ruthless to get what they want."

"Now that I do not know," she said. "I am not sure if they are trying to make an ally out of her, or leverage her abilities for something specific. If it's the former, she is probably in no danger. If they have something they want from her, or some task they want her to help complete, then there may be a timeline they have to meet, or they may be somewhat desperate. Unfortunately, there's no way to know which it is without asking them."

"Like just ASK them? Would they tell me the truth?"

She chuckled. "Not the whole truth, certainly. Claudia is the Arcana, as far as I know, but I don't know the exact method by which the Tower works. There are many branches in that particular family tree. Some of them have thorns, and some have flowers."

"But you think I should talk to them?"

"I suspect you will end up speaking to them whether you intend to or not, because they haven't gotten an answer from you yet. What I would advise, though, is that you learn some methods of self-defense so that they cannot influence you or take advantage of your lack of experience."

"I think she has to touch me in order to influence me. I felt really strange when I was talking to her, and it took a lot to cut through the fog in my head. When I pulled my hand away from her, it was easier to think."

"Ah, that's very good," she nodded. "It means that she already has limited power over you, but it also indicates that you have some natural resistance to her influence. That would stand to reason. The Moon has deep roots in influence and illusion, so it would be very difficult to use that power against you. I imagine she would have tremendous sway over someone with no immunity at all."

The thought of that chilled me. "That seems like an unfair advantage to have over people." I felt awash with shame; I had done something similar to Alex, even if I hadn't meant to.

"Unless I miss my guess, my dear, you have already paid a price for such a skill."

Aunt Kitty looked at me quizzically, and I dropped my eyes. "It was an accident. There was a boy I really liked, and I might have made him fall for me without meaning to. Once I knew what I was doing, I made it stop. Now he barely knows I exist, just like before I found the card."

Mary looked at me with compassion, and Aunt Kitty squeezed my forearm.

"That speaks well of you, Lia," my aunt said. "You valued his free will over your own desires. You were willing to lose him rather than control him."

"Well, of course. What good is someone's love if they don't give it freely?" I felt hot tears threatening to fall. I couldn't look up from the floor and meet their sympathetic gazes. The last thing I wanted to do was to break down in front of them.

"Your spirit and heart are strong," the Empress said simply, and I appreciated the fact that she refrained from comforting platitudes. They would have been wasted on me right now, and I thought she must have realized that. "One thing I can do for you is to place a blessing of protection around you. Protection is one of my goddess' strongest gifts, and her blessing will enhance your own natural resistance to the Tower's influence. It will also make the thought of harming you seem distasteful to those who might try."

"Which is your goddess?"

"She has many names, but for me, she is Isis. She is the Great Mother, which is the Empress' aspect of deity."

"I thought Gaea was the mother goddess." The words were out of my mouth before I realized that they might appear disrespectful.

"Gaea is also the essence of the Mother, and for other Arcana before or after me, that may be how she appears. But for me, she is Isis."

"So Selene isn't Selene for everyone?"

My aunt responded. "For me, she was Selene. For you, she is Selene. I don't know how your grandmother saw her, nor do I know how generations before saw her. What I do know is that my relationship with the Moon was very different from Grandmother's. And I suspect yours will be somewhat different from mine, because you are somewhat different from me. Since you have chosen this path, at least for now, I've brought you my journals. They may provide some guidance for you, even if there are some differences in how the power comes to you."

"Thanks, Aunt Kitty." I wrapped her in a hug, grateful not to have to go through this alone, as she had until the Empress came into her life.

"You have your aunt's pure heart," Mary smiled. "I can see why Selene thought you worthy." I thought that was, perhaps, the greatest compliment I had ever received. "Come here, child," she instructed. It struck me that coming from her, being called a child was in no way patronizing, because all of us are children in the eyes of the Great Mother. I slid off the couch and knelt at her feet instinctively. She placed her right hand on top of my bowed head. I felt a gentle buzz of electricity slide over my skin, radiating from her hand and enveloping me slowly. I imagined she had given me a second skin of static electricity, pulsating outward.

She murmured quiet words that I could not understand. As I held the image of that glowing aura in my mind's eye, I felt something within me stirring, and a light from inside me rose to meet the one the Empress had placed around me. I wasn't sure how I knew, but when the two lights met, hers full of warmth and sunlight, mind radiating cool as moonlight, they swirled together and I felt as though I had a psychic alarm system with all the bells, buzzers, and whistles. I slowly opened my eyes and looked up at her, and her kindly look had turned into something like surprised respect.

She took a deep breath and let loose a peal of genuine laughter.

"It would be very unwise for anyone to underestimate you, my dear."

Chapter 20

It was three more days before I spotted Claudia and John again. I saw their SUV in the Walgreens parking lot when I was on my way home. I didn't think it was coincidence. I figured they were waiting for me to pass so they could follow me the rest of the way, and they had the misguided notion that this was more subtle than sitting in a driveway across the street from my school.

This meeting would be different...I wasn't filled with fear any more. I still didn't know a whole lot of magic, but the Empress' confidence that I was safe for the time being made me feel much better. This time, instead of fleeing to a public place, I pulled into my driveway, then got out of the car and leaned on the trunk with my arms crossed until they drove by.

I'm pretty sure they weren't expecting this posture out of me. When they drove by, just a little too slowly, I waggled my fingers in a petulant little wave. They pulled over by the mailbox and got out after a brief conversation.

"I guess you were expecting us?" Claudia asked cheerily.

"I figured you'd show back up eventually, yes."

"Good to see you again, Lia," she said, extending to shake my hand.

"Yeah, I don't think so." I kept my arms crossed. "I'm going to take a hard pass on mind control attempts today, thank you."

She blinked at my boldness and slowly withdrew her hand. "Well," she said, "you can't blame a girl for trying."

"Agree to disagree on that. Look, I'm willing to hear you out, but no more of the sneaky manipulative shenanigans. I've been doing some research, but that only goes so far. You want me on your side, and I want straight answers. Can you play fair, or do we part ways here, and you can drive your Range Rover back to wherever you came from?"

"Well, well. You seem to have found your sea legs."

"You could say that," I said in annoyance. "What's it going to be?" Honestly, I was surprised at my own bravado. Rudeness wasn't usually part of my repertoire.

"Your candor is rather...brave." She hesitated, and I wasn't sure if she was reassessing how to deal with me, or trying to figure out how to hide my body. "Sure, let's talk."

I gestured toward the Adirondack chairs by the large angel oak in our front yard.

She nodded curtly and started walking, and John followed, giving me side-eye the entire way. She made a face when she noticed the less-than-pristine condition of the chair, but forced herself to sit on the very edge, rather awkwardly. John followed suit, and I plopped myself in another.

"So, I take it you have considered what we discussed last week?" she began, seeking to regain the upper hand.

"I have indeed. And upon reflection, I concluded that you focused more on intimidation than you did your actual message. So why don't we try this again, and you can explain to me exactly what role you are asking that I play in this great revolution of yours."

"Indeed. Well, you should know that we represent a very powerful family…"

"Yes, The Tower. Janus. I know."

Her wide eyes betrayed her. She hadn't expected I'd known even that much. It set her off balance.

"Yes." She cleared her throat, seemingly unsure of what to say next. "It appears you've done some homework since we last met." When I didn't respond, she continued. "The fact is that we are very interested in the political climate. Florida is a battleground state in federal elections, and also a good test case for other goals that interest us, because your electorate here is fairly evenly divided along political lines."

"And my role?"

"The exact details remain to be seen, of course, but as the Moon, and also as a Floridian, you are in a unique position to help us ensure that elections tip in favor of someone who shares our values. Without knowing exactly what your abilities entail, it would be difficult to define your role exactly."

"I see." My gut told me that she was being largely truthful, even if she wasn't sharing the whole plan. "So you don't exactly know what you want me to do. You just know you want me and whatever abilities I may manifest to be on your side."

"That's it, in a nutshell. We want to know we can count on you for the greater good."

"Who decides what the greater good is?"

"In most cases, it's pretty obvious what the greater good is," she replied flatly. "But some people in power can't be bothered with it because their greed blinds them. We think that if they could be made to see reason, made to see the Universal Pattern, then it would benefit everyone. We aren't talking about killing anyone. We're talking about persuasion."

Sounded a lot more like mind control to me, but I didn't say it.

"I'll tell you what," I said, standing. "I'll give what you said some thought. I don't want to dismiss your proposal entirely just because I don't appreciate your tactics. Why don't you leave me with a number, and I'll contact you if I have questions. Then you can contact me like normal people do if you want to share information."

Claudia was displeased at what was clearly a dismissal. I had called her intimidation bluff, and it appeared that Mary had been right: they had no intention of harming me at this point. She dug in her purse, pulled out a business card, and held it out to me as she stood up. I still didn't want her fingers that close to me, though.

"Just leave it on the arm of the chair. I promise to pick it up."

"This has been a very interesting and, if I'm honest, surprising conversation," she said. When I didn't reply, she nodded to John, who had slightly more difficulty rising gracefully from the low chair. They turned back toward their vehicle.

"One more thing," I called. Claudia looked at me over her shoulder, curious. "Don't follow me anymore. It's creepy."

She chuckled, and as they got in and drove away, I realized that I had pulled off the greatest illusion of all: courage.

Even a full day after my showdown conversation with Claudia, high school drama seemed like pretty small potatoes. I wasn't sure exactly what abilities The Tower extended to Claudia, but I knew that its primary interpretation in most card readings, according to my research, was chaos and destruction, and somehow that seemed like all kinds of not-good.

The halls of St. Augustine High School seemed pretty mild in comparison. I felt like I was sleepwalking through my day, just waiting for lunch so I could talk to Treigh and hear about normal teenage gossip and normal teenage problems. On the first count at least, he did not disappoint.

"This boy…" Treigh collapsed dramatically onto our bench. "He's going to be the death of me."

"How is it that you don't have Michael eating out of the palm of your hand already?" I asked. "You're slipping, brother."

"Don't even say it. I'm having all these feelings…" He made a face like he had stepped in something gross.

"And he's not? I can't believe that!"

"He doesn't know WHAT he wants. I'm not sure he's ever actually been in a relationship, and I think he doesn't know if he wants to deal with all that mess in high school. He's cool in private, but in public, it's like we barely know each other."

"That sounds alarmingly familiar," I sighed.

"I know, right? What is it with these men? Are they sharing notes?"

I almost slipped up before biting back the truth about what had happened with Alex. I wasn't even sure why I was resisting the urge to tell Treigh about our break-up. He already knew about the fact that I had manifested abilities; he just didn't know about this one.

"It's just so unfair. I know he wants us to be a thing," Treigh continued, "but he just won't commit. It's cruel irony. Usually I'm the one allergic to commitment."

"You really like him that much?"

Treigh sighed, and not with his usual flair. Just genuine heartache. "Yeah, I really do. I wish I knew what the magic words were to get him over whatever is stopping him from being with me."

I'd never seen Treigh so sincerely vexed about anyone. "I wish I could help somehow."

"Yeah, me too. Will you help me do something pathetic?"

I arched an eyebrow. "Like what?"

"Like walk up to the lunchline with me to go buy some random thing, and tell me if he notices me walking by."

"That I can do," I said.

I fished a dollar out of my pocket to buy some chocolate chip cookies for Treigh and I to share. As we crossed through the cafeteria, I kept a side-eye on the table where Michael sat with a couple of his friends. He definitely took note of Treigh passing by, and he was definitely trying to look like he hadn't noticed. As we stood in line, Treigh kept his back to Michael so that I could cast sneaky glances toward the table. Each time, I would catch Michael's surreptitious looks in Treigh's direction. And yet, as we made our way back past the table, cookies in hand, Michael kept his eyes focused on anything but my friend. It was all I could do not to call out an obnoxious greeting.

When we got back to the bench, Treigh claimed a cookie and demanded a full report.

"He was definitely checking you out," I said. "Why didn't you say hi or anything?"

"I was trying to see if he would."

"This is too complicated," I complained. "Are you sure he knows YOU'RE interested?"

"Girl, yes. He knows."

"Are you sure?"

"He'd have to be dead not to notice. I text him on the way to school every day."

"Not that I'm an expert on relationships, Treigh, but I can testify that boys can be pretty dense about hints. Maybe you should just ask him out for coffee or something."

"I tried that. He said he had to get home and change to go to work."

"Oh, well, I guess that's possible. Did you try for a different day?"

Treigh gave me a belabored glare. "It's his turn to ask. I already put it out there."

"You're giving me a migraine. I can't keep up with all these sneaky dating rules." The truth was that I couldn't keep up with any dating rules, apparently. But there was no point feeling sorry for myself about something that was my own fault.

We had a substitute in drama. It was like a gift from on high. I loved drama class, but I was mentally exhausted. Mr. Adams had left lesson plans, but like most subs, this one had no intention of making us do the assignment, as long as we behaved ourselves. I lay down on the corner of the stage apron and closed my eyes. I'd never been any good at napping, but today felt like I was going to break tradition.

I am sitting in a canoe on the ocean. The water is like undulating glass; the moon above me is reflected on its surface and creates a brightness that blinds like cool daylight.

I am not alone. Selene sits with me, at the far end of the small boat, her gaze fixed out to sea.

The horizon stretches out before us; the shore is in the distance behind us. I look down to discover a pair of oars in my hands.

'Where to?' I ask her, but she does not answer.

'I'm not sure which way to go,' I say, and this time she turns to look at me.

'It doesn't matter to me which way you go,' she shrugs. 'I will ride along with you in whichever direction you choose to take.'

'How will I know if I'm going the right way?'

'There are many right ways.'

'That's not very helpful,' I pout at her.

'It is not my duty to help you, though sometimes I will.'

'Can't you give me any advice?"

'Only this: if it harms none, do as you will.'

'Well, of course, I wouldn't harm anyone on purpose. I didn't know what I was doing to Alex. Was that harm?'

She shrugs again. 'He is not damaged. Are you?'

I don't know how to answer that. In the distance, the foghorn blasts forth from the lighthouse.

I woke with a start as the foghorn in my dream morphed into the dismissal bell. Shaking the cobwebs out of my head and trying to process what I suspected was not completely a dream, I gathered my things and headed for home.

The goldenrod envelope stood in stark relief on the Adirondack chair. Without opening it, I knew it was a message from the Tower. To my surprise, though, it was from John rather than Claudia.

Lia,

I know Claudia can be a bit much, and often comes off as someone with nefarious motives. I would like to give you an opportunity to see first hand what types of things we can accomplish by working together.

If you are interested, meet me at the place where you and Claudia first spoke. I will be there from 4:00 to 4:30. I don't have Claudia's ability to influence you, but I do believe in the good we can do. I hope you will come.

John

I wondered if she knew he was meeting me without her. For that matter, I wondered if this was some type of trap. I should have been suspicious, but somehow I felt like his intentions were genuine. I checked my phone for the time. 3:42. That gave me time to consider his offer carefully before meeting him, if that was what I decided to do.

I took the card inside and up to my room. One thing Aunt Kitty had taught me was the importance of quieting my mind when it came to using the abilities I was learning to control. I lay the note on my bed, set the Moon card next to it, and sat cross-legged in front of them. I practiced the deep-breathing technique I'd learned.

In my mind, I stood in front of the closet filled with boxes, each skill I'd gained clearly labeled in front of me. I studied them one by one, weighing which ones would serve me the best in this situation. I took down the boxes labeled **intuition** *and* **influence***. I took the lid off of the* **intuition** *box. Inside I found a headband with a crescent moon symbol embroidered silver on black velvet. I lifted it out and positioned it carefully on my head.*

Next, I selected a box labeled **influence***. I cringed at the thought of Alex, but thought it would be very important to have the ability to convince John not to harm me if, by chance, his motives were less than pure. Inside the box was a tube of lip gloss and a pair of binoculars. I painted my lips, then placed the gloss back in the box. I hung the binoculars around my neck. I wasn't* *really sure what to do with them, but I felt like their use would become clear if I needed them.*

I was reaching to close the closet door when I heard her voice.

You're forgetting something*, she whispered. Suddenly, there she was beside me, smiling mysteriously. She stepped toward the closet and pulled out the box labeled* **illusion***. She reached inside and pulled out a pair of sunglasses.* ***You should always have these with you****, she advised.*

No disrespect*, I said carefully,* ***but do you think you could maybe give me a little useful information here? Is this meeting even a good idea? Should I stay away from these people?***

She shrugged. ***Your choices are your own****, she said.* ***Trust your instincts. Not all steps on the pattern are predetermined. Good or ill can come from any choice.***

That's unnecessarily cryptic*, I complained.*

I'm Mistress of Illusions, *she replied simply, patting me on the head as she walked by.* ***Cryptic is what I do best.*** *When I turned to reply, she was gone.*

I opened my eyes and walked over to the mirror. I couldn't see any of the items I'd taken from my mental closet, but I could feel their weight as though they were physical. I checked the time again. 3:58. With a deep breath, I centered myself and prepared to hear what John had to say.

Chapter 21

When I walked into the doughnut shop, I found him sitting at the same table where we'd been before. He was sipping on an iced coffee, and at the empty spot across from him, a chocolate cake doughnut sat waiting for me. He stood as I approached the table.

"I'm so glad you decided to come," he smiled. His voice was smooth and cool, like polished stone, but I didn't detect any hint of manipulation in his words or his tone. He motioned for me to sit in the vacant seat.

"I was intrigued by the honest approach."

"That was my hope." He directed his gaze to the rather worse-for-wear man in the booth by the main entrance. "Do you see that man? His name is Blake Freeman. He comes here every Thursday at this time."

"Okaaayyy…"

"Mr. Freeman has some, shall we say, chemical problems. He's addicted to a variety of substances. He has a family. He also has, for the moment at least, a good job at a law firm. He is teetering on the edge of losing all of that. He is mere months away from a binge that will get him fired and endanger his son, which will also cause his wife to leave him."

"How do you know this?" I asked.

"Let us just say that there is another member of the Arcana who has brought Mr. Freeman to our attention. He comes here because there is a church a couple of blocks from here that holds a Narcotics Anonymous meeting at 5:00. He has never gone, but he comes here and gets coffee and thinks about it. He watches ones of the sponsors come in every week and buy doughnuts for the meeting. A part of him wants to follow the sponsor out, follow him all the way to the meeting. But he's afraid."

"Afraid of what?" I was intrigued by the story.

"Failure. Disappointment. Judgement."

"What is it you want from me?"

"I want you to influence him to attend the meeting. Help him find the courage he can't find in himself."

"That's it?"

"That's it."

"Why do you care so much about this guy?" I was skeptical. I found it hard to believe that this was pure altruism.

"Ah, an excellent question. If Mr. Freeman manages to get his life together and keeps his job and his life, he will play an important part in a legal decision that will set a very important environmental precedent. If he loses everything, he won't be able to do that, and the case may be lost." I had to give it to John. His candor was very convincing. "You can help him, Lia. And by doing so, you can help his family, and the environment."

A man came into the shop with a rumpled plaid dress shirt and khakis. His hair was somewhat wild and disheveled, but his eyes were kind. Freeman's eyes followed him up to the counter as the man ordered a mixed dozen and dug through his wallet.

"If you're going to help him, Lia, you only have about 60 seconds," John said, and then sat back in his chair, waiting for me to make my choice.

I wasn't sure what to do. All I could do was picture his poor man leaving in shame week after week. I closed my eyes.

In my mind, the doughnut shop began to move in slow motion. The girl at the counter was chatting and laughing with the sponsor as she selected tasty pastries from the case. I raised the binoculars I wore around my neck and studied Blake Freeman. I studied the pain behind his eyes, the shame in his heart. The tiny kernel of hope surrounded by fears and insecurities. I focused on that hope, examined it closer. It took the shape of a locket with a photo of a dark-haired woman holding a laughing, chubby toddler. I looked closer and closer, focusing the binoculars to see the sadness behind the smile, and behind that sadness, I found love, faith, and hope. I concentrated, pulling her light out through the photo, bringing her glow to envelop the locket, making its intensity brighter and brighter until it was nearly blinding.

I pulled the binoculars away. The light was so bright now, I didn't need them anymore.

I opened my eyes just as the sponsor was taking his receipt from the girl. He made his way toward the door and Blake Freeman stood, tears streaming down his face. He stepped into the sponsor's path, and though I could not hear their words, I could sense the topic of their discussion. The sponsor reached out a hand and placed it on Blake's shoulder. The two men walked out together.

I felt exhausted, both physically and emotionally. I turned to look at John, whose mouth stood agape as he stared at me.

"Well done," he said after a moment.

"Thanks," I said, feeling slightly conflicted but also accomplished. I picked up the doughnut and bit into its iced goodness. I had definitely earned it.

I was still feeling pretty accomplished the next day at school. My experience with John was really causing me to re-examine my black-and-white point of view as far as influence and free will was concerned. It was better for people to make their own decisions, to choose the right path on their own. But what if their judgement was impaired? What if they weren't able to see the right path, or lacked the resolve to take it, even if they wanted to? It was a lot to think about.

It's not like I was going to go around micromanaging everyone's life. But some people might need help. Was that my obligation? Is that what these gifts were for?

I saw that Treigh had reached our lunch bench ahead of me. He was deeply engrossed in scrolling through his social media, pretending to read it as a way of hiding his distraction.

Even after I sat down beside him, Treigh was uncharacteristically quiet. "This boy's really got me twisted."

I placed my hand on his leg. "I'm sorry. Why do you think he's being so aloof?"

"I don't know. I don't think he's ever been in a relationship, and maybe he doesn't know how to do it."

"Do you think he's afraid to be Out?"

"Maybe. But you'd never know it from the way he talks on the phone. And it's not like it's some great big secret. He joined GSA! He wears the wristband everywhere. I mean, people KNOW."

"Do you think he's not sure how you feel? Maybe he's afraid of rejection."

"If I flirted with this boy any harder, I'd get arrested."

"But you're flirtatious all the time. Maybe he thinks you're like that with everyone."

Treigh gave me a flat look, ending my commentary. He evidently thought he'd made his case clear as crystal. But I suspected otherwise. I'd seen how garishly flirty Treigh was. Michael might have no idea how much Treigh liked him, because it took a long time to get past Treigh's charming defenses enough that you got to see the raw, unvarnished guy beneath all that designer fashion.

I stared hard at Michael across the courtyard. He had snuck a couple of looks at Treigh, and then turned a quarter-turn, probably so he could see us out of the corner of his eye without risking getting caught. I hated to see Treigh this torn up. He already had trust issues. Either Michael was blind to Treigh's interest, or he was playing an unfair game of hard-to-get. Regardless, I knew that if I wanted to, I could change that.

The idea hit me all at once. If Michael did, indeed, already have feelings for Treigh, what harm could come of giving him a teensy boost of courage? They would both be happier with a little nudge in the right direction. And if he didn't have feelings for Treigh, at least Treigh would know and the games would stop ripping his heart apart.

"I'm going to go get you a cinnamon roll," I announced. "Stay here."

"You are an absolute angel," Treigh said sadly, resting his head on his arm on the back of the bench. "Sugar therapy to the rescue."

I patted his cheek and walked across the courtyard and into the lunchroom. I turned to look back out the window once I was out of Treigh's line of sight. Instead, I focused my attention on Michael. He had noticed that Treigh was now alone, and looked quickly around before turning back toward his circle of friends who were totally engrossed in video games on their phones.

I closed my eyes and lifted the magical binoculars.

I focused on Michael, on his heart. In my mind, a dark sphere appeared at the center of his shirt. I increased the magnification, and saw that the mass was a dark bird with its head under its wing. I knew this represented his fear. I imagined the bird's feathers changing, one by one, from near-black to a bright yellow. As the last feather transformed, the bird pulled its head from beneath its wing and looked around. Michael mirrored this movement, and his gaze landed on Treigh, whose eyes were still closed in the November sun.

The bird cheeped and stretched its sunny wings outward. It hopped forward onto the table in front of Michael and cheeped loudly at him, nagging him to take action. He stood slowly, and the bird took triumphant flight into the sky. As it climbed out of sight, Michael moved in hesitant steps toward the bench.

I opened my eyes. Michael's back was to me, but I saw Treigh react to what must have been an awkward greeting. The smile that spread across Treigh's face was like watching the sun rise, and I felt its warmth to the tips of my toes. Somehow, I didn't think Treigh was going to need that cinnamon bun anymore.

I got the full report on the way to the parking lot a couple of hours later.

"Oh, sweet Lord, Lia, I cannot believe this is happening!" Treigh was gushing about how Michael had come up to him at lunch. "I think maybe, that whole time, he was waiting for me to be alone, you know? Because you were gone less than two minutes, and he came right over and said hi!"

"What else did he say?" I was on a high of my own. I had helped create this joy for my friend, even if he didn't know it.

"Not much at first, to be honest. It's like hello was the only part he planned. It was actually kind of cute."

"I'm really happy for you, Treigh. Now at least you can feel okay about moving forward a step or two, right?"

"Exactly. I just have to keep my Libra-ness in check. It's like the floodgates have been opened, but I don't want to lose my mind and start picking out china patterns. I don't want to scare the man. He already seemed a little shell-shocked that he had taken the first step."

I laughed. "Wise choice. Take it slowly, or at least normally. Clearly, he just couldn't deny his feelings anymore."

"Me either," Treigh grinned. "I think I might ask him out on a proper date in a couple of days."

We had arrived at Treigh's car, and I could tell he wanted to hurry and leave campus, probably in the hopes that Michael would call.

"I think that's a great idea. Text me later?"

"I will, I will. Ahh! I cannot beLIEVE this day!" He gave me a tight squeeze and jumped into his vehicle. I waved and watched him back out of his parking space.

I had to admit that I was feeling pretty good about myself after seeing that look on Treigh. I still had some reservations about the fact that I had nudged things along, but if Michael had really just lacked the littlest bit of courage, then what was the harm? It wasn't like what had happened with Alex, because Alex never had any intention of approaching me without having been influenced to do so. Honestly, I had probably just saved them both a week of wasted time, and Treigh a week of agony, wondering about Michael's intentions. There was really no downside.

Still, there was something nagging at me. I just couldn't put my finger on it.

I sat on my front porch, enjoying Florida's version of late fall and working on some Trig homework. My phone started buzzing. I looked down to see a series of texts coming through from Gemma.

hey, trina n i had an idea
do u wanna have a friendsgiving next wk?
not on thxgiving, but maybe weds?
we could do it @ my house.
what do u think?

Friendsgiving? I had heard of it, but I had thought it was just something some tv show had invented. But sure, why not?

Sounds good.

And then I had a thought that set my stomach doing flips.

Whos coming? Can I invite ppl?

not sure who yet? who do u want 2 invite?

Treigh and maybe his +1

yeah thats fine. I should tell u that alex will prb b there. Is that ok?

Ugh. Kill me.

Ill be fine. Just warn me if hes bringing a date.

Kk this will b fun! I promise!

This was followed by a ridiculous and random series of emojis. This might be the king of bad ideas. But if Gemma was still calling me to do things, it at least meant that our friendship wasn't based on my influence. Somehow, the thought of that brought me some comfort.

My phone buzzed again, but this time it was the ringer, not a text. Aunt Kitty was calling. As much as I had to tell her, I thought I'd better wait until I finished my homework, so I let it go to voicemail.

After homework turned into after dinner.

After dinner turned into after I had a chance to relax and watch a couple of streaming shows. And then it was too late to call. It's rude to call someone, like an adult someone, after ten p.m., right? Or maybe I was avoiding telling Aunt Kitty about my meeting with John. In my gut, I knew she would disapprove in her characteristic non-judgmental way. Still, I had a lot to think about. I wasn't sure exactly where I stood on this whole Arcana faction business, and frankly, I wasn't sure I even needed to take a side. Why couldn't I just stay neutral? Uninvolved? That seemed like the best course of action to me. I didn't want her raining on my parade and telling me that was impractical.

Treigh wasn't in Trig the next morning, and he also hadn't texted me to tell me he was staying home. I sent him a message saying that he'd better explain himself before lunchtime, and made my way to English. When I got there, Gemma met me at the door, brimming with excitement.

"So it looks like we have eight people coming to Friendsgiving. Ten if Treigh and his date--it was a date, right?--come. Here's a list of dishes...what do you want to bring? We don't have anyone with food allergies, as far as I know. You don't have any, do you?"

I blinked at her barrage of words. So. Many. Words.

I looked at the list. It looked like all the things that were actually fun to cook had already been taken. I wrote my name down to bring a vegetable side dish.

Alex hadn't listed a date. I breathed a sigh of relief. It would still be awkward, but at least it wouldn't be actual psychological torture.

"What does one actually DO at Friendsgiving?" I asked Gemma. "I don't know how to dress or what to expect."

"Oh, it's literally just a meal. Everyone arrives maybe 30 minutes before we eat, so maybe like 5:30, and then we have a nice meal and sit around being grateful for one another."

"That sounds pretty easy. So just sort of nice dinner clothes?"

"Exactly. Maybe a step up from regular clothes, but not super fancy."

"Okay, let me know if you need any help or anything."

"I've totally got it handled, but thanks!"

Lunch was truly boring, sitting alone on the bench, but on the bright side, I did manage to finish my English homework, which would have been impossible if Treigh had been there to talk with. He texted me about halfway through to let me know why he was absent:

Hey, hunty. Decided 2 stay home today bc I'm nervous about my black belt test and I want 2 practice.

When is that?

Thursday. UR coming, right?

Wouldn't miss it.

Kk. Call me later!

Will do! Xoxo

And I did call him later, and told him all about Friendsgiving, and the fact that he absolutely *had* to come with me so I wouldn't have to face Alex alone. He said he'd talk to Michael about it, but it was a week and a half away, so he might just wait a day or two to mention it, since they had really just started talking to each other for real yesterday. Fair enough. I hung up and went to raid the kitchen for a snack.

Chapter 22

When I got back to my room, I checked my phone and discovered a text from Aunt Kitty. DANG. I had forgotten to call her back. The text was a simple three-word directive: *Unpack a box.*

Ah. She had told me that I needed to maintain my mental closet, and so far, I'd only paid attention to it once. I guess I was going to need to work on my mental discipline when it came to things like that. I sent back a heart emoji and a gift box emoji to acknowledge her advice. I wasn't really ready to talk about my internal struggle to figure out where I fit into the Arcana philosophically, but she was the only person I fully trusted to help me understand my new skillset.

I propped myself up in bed, closed my eyes, and pictured the shelves of boxes. *There were more of them than I remembered, but I couldn't read all of the labels for some reason. I scanned the boxes I could read, trying to decide which one to study.*

I thought back to the sad little girl I'd seen by the graveyard on Halloween night. She was the first ghost I'd ever seen, and she had been so clear, so strong, that I had mistaken her for a living, breathing girl. I knew almost nothing about the ability to see and communicate with spirits. Maybe now was a good time to learn.

I opened up the box and pulled out a pair of retro cats-eye glasses. Stylish! Now to figure out how to use them properly. I put the glasses on and opened my eyes. As had been the case with the binoculars, I could feel the weight of the glasses on my face, though they were invisible to ordinary eyes.

"Now what?" I said out loud. Despite living in one of the most haunted cities in the United States, I had no idea where actual ghosts hung out, as opposed to just where tourist attractions had popped up. I didn't really feel like going out, especially with night falling, but I was pretty sure there weren't any ghosts here in my house, certainly not with Aunt Kitty's wards up in full force.

I decided to go to the only place I personally could guarantee there was at least one ghost: back to the Huguenot Cemetery. The drive wasn't a particularly long one, and I was hoping to score some easy parking at the Visitor Center. I threw on a hoodie and headed down to the car.

I plopped myself into the seat and twisted to buckle my seat belt, which I had a little trouble with, because my oversized hoodie kept getting in my way. I straightened up and about jumped out of my skin.

A woman was sitting in my passenger seat. She was wearing white pants and a coral blouse, looking like she had come from, as she would call it, "the hairdresser."

My grandmother.

I didn't have many concrete memories of her, because she had died when I was six, but she looked exactly as I remembered her. She stared straight ahead with her head cocked to one side, like she was listening to something.

"Uh...Grandmother?"

She turned her head slowly to face me, looking somewhat startled that I had spoken. "You can see me?"

I nodded, unable to find the right words for this occasion.

"Well, it's about time," she said, and as she spoke, I noticed that her lips were slightly out of synch with the words I was hearing, like watching an old Godzilla movie like the ones my mother loved, where the dialogue had been dubbed with English over the original Japanese. "I see the Moon has found its way to you."

I nodded again. She seemed moderately annoyed, though I couldn't really tell why. Maybe she felt she had been disturbed somehow when the Moon card had somehow managed to transport itself out of her grave and into my aunt's grimoire for me to find.

"Why are you here now? Did I disturb you by awakening the card?"

She continued to stare out the dashboard as if watching some action unfold on the hood of my car. The effect was a little chilling. "I've been trying to talk to you since you drew down the moon. I don't have much concept of time, but it took you long enough to hear me. I can only manifest enough to talk to you for short periods at a time."

"I, uh, I'm sorry, Grandmother. I didn't know how to hear you before now."

She thought that over and seemed to find that explanation acceptable. "I can't get into the house," she said simply.

"Yeah, Aunt Kitty set up wards a long time ago."

"Well, I suppose that makes sense. Can't leave the place unprotected. Certainly your mother wasn't about to learn to cast them. I guess it's good that someone did, though."

"Grandmother," I began, "I have an awful lot of questions about the card and about Selene, and everything that's been going on. Is that why you're here?"

"You need to know about the other Arcana. About what they are capable of."

"I've met two: the Empress and the Tower."

She nodded. "Mary will help you. She and I didn't get along very well, but she looked after Kitty well enough, and she can be trusted."

"But the Tower can't?"

"I do not know this Tower. The man who held the card in my lifetime was trustworthy, as long as it suited his interests to be."

"That's not exactly a ringing endorsement," I commented.

Suddenly she fixed her gaze on me with a disturbing intensity. Her eyes turned as dark as the night sky. "You must beware the Magician. He is powerful and ruthless, and will not stop trying to harness your will. You must not give in to him, no matter the cost."

"I...uh...how will I…"

She began to fade. "Do not...you must…" and then she was gone, and I was chilled, not from the outside temperature, but from a cold that seemed to radiate from inside my bones.

It was time for me to woman up and quit avoiding my aunt's calls and messages. As soon as I was back in the house, I mentally took off the ghost glasses and put them back in the box in my mind's closet. Then I dialed Aunt Kitty's number.

"Well, there she is," she quipped, giving me just the smallest bit of a hard time for not responding to her sooner. "How is everything going?"

I took a deep breath. "Um, well...Grandmother says hello."

That took the mirth out of her voice. "I beg your pardon?"

"I, um, I took your advice and tried exploring one of the boxes. I chose the one that involved seeing ghosts."

"Seeing ghosts? You never mentioned that!"

"I know I didn't...it had only happened one time, on Halloween."

I could tell she was exasperated with me. She was trying to teach me about what was happening to me, and here I was, holding back information. "Tell me what happened."

"On Halloween, or today?"

"Let's start from the beginning. What happened on Halloween?"

"I went on a ghost tour with this boy I'd been kind of dating, and I saw the ghost of a little girl by the Huguenot cemetery. I didn't realize she was a ghost until I tried to talk to her. She kept pointing toward the Old City Gate, but she didn't actually say anything. And then she was gone."

"And she was the only one you saw?"

"Until today, yes. Today I decided to study that ability, and was going to go back and see if I could find her again. I got in my car to leave, and there was Grandmother. She told me she couldn't come inside because of the wards, but she'd been trying to talk to me. She seemed sort of angry. And she said to beware of the Magician."

"How long ago was this?" The alarm in her voice was apparent.

"I don't know, maybe ten minutes ago?"

"Okay, I'm glad you called me right away. Are you back inside the house?"

"Yeah, I felt like I'd better get back inside the wards."

"Good decision. Let me try and sort through this a little bit. I guess if you were going to be able to see ghosts, it would make sense that it would start on Halloween, because that's when the Veil between this world and the unseen world is the thinnest. It's still a rather unusual set of circumstances that you would have full sight right out of the blue, but I guess it's not unheard of. And it sounded like that little girl was not harmful, more just stuck in time, mourning maybe."

That seemed reasonable...or, at least, as reasonable as anything was sounding these days. "What about Grandmother, though?"

"Well, your grandmother was a bit of a cantankerous sort when she was alive, and it seems like crossing over didn't improve her disposition. I don't know what to make of the warning about the Magician. I don't know who holds that card, and I've never actually met anyone who does, as far as I'm aware. I'll see if Mary knows anything. But I want you to be extra careful. Those who have crossed over fully don't make appearances on this side of the Veil lightly. It's very difficult, I'm told, and therefore fairly rare. She must have thought that warning was terribly important."

"So Grandma never appeared after she died?"

"Well, no, but then I had buried the card with her. I never developed that kind of Sight as an ability, though sometimes I would hear spirit messages."

"You never saw ghosts?"

"No. Full Second Sight like you described is an incredibly rare ability. Many people who are sensitive can feel the presence of spirits, can even receive messages. But very few see ghosts as a physical presence."

"Why is it that I can see ghosts and you couldn't, even when you were the Moon?"

"That's an awfully good question. It may be that you had latent ability, even before the card came to you."

"What does that mean?"

"It means that maybe you would have developed some psychic abilities on your own, even without becoming Arcana. Now that you are the Moon, whatever abilities were in you to begin with may be heightened. Of course, I'm just theorizing. But either way, I think you need to focus very specifically on protection. You remember that orb of protection that the Empress helped you manifest around you?"

"Sure, of course."

"I want you to focus on it, strengthen it a couple of times a day. Make it very strong. Your grandmother apparently feels like you might be in danger. It would be...unwise...to ignore a warning like that."

"Should I tell Mom about this?"

"At this point, I think you'd better. There is something to be said for protecting people who are non-magical, but when someone is very close to you, there are certain things you need to share in order to keep them aware and out of danger. You also should keep her informed as your confidante. There's no one you can trust more than your mother. Your well-being is her top priority, so you shouldn't keep her in the dark about this."

I considered this, and realized I had more than one person I could trust. "In the spirit of full disclosure, I think there's something else I need to tell you."

She paused. "I feel like I'm not going to like it."

"Well, maybe not. But maybe it will be neutral. I just feel like you should know." I told her about John's note and our meeting at the doughnut shop. I told her about Blake Freeman.

She let me finish the narrative without contributing any commentary. I wasn't sure what she was thinking, but I was fairly sure she didn't approve.

"Lia, you are wading into some dangerous waters. It's very dangerous to interfere in someone's free will, even if you have the best of intentions."

"But Aunt Kitty, even if I didn't care about the supposed legislation this guy will help with, even if I don't buy that part of the story, isn't it better that he's getting help with his addiction?"

"It certainly seems so on its face. IF this man is who John says he is. IF he can stick to his recovery attempt, which will be harder to do than if it had been his own idea. The problem is that there's no way of knowing how much his path has been altered. What is clear, though, is that your intentions were pure. I don't fault you for your compassion. But just remember that free will is a precious thing. Our spiritual growth is dependent on it. Think and weigh very carefully before you trifle with something like that."

I didn't like the fact that I had done what I thought was a good thing, and yet was being made to feel guilty about it. Or maybe I didn't like acknowledging that I might have been manipulated, or even duped. Either way, I was feeling grumpy. I pouted and didn't respond.

"I'm not going to lecture you, Lia. Your choices are your own. I would just advise you to remember that other people's choices are their own as well. Your abilities come with a lot of temptations. One of those temptations is that you might tend to see yourself as...MORE...than non-magical people. Once you put yourself above them, it becomes easier to feel okay about manipulating them, making decisions for them, even using them. That's not the kind of person you are naturally. Just be aware."

"Okay. I promise to keep it in mind. I've got to go now. I have some homework I need to do, and it's my turn to make dinner."

"Alright. Thanks for calling me. I'll reach out to Mary and see what she can tell me about the Magician."

We said our farewells and hung up. I was still grouchy about her taking me to task about helping Blake Freeman. But it was more than that. I was grouchy because she had read me correctly. I had felt so proud of myself for making Blake choose what seemed like an obvious right path. I felt like I had saved him, and had fancied myself a sort of superhero.

I had liked that feeling so much, that the very next time an opportunity had presented itself, I had tweaked someone's free will again, all in the name of what I thought was the right path. I had made Michael go and talk to Treigh. I had interfered in Michael's decision making, even if I thought I had done it for all the right reasons. I just wanted my friend to be happy. But would he be happy if he knew WHY Michael had found the courage to finally go up and say hello?

I knew very well the answer to that question. He would not be happy. Not at all.

Chapter 23

And so began moral quandary number...how many was this now? I'd lost count. Three? Five? But this one actually scared me. The more I thought about the implications of what I'd done by influencing Michael to get over his fear and talk to Treigh, the more I realized that even if my intentions were good, what I had done was wrong. And I was deeply afraid of what would happen if Treigh knew.

So did it compound my sins if I just didn't tell him? I mean, if everything worked out with
Michael, he never needed to know, right? But I would know. And I would feel like I was intentionally deceiving my best friend. Was it better to tell him the truth, or was that just for my peace of mind, so that I could feel like I had confessed myself?

The whole internal argument was giving me a headache and making me miserable. My mother eyed me suspiciously over the lasagna I was poking at, but not eating.

"Spill it," she said. "What's going on?"

"Huh? No, I'm fine. I'm just..."

"Horsefeathers." That was my mother's favorite euphemism for BS. "You usually INHALE lasagna. What's wrong?"

"I...uh..." And then the floodgates opened. I told her about John and about the ethical dilemma he had presented. I told her about Blake Freeman, told her about what I'd done to influence Michael. I told her about how guilty I felt, and how I wasn't sure if I should spill my guts to Treigh or not. By the end of my narrative, my lasagna was cold and my cheeks were wet.

Without comment, my mother got up, pulled me out of my chair, and hugged me close. I started bawling. In that moment, all I wanted was for someone to make all these grown-up decisions for me and absolve me of all responsibility. She held onto me until I ran out of tears and was left with nothing but heaving breaths and sniffles. I sat back down and gulped down a glass of water while she heated up my lasagna in the microwave.

"So," she began as she set down my plate. "You've screwed up pretty royally here, and I think you know it. But that's the nature of learning to navigate the world on your own. You will mess up sometimes, and you have to do your best to try and make it right. And the truth is, that might not be easy, and you might not be able to fix it. But I raised you to be a woman of principle and honor. So you have to try."

"But what if Treigh doesn't forgive me?"

"He might not. But that has to be his choice. You already took someone's choices away. You have to give them back."

"I'm scared."

"You should be. Treigh loves you, and I suspect he'll find his way back to that, but what you did to him was wrong. The pain of that choice is what leads you to not repeat the mistake."

"I feel it badly enough now. I won't make that mistake again."

"I believe you. Do you think it's right to hide this information from him?"

I paused. I knew the answer, but I didn't want to face it. "No, it's not right."

"Then you know what you have to do. Treigh deserves the truth, or you disrespect the trust he has in you."

"The trust I betrayed."

"Actually, yes. But you can't make it right by hiding from the truth."

Darn her logic. She was right. *Ugh.*

Deciding to tell Treigh and actually telling him were two different things. It wasn't the kind of conversation to be had on the way into a class or walking in the hallway. I thought maybe lunch had some potential, but Michael was also at the bench when I got there. They seemed happy enough, and it was casual and comfortable, so even though I knew I was just postponing the inevitable, I hung out with them for a little bit, and then made my excuses about having to go to the restroom.

Drama was actually quite busy with the announcement of an end-of-semester individual performance showcase. Everyone was digging through script files either in old gray file cabinets or online script archives, looking for what five-minute performance they wanted to choose for their final grade of the term. I knew I should care about that, knew I should be excitedly planning and choosing, but I couldn't bring myself to be motivated. All I could think about was Treigh.

"Hey, Lia, want to do a duet performance with me for the showcase?" Gemma plopped down beside me in a folding theater seat.

I tried to look engaged. Truthfully, I appreciated her offer, because having her as a partner would force me to be accountable. "What did you have in mind?"

"I'm not sure yet. Probably something serious. I don't really feel like doing comedy. I haven't even looked at the script box yet. But I could sing...we could even do a musical!" She was clearly getting excited about the prospect, and her eyes lit up with an idea. "How about a cutting from *Wicked*?"

It actually sounded fun, but I couldn't help feeling like I'd been typecast. My own fault, really.

"Yeah, sure, I'm game. But I suck at cutting."

"Oh, don't worry about it! I love cutting! I'll pull something together tonight and text you a copy."

"Cool, thanks. I appreciate it. I had no idea what I was going to do. This really helps me a lot."

"I'm so excited!" She studied me for a minute. "Are you okay? You look...off."

"Yeah, I'll be fine. Just not looking forward to a chat I have to have with someone later. I'll survive. Probably."

"Want to talk about it?"

"Not really. I'll just be glad to get it over with. Thanks, though."

"All right, I'll leave you to your brooding, then. But I'm here if you need me!" She patted my knee and then skittered off to see what scripts other people had chosen.

Brooding indeed. As much as I didn't want to have this talk with Treigh, I rationalized that he would probably appreciate that my intentions were good, and that I felt like I had to come clean. Surely that would count for something. I texted him to ask if we could walk to the parking lot together, and he replied with a *yes* and a heart emoji.

When the bell rang, I gathered my things and dragged myself out the auditorium door. My heart was in my throat as I watched him stroll across the courtyard.

"Hello, darling! What's up that you needed an escort today? Everything okay?"

"Yes, well, sort of. I wanted to talk to you about, you know, some of this woo-woo stuff that's been going on. Some stuff you don't know about yet."

His eyes brightened with excitement. After the initial conversation about my ability to move objects had sunk in, he had gotten over his trepidation, it seemed.

"So, you know that Alex and I sort of broke up..."

"Yes, honey, and I will never forgive him."

"Well, you might, see, because it was kind of my fault. I mean, it was my fault." Treigh looked perplexed. "I mean, he probably didn't really like me all that much in the first place. See, there was this thing like a month ago, and I was on the beach and Selene was teaching me some stuff about what I could do and I made a wish and then all of a sudden Alex liked me. And I didn't really realize it, but by making that wish, I sort of interfered with his free will. Not sort of. I did. And once I realized it, which was after the Halloween party, I sort of took the wish back, because it wasn't right. And then he didn't really like me that much anymore." I stopped to take a breath, and Treigh was looking at me sympathetically.

"Aw, honey, I'm so sorry...you didn't know. It's not your fault..."

"No, but wait, there's more..." The words were rushing out in a flood now. "There was this guy, John, who also knows about this stuff, and he showed me how I could use my will to influence people to make good choices, and I wasn't too sure about that, but the more I thought about it, the more I thought that there might be a way to accomplish some good, you know..."

"Uh huh..." He was starting to look a little more skeptical. I rattled on.

"So then we were at lunch, and you were all sad, and I saw that Michael was looking at you on the sly, and I thought maybe he was just shy or something, and...well...I might have given him a little boost of courage so he'd come over and talk to you." Treigh stopped walking and his eyes got wide. "I didn't force him or anything, I just sort of...mentally encouraged him."

"You. Did. What?"

"Nudged him. A little."

"So it wasn't his idea to come talk to me the other day?"

"Well, he was probably thinking about it already..."

"Probably?"

"I'm pretty sure he would have anyway. I just wanted to help."

"Pretty sure? Lia, how could you DO this to me?" His voice was rising in both volume and pitch. "How can I trust anything that happened between him and me after that? How can I be sure he wants to hang out with me at all?"

"Oh, I'm not influencing him now, not at all..."

"How can you possibly know that for sure? How? You have literally no idea what you're doing! You can't go messing around in people's lives like that! What if he never would have come up to me? Maybe he and I aren't supposed to become anything at all! Did you ever think of that? Like maybe there was another purpose other than becoming a couple? And not only that, I had this beautiful memory of him overcoming his shyness because I was that important to him...and you've robbed me of that! I wasn't that important to him! That beautiful memory is a freaking LIE!"

"I...I just wanted you to be happy...Treigh, I'm so sorry...the more I thought about it, the more I regretted it, and I felt like I had to be honest with you about what I did...I'm so sorry..."

"You should be sorry! How can I trust you now? How do I know you aren't working some other kind of mojo on me, or on him? Or on anybody? How can I even trust what I feel around you? Like EVER?"

"Oh, don't say that! I swear, I learned my lesson! I've felt so guilty…" Tears were welling up in my eyes.

"Well, boo hoo for you! Cry me a damn river! Of all the people in this world, I never thought you would do something like this to me, betray my trust like this! You were literally the persona I trusted most in the world! You are the one I tell all my family drama to! You're the first one I came out to! And now you do this? I can't even look at you right now! I'm going home, and I don't want you to text me or call me. I don't even know how to process this." He stalked off toward his car, leaving me a sobbing mess.

Chapter 24

Not calling or texting Treigh took all my willpower, but if I had any hope for a chance at forgiveness, I was going to have to respect his wishes. I snuffled and blubbered all the way home, and dragged myself up the stairs and crawled immediately into bed to blubber some more. It seemed like I was doing an awful lot of crying lately, and I hated it. I just wanted to stay in bed for a week and wish it all away.

I am floating on my back in the ocean, looking up at the moon. I have a sense that the ocean is made up of all the tears that have ever fallen. Selene's voice is all around me.
Your friend is ungrateful. In the past, people would have offered blood sacrifice in exchange for what you gave him for free.
He didn't ask for my help. It wasn't my right to step in.
Her vexed sigh is the breeze across my skin. ***Humans make no sense.***
And then I float away into a blessedly dreamless sleep.

Literally the last thing I'd wanted to see this morning was a tell-tale goldenrod envelope under my windshield wiper as I slid into my driver's seat. With an internal groan, I pulled out the card inside.

Lia,
    Haven't heard from you in awhile. Would like to touch base. Give us a call when you can.
John and Claudia

Awesome. More confrontation. This one possibly laced with danger. Even though I was in no condition to find strategic ways to handle the Tower, I knew that if I didn't get back to them today, they were likely to show up somewhere inconvenient. As I drove to school, I tried to work out what to say to make it clear that they weren't going to get my help, but at the same time not invite their wrath. By the time I parked, I came up with something I thought might serve.

> **Hi, John and Claudia, it's Lia.**
> **There has been a lot going on lately, and I think it's very important that I better learn to control my abilities before putting them to any kind of use. I would like to stay in touch, but I hope you will respect my decision to figure out what my skills are and how to use them safely before trying to include me in any plans you might have. I have sent this by text so that you will have my phone number, as a show of good faith.**

It seemed a little bit risky to let them know how to contact me, but how does the saying go? Keep your friends close and your enemies closer? I didn't know which category they fit into, and I didn't want to completely cut them off just yet.

Across the parking lot, I heard the annoying peal of the first warning bell. I had ten minutes to get to Trig. I gritted my teeth at the thought of it, and for once in my life, I was glad to be in a class that had assigned seats. I was pretty sure Treigh wasn't going to welcome me to sit next to him, and since my seat was a couple of spots away, it took the stress out of that first-of-many awkward moments.

He didn't even look up as I entered the room; he just kept scrolling through his social media account. I averted my eyes and slunk to my seat. Class was half lecture and half bookwork, and when the bell sounded to leave, he got up and walked out without a backward glance. I don't know what I expected, but the sense of isolation I felt was profound.

I walked alone to English, and the usual scene of Alex talking to Gemma and Trina awaited me. Gemma and Trina looked up and smiled, but Alex's eyes only darted in my direction for an instant. My loneliness deepened, and I thumped into the seat and put my head down, waiting to be saved by the bell yet again.

When second period ended, Gemma caught me on my way out the door.

"Hey, Lia, here's your script! I hope you're okay with playing Elphaba? Cool! I'll talk to you in drama!"

I hadn't managed a single word before she was gone.

That's pretty much how most of the day went. Other than "excuse me" or "I'll have a Cuban sandwich, please," I made it to the end of the day without actually holding a conversation with anyone. In drama, Gemma and I ran our lines and talked about the script she had cut together, but managed not to engage in much social conversation. Then, at the end of it all, I made my way back to the car.

In the midst of my gloom, I had one of those random revelations that comes in times of quiet reflection. I realized that there were probably dozens of students at St. Augustine High School who spent every day as I had just spent this one: without any meaningful connection with anyone at all. No friendly banter, no flirting, no venting. Nothing but functional conversations with no purpose other than to get a bathroom pass or complete an assignment. It seemed to me a very empty way to live, especially if the isolation was imposed by social groups and cliques who wouldn't accept you for whatever reason. I wasn't sure what I was going to do with or about this new perspective, but it also seemed too important to ignore.

Once I got home, I started looking through the script cutting Gemma had put together. Looked like it would run about seven minutes, which seemed pretty good for a duet scene. It seemed to highlight the evolution of Glinda and Elphaba's relationship without really delving into much of the rest of the story. The highlight, naturally, was the two of us singing "For Good". I pulled the song up on YouTube and tried practicing my parts, but the more I sang it, the more I thought of Treigh, and it made me feel that much worse. I threw on my sweats and decided to go for a walk.

I was tired of feeling so alone, and yet my coping mechanism was to be...alone. Yeah, it made no sense, but my life didn't make much sense right now either.

I wandered through my neighborhood, just trying to empty my mind of all the emotional clutter that had been pelting me for days. I couldn't exactly feel sorry for myself, because I'd largely made my own bed, but I also didn't know what to do. I felt lost without Treigh, and even my traditional escapes of reading and music weren't offering much relief. Sleep wasn't much better; Selene might decide to do a dream fly-by at any moment, and so far, that hadn't exactly brought much in the way of comfort. I got the feeling that comfort wasn't really her thing.

When I arrived at the median bench where Treigh and I had sat eating ice cream drumsticks just a few days ago, I plopped down and tried to wrack my brain for a way to make things right with him. There had to be a way; we had been through too much together. But the ideas weren't coming, and the cold from the stone bench was seeping slowly through my Slytherin sweatpants.

Out of the corner of my eye, I saw someone approaching. I turned and saw the man who had come to my door (Was it two months ago? It seemed like an eternity.) and returned my folder. He was out walking two black German Shepherds. He spotted me and waved in greeting. I didn't want to appear rude, so I waved back, and then the unthinkable happened. He headed my way to chat.

"Well, hello! Long time, no see! Lia, wasn't it?"

"Yes, excellent memory. I'm sorry...I don't think I ever got your name."

"Dominic Quinn. Forgive me for not shaking hands. Darcy and Tess are two hands full." The dogs began sniffing around the grass on the median. "Are you waiting for someone?"

"Oh, no. I just was out for a walk, and decided to sit for a few minutes." It occurred to me, a second too late, that I probably shouldn't have told him that.

"Sort of gloomy weather for a walk," he remarked, looking up at the cloudy gray sky.

"I suppose so," I replied, "but I like it. Makes the cup of tea waiting for me seem that much more appealing."

"I imagine it would," he smiled, revealing dazzling white teeth. There was still something nagging at me, something familiar about him that I couldn't place. One of the dogs, Tess or Darcy, I'm not sure which, was marking territory on a small sapling while the other sniffed around my feet. Instinctively, I reached down and pet the dog's head. It leapt back, startled, and then started hopping around its master's legs. "There, there, Tess. She was just being friendly." He patted the dog's flank, and she settled down, but continued sniffing the air in my direction. "Well, then, I suppose we'd better get going. Good to see you again, Lia."

"You, too." I watched as they walked down Rainey Avenue, and then turned a corner out of sight. Once they were gone, I stood up and headed for home. Suddenly, drinking a cup of tea while safely inside my warded kitchen sounded like the best idea I'd had in days. I chided myself for being so jumpy, but my nerves didn't settle until I'd locked the kitchen door safely behind me.

The next couple of days were no better. I fought through *Wicked* practices with Gemma, and despite the emotional challenges of doing a scene about friendship while my most important friendship was in turmoil, the performance was improving. Maybe my emotions were adding to it, I wasn't sure.

But on Thursday evening, the night of Treigh's black belt test, I couldn't think of much else. I knew how hard he'd worked on it, and I hoped he'd do well. I wondered if his family would ask why I wasn't there, and what he would tell them if they did. I wondered if Michael would be sitting in the seat where I should have been.

Unable to just let the event pass unmarked, I pulled a blank notecard out a box I'd had for probably three years and wrote a short message:

Treigh,
 I wish I could have been there tonight, but I know you did great. I just wanted to let you know I was thinking of you and wishing you well.
Love, Lia

He lived about fifteen minutes away, so I drove over there, knowing no one would be home. His car was in the driveway, since his parents had no doubt driven to the karate school. After the test ended, they would all go out to dinner. I sighed and put the note under his windshield wiper for him to find in the morning. Then I headed back home.

In an age when cookie-cutter neighborhoods have all their announcements on some social media page, my neighborhood is old school. When something important is going on, we still staple notices to the wooden telephone poles that dot the streets. It's endearing, really, even if the flyers don't last very long. It usually only takes a day or so before some property-value do-gooder comes by and tears them down because it "makes the neighborhood look junky".

As I slowed down to pull into my driveway, I passed one of these flyers in front of the house next door to mine. I couldn't read the text, but I could clearly see a photo of one of Dominic Quinn's dogs taking up the center of the flyer. After parking, I walked over and read the text: **Lost Dog. This is Tess. Her brother and dad miss her. If found, please call the number below.**

Aw, that made me sad. I made a note to keep an eye out, hoping that Mr. Quinn found her soon.

Despite not being a particularly religious household, Sundays were always the most low-key day of the week. Mom and I would usually have a nice brunch and then tackle various household or homework tasks in a relatively leisurely way. This weekend was no exception. I made some corn muffins and set out some pepper jelly while mom cooked up some Canadian bacon and eggs.

"Treigh's still not speaking to you?"

"No, not really, but he acknowledged my presence on Friday. Actually made eye contact. I count that as progress."

"Aw, honey, I'm sorry. Maybe he just needs some time."

"I hope so. This sucks." I bit into a gooey-spicy-sweet corn muffin.

"You going anywhere today?"

"Nope, no plans. Gemma and I did our rehearsal stuff yesterday because she had some family obligations today. I'm just going to do my laundry and maybe clean out my closet and pull out stuff to donate. Maybe watch some movie or other."

"Sounds like a good day. How about a movie night later? Some old monster movie from the '50's?" Mom had gotten me hooked on golden-age monster movies before I was ten.

"That sounds excellent. Especially if it's popcorn-for-dinner night."

"Consider it done. I'm going to make a quick run to the grocery store and the ATM. Do you need anything?"

"Probably could use some toothpaste. Other than that, I'm pretty well set."

"All right," she said, standing and taking her dish to the sink. "I should be back in about an hour. Could you take the kitchen trash out to the can? It's starting to reek a bit." She patted me on the head.

"Sure, no problem. See you soon."

After cleaning up the dishes, I tied up the trash bag and slipped some shoes on so I could take the bag out to the small enclosure that housed the large trash cans. I hoisted the bag into the large plastic bin, and as I turned to go inside, something dark streaked across the end of my driveway. I stepped out from behind my car and saw Tess the dog sniffing around the chairs in my front yard.

"Tess! Hey, Tess! Here, girl! Come here, Tess!" The dog looked up at me and sniffed the air. She cocked her head to one side and sat down.

"Oh, you're going to make me work for it, huh?" I slowly moved toward her, remembering how jumpy she could be. I extended my hand and spoke in a soothing tone. "Hey, sweet girl. Your daddy is missing you! Wouldn't you like to go home?"

I could see that she was still wearing a red collar. All I had to do was get a hold of that collar, and then I could figure out how to contact Mr. Quinn and return her. I cursed the fact that I had left my cell phone on the table when I was taking out the trash.

Almost there...I was only about two feet away from grabbing her collar when she suddenly barked and started trotting off in the other direction. "Gah!" I exclaimed, and started after her. "Come back here!" She wasn't moving at a full run, but it was just fast enough that I couldn't quite catch up. She stopped here and there to smell the grass, always popping up and skittering away before I could grab her. I'd followed her for about a block and a half, and I had resolved to go back and get my phone, call the number on the flyer, and alert Mr. Quinn to where I'd seen her headed. She started pawing at something in the gutter next to a burgundy van.

"Find something interesting, girl?" She seemed very intent on whatever she had found, but more importantly, she was holding still. "Whatcha got there?" I reached out slowly and started slipping my fingers under the back of the collar.

Before I could get a solid grip, the sliding door on the van whipped open behind me. Strong arms encircled me, pinning my arms to my side, while simultaneously something, a pillowcase maybe, was dropped over my head. I was lifted off my feet and started screaming and kicking as I was being pulled backwards into the van. I heard the van door slam shut and a sickly sweet scent filled my nostrils. Something laced with the scent closed over my mouth and stifled my screaming. I fought with all my strength, but I could feel myself losing consciousness. As my mind went blank, my last memory was the sound of Tess barking as the engine in the van sprung to life.

Chapter 25

I awoke sometime later and found myself on a bed with my wrists bound behind me and my ankles tied together and tethered to a bedpost. There was something in my mouth that felt a bit like a washcloth. The room was dim, and my foggy brain tried to make sense of my surroundings. There wasn't too much furniture, just a bed, a nightstand, and a couple of chairs, but it appeared to be clean. The pillow had a fresh fabric-softener smell. The light filtering around the edges of the window shade across the room told me that it was still well into the daylight hours.

I tested my bonds. My ankles were zip-tied, so it stood to reason that my wrists were as well. Not much hope of pulling those loose. I couldn't see anything sharp within my reach, so I couldn't saw through the plastic like I had seen captives do on film. Panic was replacing the fuzziness in my mind, and I thrashed my feet, trying to yank the rope free that acted like a leash to the bedpost. No luck there either, but I had made sufficient noise that I appeared to have attracted someone's attention. I could hear a shuffling movement on the other side of the closed door.

There was no point in trying to pretend I was still unconscious, because I'd made such a racket. Instead, I struggled into a sitting position so I could my kidnapper in the eye. That wasn't much protection, but false bravado was all I could muster. I could hear a man's voice humming something that was vaguely familiar, but my clouded brain couldn't quite place it.

The doorknob turned and the door swung open.

There, facing me, was a smiling Dominic Quinn, flanked by Darcy and Tess. Somehow, that was not much of a surprise.

"Ah, Lia. So sorry to have to do things this way, but I don't think I have much choice. You needn't be afraid; I have no intention of doing you any harm at all. We just need to come to an understanding about a few things.

I mumbled incoherently into the washcloth. It wasn't incoherent in my head, though, and I think under the circumstances, my mother would have forgiven me for my colorful vocabulary.

My mother. She would be so worried…

My fear was transforming itself into anger and I felt a familiar prickle along my skin. How had I managed to forget that I had a whole new skill set that could help me with this predicament? The substance he had used to knock me out had not fully left my system, and I was having a little trouble focusing my attention. I centered my thoughts on the prickly feeling, willing it to become lightning.

"Now, now, we can't have any of that," Quinn said reproachfully. He produced a small syringe from his pocket and, like a flash, jabbed it into my shoulder and pushed the plunger. "This won't harm you, but it will calm you down a little bit. The effect will also dampen those lovely abilities of yours. Can't have you throwing a chair at me while we chat, now can I?"

I thrashed about again, more out of frustration than anything else. He just smiled and patted my leg. He knew who...what...I was! I wondered if this is what Claudia had meant with her veiled "one way or another" threat the first time we met.

"I'm sure this is quite a stressful situation for you, but it has to be this way because I need you to be completely focused on what I have to say, a 'captive audience' if you will. I should begin by telling you that may name isn't Dominic Quinn, though I think I'll refrain from giving you the real one for the moment. I have been keeping an eye on you, so to speak, for quite some time, because I was quite sure that it was only a matter of time before the card came to you and you became the Moon. I confess I expected it to be later, once you'd gone off to college somewhere, but it appears that the magic in your blood had other plans. Took me quite by surprise, you accidentally doing Blood Magic. That bodes well for how strong you will become in time."

He paused here and examined my eyes. He seemed satisfied that the injection was having the desired effect, and he was right. The prickling feeling had all but stopped, and I was feeling a bit foggy again. Nothing a nap wouldn't fix...

"No dozing off on me, now," he chided. "Don't be rude. Where was I? Oh, yes. Your play. It wasn't a bad attempt, from a literary standpoint, by the way. Anyhow, I knew it was only a matter of time...vacancies in the Arcana don't last forever. After your aunt relinquished her place, I rather wondered how things would play out, since your mother had no interest at all in her magical lineage. Seemed only logical that someday the card would find you. They do like to stay within the bloodline if they can."

In the very back of my mind, all sorts of alarm bells were going off. He knew my aunt, my mother, my family history...and he sure knew an awful lot about how the cards worked. I wasn't sure how I should feel about that, and the drugs in my system were making it hard to feel much of anything.

"I'm sure you have a lot of questions, my girl, and if all goes well, I have all the answers you seek. But as I said, we need to come to an understanding. There is too much at stake for me to have you and your powers out there spitting into the wind, if you'll pardon the metaphor. Your aunt seems somewhat content to let you discover your skills and develop them in a somewhat random fashion, but that is messy, and it just won't do. You play an important role in the Pattern, Lia, and you need to be properly trained to do your part."

The more he talked, the less I felt afraid. Part of that was probably whatever he'd shot into my arm, but part of it was something else. I just wasn't sure what. One thing I did feel certain about, though, was that he truly didn't want to hurt me. He seemed to feel like I was...necessary.

"There, now, it seems like you've calmed down quite a bit. Can I trust you not to scream if I take that cloth out of your mouth?" I nodded slowly, and he smiled. "Excellent. I'm pleased to see that you can be reasonable." He pulled the wadded up washcloth (I'd been right about that) out of my mouth, and I worked my cramped jaw around a bit.

"Can I have some water?"

"Certainly, in a couple of minutes. Let's try to establish some ground rules for our conversation first, shall we? We have much to discuss."

"Did Claudia send you?" I asked, trying to give him as jaded a stare as I could manage. I was startled when he responded with laughter.

"Good Lord, no. No one sent me. As I told you, I've had my eye on you for quite a long time. She and her brother never would have found you, had they not managed to get a decent clairvoyant working with them. Alright, my turn. Did your aunt give you the card?"

"Not exactly. I found it in some of her things, though she said...she had not put it there." I had almost told him about her burying the card with my grandmother. I wasn't sure why, but I felt like I shouldn't share that. "If you're not with the Tower, what Arcana are you?"

He studied me intently for a moment. "I am the Magician, my girl." My eyes must have widened a little bit, because he added, "I see my reputation precedes me. I hope you will give me the benefit of the doubt and draw your own conclusions."

"I don't know anything about your reputation. Just that my grandmother doesn't trust you."

This time HIS eyes got wide. "Doesn't she? Interesting. And impressive." I knew I was oversharing, but I couldn't seem to put a filter between my brain and my mouth. "Why don't I get you that water now?" He stood and slipped out the doorway, the dogs padding after him. Within a minute, he returned with a bottle of water in his hand. He opened the top and tipped it to my lips. I drank greedily, grateful to get that horrible dryness out of my mouth. After gulping down half the bottle, I pulled back for a breath.

"Thanks. But why the restraints? Why couldn't you just introduce yourself to me and have a conversation like a normal person?"

"Well, I suppose neither of us is exactly normal, wouldn't you agree? But the fact is this. I have some rather ambitious, rather important plans, and I want you to be part of them. I needed you to hear me out without interference from anyone else. And I need you not using any of your own abilities upon me while we talked."

"Seems a little unfair. You can use yours."

"Well, I certainly could. But at the moment, I don't really need to."

"But you needed to pull me into a van and drug me."

He smiled. "It's a fair criticism." He set the chair at the foot of the bed and sat down.

"Look, I'm feeling awfully sleepy because of the sedative you gave me, so I don't really have a lot of bandwidth for being polite. What is it you WANT? What's the bottom line here? Is that about that same political stuff Claudia and John wanted me involved in? Because I don't really think I'm going to do a lot of messing with people's free will anymore. I've made a mess of things, and I've learned my lesson about that."

"I appreciate your candor. Your boldness may be a little ill-advised, but I can forgive that for now." He paused, perhaps considering how much to tell me. "I'm not particularly interested in politics in the sense that the Tower is. My politics are more personal, you might say. Let me ask you this: with what goddess have you aligned yourself?"

"Selene." Dangit. I hadn't meant to tell him that.

"Ah, yes. Illusion, insight, gravity? I take it your abilities are connected with hers?"

"I suppose. Who are you aligned with?"

"Mercury," he said simply.

I struggled to remember what I knew about Roman gods. "So...the messenger. Communication? Speed?"

"Yes, you could say that. I can be quite persuasive. Mercury also has excellent business sense. That, as you might imagine, has a variety of benefits."

"So this is about money?" I asked.

"Nothing so base. Think about this for a moment: What if Mercury's skills and Selene's were combined? Skilled communication plus intuition plus business acumen. The ability to move quickly combined with the ability to move objects. It creates some interesting possibilities, does it not? Begs for experimentation, wouldn't you agree?"

"I don't understand."

"Think of this: what might be accomplished if all the Arcana could be assembled in one place? The powers of so many gods at my...OUR fingertips. What might we accomplish? What might we create?"

I blinked at him. I knew there must be quite a lot that the power of 21 deities could do. But it seemed to me that it could do as much--if not more--harm than good. I was pretty sure he didn't see it that way, though. His eyes were alight with the promise of that much power.

He looked as though he was about to say something else when his chest pocket started buzzing. He pulled out his phone to check the identity of the incoming caller, then abruptly stood up.

"I have to take this call, my dear, but we can continue this conversation in a little while. I'm sorry I have to do this..." He shoved the washcloth back into my mouth and strode out the door, closing it behind him and the dogs. With the combination of the quiet and the sedative, it wasn't long before I lapsed back into darkness.

There was no way of knowing how long I had been out, though it must have been a few hours because the light had shifted measurably, and a dusky twilight filled the room. My head felt like it was full of cotton...with a few toothpicks thrown in for good measure. Whatever he had shot me up with, I definitely didn't want any more of it.

Think, Lia, think, I told myself. *There has to be a way out of all of this.*

I tried to concentrate on my senses and filter out the headache. I closed my eyes and focused on what I could here. Every few minutes, there would be the very faint hum of a vehicle driving by. If there had been any noise in the room at all, I would not have heard it. So that told me that there was a road nearby that was regularly traveled. That was good. I also couldn't hear movement anywhere else in the house, so that was also good. It was possible he had gone out for some reason, once he realized that I had passed out again.

The sense of smell wasn't much help. The fabric softener was strong enough to drown out all other smells, as well as to add to my headache. I also couldn't see much other than this room, since the door was closed. I couldn't do much with my fingertips either...or could I? Slowly and quietly, I tried to roll from my side up onto bent knees, hoping I could reach the rope and fiddle with it enough to untie it. I made maybe ten attempts before coming to the conclusion that physics had beaten me on this one.

I wondered if my head had cleared enough to use my abilities. I concentrated on my mental closet, and found it very dark. The labels on the boxes were hard to read. I looked at each, squinting, trying to make out which box was which. Frustrated, opened my eyes and tried to remember how it had felt the first time I had levitated things without meaning to. That time, I had just *willed* it to happen. Maybe I could do that again.

Despite the stabbing pain in my temples, I focused hard on the light switch. *On.* But nothing happened. *ON.* Again, no luck. I felt the rage and vexation rising in me. One more time. *ON!* Third time was the charm, and I was rewarded with a satisfying *click.* Ironically, nothing turned on, because there were no actual lamps in the room. It didn't really matter, though. The important thing was that my mojo was working.

I stared at the knot in the rope tying me to the bedpost. Slowly, and very painfully, I pulled the short end of the rope through the knot, loosening and eventually completely untying it. The rope fell away from my ankles and I was able to sit up and swing my legs over the side of the bed. Too bad I couldn't work that same magic on zip ties. I stood up and very slowly hopped my way to the window. Quinn may have gone out, he may well have been sitting across the room, reading a book and waiting for the dogs to alert him to any movement coming from the room where I found myself.

I finally made it to the window and used my nose to scoot the blinds out of the way. Just my luck; the window faced the fenced-in backyard, so there was no chance anyone would see me and send for help. Still, I had made a little bit of progress. I knew that I was in a residential neighborhood. My mind was clearing a little bit from the adrenaline now pulsing through me. I had committed myself to an escape attempt; there was no way to quickly re-knot the rope around my feet, so I needed to think of another plan.

I slowly hopped my way across the room to the door and laid my ear against it. I couldn't make out any sound of movement. *Selene*, I thought. *How about a little help here?* There was no response, which flared the anger in me anew. I used telekinesis to turn the knob millimeter by millimeter, then to pull the door open just the tiniest crack. I could see that I was at the end of a hallway, and that there were two rooms on the opposite side. The one directly across from me was closed, and the one a few feet away was cracked open. I used my chin to open the door just a little bit wider and poked my head out into the hall.

From this angle, I could see that the hall was actually a fairly short one. It opened out into a larger room maybe twenty feet from where I was standing. I could see the back of a brown leather couch, and there didn't appear to be anyone seated on it. Maybe he really wasn't here. The dogs probably were, though, and that would mean big problems for me.

I knew I had to risk it, so I opened the door enough to slide myself out into the hall. Even though my headache remained, my head was no longer full of cobwebs. I willed the doorknob across the hall to turn, and the door popped inward just a crack. I moved at a snail's pace across the hall and peered into the room directly opposite my prison. It was dark, and it took my eyes a moment to adjust.

I couldn't believe my good fortune...it was a garage. Maybe I'd be able to find something sharp to cut the zip ties with! I nearly toppled over crossing the threshold, because I had missed that there was a two-inch drop onto the concrete floor, but I managed to catch my balance by throwing my weight against an old refrigerator which was positioned just inside. My shoulder landed with a dull but resounding THUMP.

I froze in terror. From down the hall I heard the sound I had been dreading: a short clipped bark and the clicking of dog's nails coming up the hallway. With my cover blown, I yanked the door shut with my mind. Snuffling sounds emanated from just inside the door, followed by the impassioned barking and howling of the dogs. I whimpered in panic and looked desperately around the garage for things I could throw with my mind if that door should open. Darcy and Tess started scratching madly on the other side, but there was no sound of footsteps rushing to investigate. I breathed a sigh of relief.

The relief didn't last long, though. Even though there was no immediate threat, I was still bound and stuck in a strange house. And who knew how long it would be before Quinn came back. A quick survey of the garage proved disappointing. Whoever heard of a garage totally devoid of tools? Two motorcycles, but no tools. I couldn't find a single sharp edge within my reach. What I did find was a side door, and bound or not, that was looking like my only option. Since it was at perfect hand-level, I was able to unlock it with my fingers and then turn the knob. I pushed with my shoulder and, though it took some effort, the door finally opened. I was overjoyed!

Until I realized I was inside the tall wooden fence that ran the perimeter of the back yard.

If I hadn't had a washcloth in my mouth, I'd have screamed.

The latch for the gate was at the very top of the fence, maybe six inches above my eye level. In itself, that wouldn't have posed a problem, thanks to my new abilities, but a silver padlock held it tightly shut. I started scanning the fence, looking for missing boards, and finding none. I couldn't believe I had made it outside, but still couldn't escape. I was no less trapped than I had been when tied to the bed.

Just then, I felt a *whoosh* in my mind and felt Selene's presence swirling around me.

About time! I thought.

Don't be impudent. Selene responded. *You've were hidden, even from me. The house is bespelled.*

It must take some pretty powerful magic to hide someone from a goddess. *How do I get out of here?*

You must stay hidden. I may be able to reach out to your aunt.

What if he comes back?

Pray he doesn't.

Consider this a prayer.

And then she was gone. I hopped a few feet and crouched down behind the air conditioning unit. If Quinn came back, it wouldn't take him long to find me, and at most this would buy me fifteen seconds, but I couldn't think of what else to do.

Night fell, and I shivered against the wall of the house, my heart thudding in my chest while I waited. It wasn't long before I heard a car pulling into the driveway. The car door opened, just one. I began to tremble, and I could hear the dogs barking inside.

Their master was home.

Chapter 26

I couldn't hear the key turning in the lock from my vantage point, but I did hear the front door open. I couldn't make out the words, but I could tell that he was greeting his dogs.

Selene! I screamed in my mind, but she did not respond. I could only hope that meant she was bringing help. I retreated to my mental closet, now brightly lit and clear. I searched for something that could be of help in my current predicament. I pulled the box for *illusion*, deciding that this was probably my best hope. I could not make the hand movements Selene had taught me, but I hoped that it would still work. In the box, I found a small paintbrush. I pulled it out, and wracked my brain for the right illusion. I knew I wouldn't have much time.

As if in response to this thought, I heard a shout from inside. He had clearly discovered my absence. He might search the house first, maybe, and that might buy me maybe two minutes.

I didn't think I had the skill necessary to make myself invisible. What might not seem out of place in a somewhat unkempt backyard? Especially something that was girl-sized? I closed my eyes tight and held the paintbrush in the forefront of my mind. The bristles were suddenly covered in a dark green paint, and as I waved the brush around, I imagined myself as a large, weedy, dandelion bush, growing waist high against the house. I had seen a few dandelions dotting the yard, so I hoped he would see me as part of the natural greenery.

I heard the interior garage door whip open.

"Lia, I know you're here somewhere. You couldn't have gone very far with those bonds. I can feel the traces of your energy. Don't be foolish. Come out now." I could hear him rustling through the garage, searching any place that might be big enough to conceal me.

He said he could feel my energy. I certainly hadn't accounted for that in my illusion, nor did I know how to. *I'm a plant, I'm a plant...* I thought desperately. It seemed like a pretty lame idea, but if magic was directed intent, as my aunt said, then it just might work.

The outside door that I had thought would mean freedom burst open. I was amazed he couldn't hear the panicked pounding of my heart. He strode out, confident and angry...and stormed right past me. I almost wept with relief. He walked the perimeter of the lawn, searching and clearly confused. He walked more slowly, retracing his steps back toward the gate. Would he walk past me a second time without noticing? *I'm a plant, I'm a plant...*

He was maybe five feet from me when I heard another car pull into the driveway. He heard it, too, and it seemed to cause him alarm. "This isn't finished, my girl. I know you're here somewhere. If you could have left, you would have." He headed back through the open garage door, and I let out a breath I hadn't realized I was holding.

Someone got out of the car and walked to the front door. I could hear the newcomer knocking forcefully. I heard the door open, and Quinn's voice saying something like, "Can I help you?"

Then I heard the most beautiful sound I had ever heard in my life. "Yeah, hi. I'm going to need to talk to Debbie, please." That voice. That gloriously sassy voice. Treigh's voice. Tears started running down my cheeks, and there was nothing I could do about it.

Quinn was clearly protesting that there was no one named Debbie here, but Treigh wasn't having it. "Look, she gave me this address, and she owes me $50. I'm going to need my money back, and I'm not waiting anymore." The argument raged on, and Treigh was clearly buying time. I didn't know what the plan was; I only knew that I couldn't help much.

A familiar tingle passed across my now-freezing skin. *Well done, Lia. All will be well now. Help is coming.* I went from weeping to sobbing. I was going to be alright! *Show them where you are, my dear.* I wasn't exactly sure what she meant, but the image of a searchlight popped into my head.

I looked up at the waning moon and imagined a beam of moonlight focused directly on me, revealing my location.

I heard more car doors open. One set of footsteps moved toward the yard gate, and the other moved toward Treigh. The front door slammed. A hand reached over the gate and felt the latch and the padlock. I heard a quiet expletive and recognized Aunt Kitty's voice. "Lia, I know you can hear me. I see your signal, but you have to stop before he sees it, too. We're coming for..."

I heard feet running toward her, and then my mother's voice. "Is she here? He slammed the door as soon as I got out of the car."

"She's here, but the gate is locked."

"The hell it is," Treigh snorted. "Stand back." A moment later, the wooden gate splintered inward. Again. Again, until there was a crack across the entire width of the gate. I could hear the three of them huffing and puffing as they worked at the boards, yanking them off of the crossbeams and creating a hole where the bottom of the gate had been. Treigh and my mother crawled through.

"Lia!" Mom called. "Lia, where are you? Kitty, I don't see her!"

I had forgotten about my glamour. I dropped the weedy illusion and revealed my hiding place behind the air conditioner.

"Oh, God!" Mom exclaimed and leapt to my side. She wrapped her arms around me and I sunk into her warmth. Treigh crouched down and pulled the wadded-up washcloth out of my mouth.

"Lia…" He looked over my pathetic condition, bound hand and foot, and his eyes filled up with tears. "Oh, darling…"

That was the last straw. Whatever piece of my nerves had been intact became thoroughly unraveled, and I began bawling.

We heard the front door slam and the barking of dogs. "Darcy, Tess! Here!" A car door opened and the dogs stopped barking. "We WILL meet again, my girl!" Quinn called, and then the car engine roared to life and peeled out, leaving the squeal of tires as his final word.

Treigh lifted me up and my mother opened the door to the garage. We passed back through the hallway I had seen before, and Treigh set me down gently on the couch. I had managed to get myself under control as we passed through the house. He went into the kitchen to try and find something to cut the zip ties. My mother went to let Kitty in through the front door, and then came and sat beside me, rubbing my arms to warm me up and trying to appear reassuring through her own tears. Aunt Kitty remained on the front step.

"Kitty, why don't you come in?" Mom asked.

"The house is strangely warded. It has enchantments all around it, especially on the doors and windows. I'm guessing Lia's powers don't work very well in there."

"You're right," I croaked. Between the gag and the crying, I was seriously dehydrated. "How did you know?" Treigh returned from the kitchen with a knife and a bottle of water.

"Turn around," he instructed, "and hold still."

"My hero." And then I stopped speaking because I was about to become hysterical again. My hands popped free, and I immediately brought them around and started rubbing my raw and sore wrists. He went to work on the tie around my ankles and soon it popped off as well.

"Who did this to you?" my mother asked.

"I don't know his real name. He called himself Dominic Quinn, but said that was an aLias. He's the Magician that Grandma warned me about." I grabbed the bottle of water and chugged it down. Ah, sweet relief. "Can we talk more about this at home? I don't want to be here anymore."

"Of course, honey, of course." My mother and Treigh helped me stand, and we all walked out to the car. Aunt Kitty was still examining something in front of the house. "Kitty, let's go."

"One second," she called back. She pulled out her phone and took pictures of the window sill and something underneath the doormat. Then she joined us at the car and slid into the driver's seat. "Sigils," she said, as if that explained everything.

The truth is, I didn't even care. I was tucked between Mom and Treigh in the back seat. I was safe. Now all I wanted was to let hot water wash this whole experience off of me, and then to be wrapped in the softest jammies and fluffiest blankets we owned, snuggled and surrounded by the people I loved most.

Once that had been managed, I was sitting on my own couch with a cup of chamomile tea in one hand, and my mom holding the other. I told them the whole story, from chasing the dog to everything Quinn had said to me while I was tied up. My aunt listened, quietly taking notes so she could tell the Empress what had happened.

Apparently, my mother returned to find me gone without my cell phone, and knew something was wrong. Not only was I missing, but the door was unlocked. Noticing that I had taken out the trash as requested, my mother had rightly surmised that someone had grabbed me after I'd gone outside. She had called Kitty and Treigh, since they were the only two people who might have a full understanding of who might have taken me and why. Like I had originally, they had assumed that the Tower had been responsible for my disappearance.

They had walked the neighborhood but had found no clues. When Kitty arrived, she had tried various location spells, but she had been terribly out of practice, she thought, and her efforts turned up nothing. As soon as I had managed to get myself out of the house and away from the warding spells, the pendulum my aunt had been using to try and locate me started swinging in the general region of Quinn's house, only about three miles from my own. They had gotten in the car at that point and started patrolling that area, and then the moon had come out. A will o' the wisp had begun floating in front of the car, and my aunt had recognized immediately that Selene was trying to signal her. They had followed the floating light until it stopped in Quinn's driveway. The rest I already knew.

By the time we had finished our respective stories, it was nearly ten o'clock, and I was having trouble keeping my eyes open.

Treigh rose to leave, but said, "Ms. Alvarez, can I talk to Lia alone for a second before I leave? We need to settle a couple of things."

"Of course, dear," my mother obliged. "I'm going to run upstairs and get the guest room ready so that Kitty can stay the night." She patted my leg, and she and my aunt scooted up the stairs. Treigh turned to face me.

"Look, I don't want you to say anything until I'm done, okay?" I nodded, and he continued. "I'm still not okay with what you did, and I might have some trust issues for awhile, but when your mom called me and told me that you had maybe been kidnapped...or worse..." His voice trailed off for a minute, but then he gathered himself. "When I thought that I might never see you again, that you might...die...with us being like we were, well, I have never felt that bad in my life. I can't go on without my queen by my side." My eyes filled with tears. "But I also have to have you promise that you will NEVER use any kind of magic on me without my permission."

"I promise," I said, my voice quivering with emotion. "Treigh, I'm so sorry." I stood up and threw my arms around him, shaking with the few tears I had left. After a minute, he sniffled and broke the hug, but he was smiling."

"I want to make something very clear here. We are off this week for Thanksgiving, and I'll be damned if some tragedy is going to ruin the best food holiday on the calendar. You are to go NOWHERE alone this week. If your mom can't take you, you call me. If I'm not available, you wait. Do you understand me?"

I nodded. "Now you have to go to Gemma's Friendsgiving."

"Fine. Two days of food is an acceptable situation."

"You can bring Michael if you want..." I tiptoed around the subject.

"He's in North Carolina for Thanksgiving. I'll have to settle for you." He winked, and I felt better than I had in over a week, even given what I'd been through that day. "Alright, go to bed, and I'll call you tomorrow and check in."

"Okay." I hugged him one more time, locked the door behind him, and then dragged my tired bones up the stairs to my bedroom.

I am lying in a canoe on the ocean, staring up at the moon. The water rocks me gently, and I am soothed by the sound of the waves lapping against the side of the boat.

The goddess appears in a beam of moonlight, floating above me.
Thank you, Selene, *I say to her.* Thank you for helping them find me.
You're welcome, child. You did well. Your mind and instincts are strong.

I've never been so afraid.

You had good reason to be, child. The Magician is powerful. Usually he is wise and just, and has the power to manifest success by sheer will. But this Magician is reversed, deceitful and greedy. He is a dangerous man.

He said it wasn't over. That he'd see me again.

I suspect he will. He is not used to failing, and he does not take it lightly. You will need to grow stronger and make allies. There are secrets that will not stay hidden for long.

What does that mean? What secrets?

You will know in time, my dear. I am the mistress of hidden things, and these must reveal themselves in their own time.

So I'm still in danger?

Certainly so. Power brings danger, I'm afraid. Your aunt knew this, as did your grandmother. You will have to decide if you will embrace the power and learn to control it, or walk away and leave it for another generation.

I am not going to walk away. I'm scared, but I'm not going to let him win.

I am glad to hear that. The truth is, he will likely come for you whether you reject the power or not.

What? Why?

All things in time, my dear. Rest now.

She floats up and becomes one with the glowing orb in the sky, and I drift into a blissful and dreamless sleep.

Chapter 27

Being back in Treigh's good graces, I was now actually looking forward to Friendsgiving. I wasn't exactly looking forward to being around Alex, because AWKWARD, but the rest of it would be okay. Despite being told I didn't need to bring anything but a vegetable, my good Southern manners required that I bake something sweet to take along, even if it didn't get eaten right away. So I baked brownies, because you can never go wrong with chocolate.

True to my promise, I waited for Treigh to come get me, and we went to Gemma's together.

"Girl, you makin' my whole car smell like chocolate goodness," he half-complained. "The buffet was set out along the kitchen bar, and looked like a feast fit for royalty. She had opted for chicken, since most of us would be eating turkey the next day, and it was golden brown and speckled with aromatic herbs. There were several side dishes of red, green, orange, and brown, and of course an astonishing array of desserts.

"All this for eight people? You're going to have leftovers for a week! You really outdid yourself! This is just beautiful!" I raved.

Gemma grinned at the praise. "I just can't do anything halfway," she laughed.

We all sat down at the table, and I made a conscious effort to sit a couple of seats away from Alex. A bit of a challenge, really, since there were so few of us, but I managed to put Trina between us, so it was all good. We said a friends-related blessing and then got up to load our plates with goodies.

Conversation focused mainly on school and low-key gossip, and a steady flow of compliments toward Gemma for the incredible meal and the beauty of the table. She was positively alight, and I was happy for her, since she had gone to so much trouble. When all the eating was finally over, I got up to help her clear the table, despite her insistence that it wasn't necessary (again, Southern manners on both parts). I took on the job of clearing the table while she rinsed off dishes and put them in the dishwasher. As I was going back for another load, she started to hum while she worked, and I stopped dead in my tracks.

My mind flashed back to my captivity, to the moment just before Quinn entered the room for the first time. He had been humming the same tune she was humming as she rinsed. They had both been humming "For Good."

My brain whirred and I had to put my hand against the door frame for balance. What were the odds? Had to be astronomical, right? And yet...

I looked over my shoulder, and Gemma was humming away, oblivious to my alarm. I darted back toward the dining room to get Treigh and tell him we needed to leave. Stat. In my rush, rounded a corner without looking where I was going and ran directly into Alex's chest. He grunted with the impact.

"Uh, hey," he said uncomfortably.

"Hi. Did you have a nice time?" Good gravy. Could I come up with something lamer to say? Not likely. But more importantly, I needed to leave. Now.

"I, uh, yeah, it was good. But listen, I kind of wanted to talk to you. Do you have a minute?"

My eyes widened. Of all the times he could choose... "Yeah, a minute...Treigh and I need to go soon, but I could chat for a sec. What's up?"

"Look, I...man, this is awkward... I feel like I've been a real jerk to you. I mean, one minute, we're practically a couple, and then we're hardly talking. I'm sorry about that."

You could have knocked me over with a feather. HE was apologizing to ME? "Hey, it's okay. I mean, things change..." What was I supposed to say?

"No, it's not okay. I don't know what happened. I guess Halloween night just overloaded me or something. I mean, it was a crazy night, right?"

He had no idea how crazy. "Yeah, crazy. But it's cool, really. Apology accepted." How was it possible that here I was, in this rare and special moment, and all I could think about was getting out of here as fast as I could?

"Great. Maybe we could, I don't know, try going out for coffee or something not crazy?"

"Really?"

"Yeah, really." He smiled and then that lock of hair fell in his eyes.

"I'd...I'd like that, yes."

"Cool. I'm glad I got to talk to you before you left."

"Me too." And I swear, I really did mean it, but...

"Oh, look at you two!" Gemma came out of the kitchen, drying her hands on a dish towel. "No wonder you didn't come back." She elbowed me and grinned. "Way to go, my girl."

My skin crawled and goosebumps popped up on my arms. "Hey, Gemma, thanks for everything, but Treigh and I have to go." He looked up at me with a mouth full of pie and eyes full of questions. "Like now. Really need to go. Sorry to eat and run." I tried to look calm, cool, and collected, but inside I was screaming.

My girl.

I didn't know how, but Gemma and the Magician were connected.

In the car, I told Treigh about the humming and the use of the endearment Quinn had used for me. He eyed me skeptically.

"Lia, as your friend and the voice of reason, I think your trauma is playing games with your mind. Are you absolutely sure it was the same song? People hum, and if they aren't good singers, they could make two songs sound alike. You've been singing that song non-stop for over a week. So has Gemma."

"I'm pretty sure, Treigh."

"But you were drugged when you heard him singing, right?"

"Well, yes, but…"

"I'm not saying you're wrong, I'm just saying you MIGHT be imagining it. You have to at least consider the possibility. My brain said he had a point, but my gut told me otherwise.

I called my aunt as soon as Treigh dropped me off at home and asked her if I had lost my marbles. She said she wasn't sure, that it could be my mind playing tricks, or it could be something else.

"There's one way I know of that we could check," she said. "We could examine Gemma's aura. That's not a 100% accurate way to determine something like this, but it's probably easier than some other methods which would be pretty hard to disguise."

"How do we do that?"

"Well, we need someone who can see auras, for one. I never was any good at it, but Mary might know someone. I'll call her and ask, and I'll tell you tomorrow what I find out."

"Okay, that sounds pretty good," I agreed. I was still freaked out, but at least we had a plan of action. "I'll see you tomorrow."

Aunt Kitty's Prius pulled into the driveway around 1:00 on Thanksgiving afternoon. She was wielding her usual basket of baked goods and rolling a small suitcase.

"Are you staying over?" Mom asked. "You should have told me! I would've washed some fresh towels, and…"

"Hold it, hold it, Maddy," Aunt Kitty laughed. "I'm not staying over. This was just a convenient way to tote along a few things I thought you and Lia might like to have. All of these scares we've had lately have made me think that Lia needs to know more about the things she can do, and also about some of our family history."

"That sounds like it violates the spirit of the holiday, however practical it may be," Mom pouted. "But we'll let you stay anyway, since you brought biscotti."

"The universal currency," my aunt smiled, and climbed the steps into the kitchen.

The meal was small but satisfying; most importantly, I felt safe, protected, and loved. I had gained a tremendous appreciation for those things over the past week. Afterwards, we sat with cups of chai latte, and my mother lit a fire in the small fireplace while we drank.

"You probably need to know a bit more about your grandmother," my aunt said at last. "She was the Moon for about 35 years before relinquishing the power to me. She was notoriously difficult, but she was also very strong and, at one time in her life, very powerful."

"What happened to her?" I asked with a sense of foreboding.

"She had a heart attack, just as you were told. There wasn't anything mysterious about her death in and of itself. But she was very much a student of Selene's magic. She was constantly testing new abilities, working at developing them and making them stronger. She had a variety of skills I never developed, but then, I never worked at it the way that she did. I was much more content to keep to myself and only use Selene's gifts on occasion."

"Mom, did you know about all of this?"

"Not really," she replied. "I moved to Jacksonville to go to school and work for awhile. I wasn't involved or interested. I thought I was being practical; I never really believed in the things my mother would talk about. I thought she and your aunt were sort of New-Age hippie pagan types like a lot of people who tend to live near here. You know, like Casadaga, the new-age community down south a ways?"

Aunt Kitty patted her knee. "Your mom was always a stark realist, Lia. She never showed much interest in magic, so we didn't discuss it with her."

"I'm sorry about that now," Mom mused. "I wish I had known more about it. I feel like I've got a very steep learning curve here."

"The thing about your grandmother, Lia, is that she used her magic in whatever way she saw fit. She wasn't a bad person, but she was...shall we say...ethically flexible when it came to things like people's free will. That's one of the reasons I was so adamant about it with you. She felt like her magical abilities gave her the duty to push things in the direction she thought they should go. She was doing the right thing, by her way of thinking, but it didn't always have the best consequences. From what the few Arcana I've met have told me, she managed to tick off just about everyone. Probably the only thing that saved her from serious repercussions is that she never really had an organized goal or approach. She just did whatever she felt like doing in the moment."

"Like what?" Mom and I asked together.

"Well, influencing Maddy's and my dating lives for one. No boy she didn't like hung around for more than one date. I didn't realize until I was much older, by the way, that that was her doing. I'm pretty sure she attended a trial or two and made herself the thirteenth member of the jury, though she never admitted as much. She got her way a lot in business, as you might imagine. It's a good thing she wasn't in politics."

"That sounds very short-sighted," Mom observed. "I mean, what if her desires weren't the RIGHT thing? And we're going to revisit this dating issue later, Kitty. I have questions."

"That wasn't a problem she wrestled with, as far as I could tell. She followed what she thought was right, and that was good enough for her conscience. Here's what I think is significant, though, Lia. Other Arcana members courted her for her allegiance, just as they've courted you. But she was older and understood her powers, so she was able to protect herself better. She refused to associate with any of them, because she didn't trust that they wouldn't manipulate her."

"That seems like a pretty reasonable assumption."

"Indeed. But she did more than just say 'no, thank you.' She repelled them, made enemies of some. I sort of flew under the radar because I didn't make much use of the power. But you've come on the scene like a house of fire, and you've been noticed. There may be grudges at play, and also those who would play upon your youth and inexperience."

"So I need to train up pretty fast."

"Yes, I think so. And I don't think you can do all of it here. You need a mentor with more magical chops than I have. The Empress can be trusted, and I suspect she can make a connection or two for you going forward."

"Well, that's good to hear. It makes me feel a little less terrified to know there are at least a couple of trustworthy members of the Arcana. Is she going to help us read Gemma's aura?"

"Not her specifically, no, but she has a student who seems to be fairly adept at it."

"One of the Arcana?"

"No, just a young woman with gifts. But if Mary says she can be trusted, then I believe her. We'll meet up with her Saturday. Your job is to find a way to get together with Gemma so that we can observe and see what we can find out."

"Yeah, okay. Can I invite her here?" I didn't relish the idea of being anywhere with Gemma that wasn't protected.

"Sadly, no," my aunt explained. "My wards will neutralize whatever magic she has, just as the Magician's wards neutralized yours."

"But someplace public," Mom insisted.

Chapter 28

Black Friday was not a shopping day in our house. It was a wear-jammies-all-day-and- eat-leftovers-and-watch-the-Harry-Potter-marathon day. In other words, one of my favorite days of the year. True to form, we never even left the house except to get the mail.

I did text Gemma and ask her if she wanted to meet at Dotz for a coffee so I could thank her for the lovely Friendsgiving party. She was quick to agree, and I communicated the details to Aunt Kitty so she could set things up with the Empress.

The next day, Aunt Kitty pulled up in the driveway with the Empress and a woman of indeterminate age (though I guessed maybe thirty) with bright purple hair. She had an easy smile and a wide array of piercings and tattoos. They certainly made quite a pair. Mary introduced her to me as Kai.

"So you see auras?" I asked. "What do they look like?"

Kai smiled like a teacher does when a student asks her first question of the school year: indulgent, patient, encouraging. "Well, you know what the corona around the sun looks like? Sort of like radiation rising from the source?" I nodded. "It's kind of like that. But different colors mean different things, and that tells you about the person. It's easiest to see if the person is in low-ish light and against a blank wall, but with practice, that's not necessary."

"So you can see mine?"

"Sure. Yours is mostly yellow, which tells me you're a pretty optimistic person by nature. But there are also some spots that are sort of gray swirling around, which tell me you've been having some negative emotions, like stress, depression, or fear. But there's this additional halo around it that's really thin of deep violet. That tells me you have great power."

"Whoa, that's cool."

"So here's the plan," Aunt Kitty interjected. "You'll go and meet Gemma as planned, and then Mary and Kai will enter a couple of minutes later. They'll stay for a few minutes, just enough to get a feel for Gemma's energy. Then they'll leave and come back here. You have your coffee and chat for another ten minutes or so, then head home, and we can debrief. How's that? Simple?"

"Works for me," I agreed, though something told me it wasn't going to be simple at all.

A few minutes later, I found myself sitting on the bench outside Dotz, waiting for Gemma so we could walk in together. Once she arrived, we placed our orders and I picked us a seat near the back wall. It wasn't a blank wall; it was covered with vinyl records, but I hoped it would do.

"Hey, I'm sorry I had to bug out so quickly on Wednesday," I began. "I hadn't been feeling all that well, and I didn't want to pass out or something and ruin your party."

"Omigosh, are you doing alright?" Her concern seemed so genuine that I was starting to feel a little foolish for suspecting her of anything.

"Oh, yeah, I'm fine. Probably just low iron in my blood or something. I'm feeling much better after a couple days of rest."

The door jingled open, and Kai and Mary entered. The young man at the register greeted them, and Mary went over and made grandmotherly chatter while Kai wandered around and looked at the coffees, baked goods, funky decor, everything. I kept Gemma engaged in small talk so she wouldn't notice when Kai staked out a seat along the window where she could sneak regular glances Gemma's direction without being seen. Mary brought some muffins to their table and they proceeded to talk in low tones about who-knows-what.

"So, you and Alex seemed friendly at the end of the meal there…any exciting news?"

I laughed uneasily. "Well, not yet. I'm not holding my breath. But he did apologize for ghosting me," I chuckled internally at my pun, given the events of Halloween night.

"See?" she exclaimed. "I told you he'd come around!"

Mary and Kai finished their muffins, thanked the cashier, and left. Gemma barely registered that they had been there at all.

We talked for a few more minutes, and ran through the lines for our duo. I was getting ready to make my goodbyes when my mother strode through the door. I was alarmed by the change in plans.

"Hi, honey! I'm so sorry to barge in on your visit, but your Aunt Kitty has had a little mishap, and she needs us to come help her right away." The tension was flowing off my mother in waves.

"Is Aunt Kitty alright?"

"Oh, I'm sure she'll be fine, but we need to go help her. She's fallen and hurt her back, and it's about a forty minute drive. So we need to get over there right away." Now I knew something was up. Aunt Kitty should be sitting in my living room right now, not lying on the floor back at home. My mother didn't lie casually, so she was clearly trying to extract me immediately because she thought I was in danger.

"Oh, Gemma, I'm sorry I keep doing this to you." I apologized.

"No, not at all! By all means, go take care of your aunt! I hope she's okay!" Again, so sincere. So what was going on? What had Kai seen? I gave Gemma a quick hug and made a quick exit, where my mother's car was waiting. What the heck?

Once we were inside and backing out of the parking spot, I asked, "So what's going on? You pulled me out of there like my life depended on it! And where are we going?"

"Oh, we're going back home, but we're going to circle around a little and then come in the back way and hide the car in the garage."

"Why?"

"Apparently there's a car a block over that's watching you. I'd better let Kai tell you the rest. I didn't fully understand it. I just know they thought you were in danger, and they said to hurry and come get you before you had a chance to start walking home."

This stunned me into silence, and I rode in quiet agitation as we wound north on Ponce de Leon, then got off and wound through back streets until we got home. We darted from the detached garage into the house. Inside, Aunt Kitty, Kai, and the Empress were waiting with the blinds mostly shut.

My mouth was dry, like it had been stuffed with a washcloth for hours. I found it impossible to speak. I just stared at them and waited for an explanation.

"Oh, thank the goddess," Mary breathed. "You weren't followed?" She addressed this to my mother.

"No, I don't think so. I took a lot of turns and retraced my steps before coming back here."

"Good, good." She walked over and took my hands, which were trembling ever-so-slightly. She led me to sit on the couch, and patted my hands comfortingly as Kai opened her mouth to speak.

"So, at first I thought it was a false alarm," Kai began. "Gemma's aura was like pink lemonade, swirling with yellow and pink. Perky, positive, girly." That sounded like the Gemma I knew. "And then after a minute, I noticed something I hadn't seen before. There was this thin energy stream of violet and purple. But it wasn't surrounding her, like auras are supposed to do. It was like a tether, an umbilical cord, linking her to something outside the cafe."

I still couldn't speak. I just stared while she continued to explain, and tried desperately not to shiver from the cold that was creeping up my spine.

"When we left, I kept watching the cord to see where it led, and it seemed to be attached to a car about a block away. I couldn't see the person in the car clearly, but it was definitely a man with a deep violet aura like yours."

"The Magician," I squeaked.

"We think so," Aunt Kitty said. "He may have been trying to recapture you. And the tether tells us that Gemma is, in fact, connected to him. But maybe not in the way we thought."

"What does that mean?" I was trying to get angry at Gemma. Anger was better than fear. I had had enough of the taste of fear this week.

"We think Gemma is unaware of the connection," the Empress said gently. "We think he's watching you through her eyes. Perhaps influencing her to stay close to you. The Magician is a master of control."

I suddenly didn't know how to feel. I wanted to be angry, but I couldn't if Gemma didn't even know she was being used. I wanted to cry, but I'd cried so much in the past month, I was dry. I wanted to jump into action, but I had no idea what to do.

All that was left was fear. Fear to leave the house alone, fear to be friends with anyone because they might be another pawn in the Magician's game, fear of losing the person I had always been.

The Empress was right. He was a master of control.

And even without zip ties, he had me trapped and afraid.

"This might not be all bad," Kai offered. "If you can figure out how he's doing this, how he's tied himself to her, you may be able to use the connection to trap him somehow. Or maybe you can at least break the connection."

"Solid thinking," the Empress agreed. "He would need a physical link to her in order to use her in that way, I should think. To the best of my knowledge, the Magician doesn't possess the power of sigils, so that sort of continuous mind control would need a physical object to anchor it to."

"A talisman?" my aunt asked.

"Just so, Katherine. Lia, think carefully. Is there an item that Gemma always has with her? It would not be something electronic, so her cell phone would not count."

It only took me a moment to think of something. "Her ring. There's this small gold band she wears on her pinky. She twiddles with it all the time."

"Ah, that is definitely a likely suspect. Jewelry is ideal for talismans. And you don't know where she got it?"

"No, we've never talked about it."

"Well," my mother chimed in, "it sounds like we need to find that out. And then figure out how to separate her from it. Get rid of it somehow."

We needed to find out where that ring had come from. There was no point in going through with some elaborate plan for some ordinary ring. If we were able to determine that the ring was likely to be a talisman, then the next step was to convince her to take it off. Then we had to neutralize it somehow.

And all of this had to be done in such a way that Gemma had no idea what had happened. If she was being unwittingly used by the Magician, then she was an innocent victim of his control, and I didn't want to hurt her.

And so we began hatching a plan.

Chapter 29

Sundays were supposed to be quiet. Have I mentioned that? The prior Sunday had been anything but, and the last thing I wanted to do was to deal with anything more stressful than homework I'd procrastinated on. So when I saw a black SUV by my mailbox, I was about ready to go to war.

Mom was making her Sunday morning grocery run, so I should have stayed inside, but I stormed out on the porch and put my hands on my hips. Claudia had already stepped out of the vehicle and was walking up the sidewalk, flanked by her brother.

"You picked the wrong girl on the wrong day," I said, seething.

Claudia was taken aback, but only for a moment. "I hardly think that's necessary. I came by to tell you we received your message. We were hoping to set up a semi-regular means of communication." Her glare betrayed her semi-polite words, and even though he was pretty slick about it, I saw John nudge her, urging her to dial it back.

"Sorry," I said through gritted teeth. "I've had a rough week, and I'm really not up to this conversation right now. You have my number to text me. What more are you asking?"

"May we speak inside?" she asked.

"I'm sorry, but no. I'm afraid I'm pretty thin on trust these days. It's not entirely your fault, but there appear to be a lot of wheels turning that I don't know about amongst the Arcana folks."

Claudia's eyes darted around nervously as she reached the bottom porch step. "That is NOT a conversation for open ears, Lia," she reprimanded me.

The truth was that she was right about that part, and even though I didn't have super-nosy neighbors, this scene might well attract unwanted attention.

"I'll tell you what, we can talk for five minutes. Right here on the porch. You're not coming inside. I don't know what kind of things you can do, and I'm not letting you in my house."

For the first time, John spoke up in his sister's presence. "Lia, did something happen?" I had to give it to him, he did seem genuinely concerned.

"You could say that." I opened the screen door and waved them to a seat on the wicker sofa. I sat in a chair a few feet away.

"Perhaps we can be of assistance?" Claudia offered. "A favor for a favor?"

"Hard pass. Like I said, I'm not feeling too trusting these days, and the last thing I want to do is enter into some kind of magical agreement on accident."

Claudia looked frustrated, but let it drop. She changed tactics. "So, you mentioned you'd like to stay in touch…"

"Generally speaking, yes. I don't trust anyone not to try and take advantage of me right now. I also don't think I'm generally on the side of interfering with free will. But I do think that you are trying to do what's right by your own standards, anyway, and I don't think we need to be enemies."

"But not allies either?"

"Not exactly, because I still feel like you have things going on behind the scenes that you aren't telling me. I don't expect you to; you don't know me either. But maybe we can see each other as sort of colleagues or something."

"Back to my original question, then," she pressed. "Can we set up a regular check-in schedule? Perhaps to let you know what we have going on, and see if you'd like to be part of it?" It was really taking a lot of effort on her part to be so accommodating. "At least until we are able to build up some level of trust?"

"I guess that would be okay. But you have to text first. No more showing up on my lawn or at my school. I look like an FBI snitch or something."

John covered his mouth in a fake cough to hide his chuckle. Claudia wasn't fooled and shot him a side-eye glare.

"I find your terms acceptable." As if it were some kind of legal proceeding. "Shall we say bi-weekly?"

"Sure, that's fine. But I don't really need a set schedule. Not as long as you text first. I'm just done with surprises from members of the Arcana."

"You mentioned something like that a moment ago. Have you had surprise visits from…someone else?"

The goosebumps on my arm told me she knew something I didn't, and she didn't want to show her hand too soon.

"Yes. Someone else." I wasn't going to show my hand either.

"I see." She shot a look at John, whose brow was furrowed with genuine concern. "Perhaps someday we can try and offer you some information to help you deal with unwanted advances."

I gave her a hard look. "I studied irony in English class. Did you?" That was both snarky and rude of me, but the audacity of her offering me assistance against "unwanted advances"…

Then she did something unexpected. She laughed. "In fact, I did. I believe our five minutes are up." She rose to go, and John followed suit, as usual. I stood and opened the screen door. "Speak to you in two weeks," she said, and led the way to the SUV.

John paused just long enough to whisper, "Be safe." as he passed me. Then they both got in the SUV and drove out of sight.

I took a deep breath once they were gone, and resolved to go upstairs and crawl into bed, and not get up for the rest of the day, except to eat or pee. I was SO done.

I told Treigh the whole Gemma-as-unknowing-spy theory on our way into school on Monday, and my opportunity for Phase One came during English class. Mrs. West had given us the obligatory just-back-from-break-so-here's-some-group-work assignment, and we were allowed to pick our own groups of four. I jumped into Gemma's group with Trina and Alex (for once, Alex wasn't my motivation for such a move). We were brainstorming ideas for persuasive speeches, which gave me an excellent chance to slip in a probing comment as we worked. As usual, she was spinning her ring around and around on her finger. I took a closer look at it. It was a simple gold band, with little triangles cut out of it at intervals.

"That's a really pretty ring," I said simply, and then I reached out with my influence, willing her to offer up information about it. I wasn't sure it would work, but I was hoping that since I wasn't asking her about it directly, the Magician's magic wouldn't catch onto mine.

I ran my hand over my front jeans pocket, where I'd hidden a small bagful of blessed hematite that Aunt Kitty had given me. Hematite crystal had grounding properties, she said, and if properly blessed, might just cancel out the enchantment on the ring. If I could get my hands on the ring, that was.

"Aw, thank you! You know, I don't even remember where I got it? I just found it a couple of months ago in my jewelry box when I was digging around for an earring. I think it might have been my mom's, but I'm not sure."

"Oh, well, it's nice," I complimented her again. "It really suits you."

I let the conversation drop at that point, because if Quinn was listening, I didn't want him to know that I had any interest in the ring other than a generic compliment. We continued our assignment, and I didn't bring it up again.

At the end of class, though, Alex reiterated his offer of a coffee date, and I eagerly accepted. We decided on Wednesday, because he didn't have to work. I wanted to be more excited, because he was actually showing interest without any influence from me, but ensuring my safety took top priority, and my focus was more on what I'd learned from Gemma.

Based on the information she had volunteered, I thought it was likely that the ring was, indeed, a talisman. Now to figure out how to convince her to take it off. I had to find an opportunity that seemed organic, but fortunately I had enough contact with her that I could probably figure something out. English class wasn't a likely time to get her to divest herself of the item, but there was always drama, and I could also probably hit her up for some final rehearsals of *Wicked* outside of school, since our evaluation was only a week away.

No natural opportunity arose in drama for me to enact Phase Two, so I asked her if we might get together Tuesday afternoon at her house for a short rehearsal. Just to make sure we were ready for our evaluation, of course. She eagerly agreed, and I wondered if I was dangling a huge carrot out there for Quinn to try and snatch me again.

"Hey, maybe Trina and Treigh could come and watch, too...maybe give us some feedback?" I suggested.

"What a good idea!" she gushed. I breathed a sigh of relief. I'd feel a little bit safer that way. At least I couldn't get snatched off the street. Besides, Treigh was my limousine service these days.

Tuesday afternoon, we all convened at Gemma's house and, true to form, she had an array of snacks out within moments. She definitely knew how to hostess, and to win Treigh's allegiance. The way to a man's heart and all that.

We rehearsed our scene a couple of times, and then performed it for our somewhat captive audience. Mostly they told us how great we were, but they also made a couple of good blocking suggestions for movement and gestures that would add to the scene overall. When we finished the practice, I started helping her gather the dishes to take to the kitchen.

"Oh, you don't need to do that!" Gemma insisted.

"I do, though! I really abandoned you last week. Let me help!"

"You're so sweet; thank you!"

I carried the stack of dishes over to the farmhouse sink, and decided this might be my chance. I slipped the idea into her mind that her parents would really appreciate it if she cleaned up not just our snack dishes, but the breakfast dishes that were still in the sink.

"You know what? I think I'm going to take a minute to clean up these dishes."

"Oh, good idea!" I replied. "You wash, I'll dry!"

"You are just the best!" If she only knew...

I sent her another suggestion: an image of her ring slipping off of a wet finger and falling down the disposal. She looked around for a moment, confused, and then slipped the ring off and placed it on the windowsill above the sink. We worked on the dishes for a couple of minutes, chatting while we worked.

"What are you two up to?" Treigh called from the other room.

"You just settle down," Gemma laughed and turned to poke her head in the other room. I took the opportunity to snatch the ring off the windowsill and slip it into the bag of hematite in one quick movement.

She walked back to the sink, and we finished the dishes. She gathered them up and headed across the kitchen to put them back in the cabinet.

I knew I had to try to distract her from the fact that she wasn't wearing her ring, so I gave her sense of urgency around getting her homework done a little nudge. Okay, a big nudge. I hated messing with her thoughts, but I didn't see any other way to accomplish what needed accomplishing. Plus, it was a matter of self-preservation. I was definitely Team FreeWill, but I wasn't an absolutist.

"Hey," she said as she closed the cabinet. "I hate to rush you guys out the door, but I have a lot of homework tonight, and a test in French tomorrow, and I really need to study."

"No problem at all," I smiled. "I really appreciate you letting me come over so we could practice. I really want an A on that scene."

"Me, too. I think we've got this!"

I agreed, "Totally! Okay, Treigh, time for us to head out! Gemma's got a boatload of homework to do!"

We all said our goodbyes, and Trina, Treigh, and I got in our cars to leave. Once we had pulled safely away from the house, I took a deep breath and let it out.

"What is that about?" Treigh asked.

"I'm not sure I can tell you just yet, but can you take me over by the train tracks on the way home?"

He cocked one eyebrow at me. "Do I even want to know?"

"Not yet, you don't."

As requested, Treigh pulled off into a parking lot off of Route 1. There were train tracks running behind the aluminum business building and, beyond the tracks, the San Sebastian River. I jogged across the parking lot and the tracks, and took off my boots and rolled up my jeans. I busted a little brush, and sunk my toes into the muck on the edge of the river. I pulled the hematite bag out of my pocket, pushed up my sleeves, and shoved the bag several inches down in the sticky mud. Then I swished my feet and hands in the water and waded back onto solid ground. I wiped the bottoms of my feet on the railroad ties, grabbed and pulled on my boots, and made my way back to Treigh's car.

He was leaning on the driver's door as I approached.

"Girl, what in the name of good sense are you doing?"

"Get in the car and take me home, and I'll tell you all about it."

When we got back to my house, he came inside and I called my mom into the room. Then I called Aunt Kitty and put her on speaker.

"Well, I'm hoping Gemma is no longer Dominic Quinn's personal livestream," I announced, and then I told them what I had done with the ring.

"That was very clever," Aunt Kitty approved. "Let's hope it works."

Chapter 30

My mission accomplished, I was able to focus my energy on what I should have been able to focus on, had I been a normal teenager anymore: my coffee date.

This time, I knew that I had not influenced Alex's interest in me. Sure, he might never have given me a second thought had I not accidentally bewitched him, but the past was the past, and I could dwell on that. It also occurred to me that if Gemma had been somehow influenced by the Magician, it was possible she wasn't the only one.

I figured it might be wise to protect against that possibility. I sat cross-legged on the floor of my room and pictured the protective energy field the Empress had placed around me. I imagined it glowing with a bright white light that would repel anyone who would wish me harm. It occurred to me that the protection spell had not kept the Magician from kidnapping me, maybe because by his way of thinking, he didn't mean me harm. Some modification of the spell was going to be necessary. I concentrated and pictured myself in front of the magical closet that held my abilities.

Beside the closet door is a full-length mirror. I face it, and I see the protection around my body like a second skin. I turn my right palm upward in front of me and reach for my own power, willing the Magician to keep his distance. A thin stream of something that looks like bright violet smoke begins to flow out of my index finger. I focus on it, put my strength behind it. 'You and your agents will stay away!' I think, infusing this thought into the stream of power. The violet energy blends in white in swirls, creating a pulsing watercolor of protection.

'Beautiful work,' says a voice behind me.

'Selene,' I whisper, and I turn to face her. 'Can you protect me from him?'

'Your power flows from me. In this way, I am always protecting you. Just as his power flows from his god. We do not manifest directly onto your plane of existence; you are our hands here.'

'So Mercury helped him kidnap me?' I am both angry and afraid. Why would Mercury give me a second thought?

She inclined her head slightly. 'Not precisely. It may be that Mercury supports his larger goal, and the ends justify the means to him.'

'Can you just ask him?'

'What have I to do with Mercury? I know his name, and that is all, just as he knows mine.'

'I thought maybe Greek and Roman deities might, you know, run in the same circles.'

'No, my dear. Gods rarely interact with each other. There was a time when each pantheon might have recognized each other, though not as much as humans always thought. We do not think or feel quite as you do. We see a much larger Universal picture and tend to focus on things beyond the minute obsessions of humans. I do not say this to belittle you, Lia. We are just...other...than you. I am bound to you by the card, and so my energy is intertwined with yours. When you are strong, so am I, and vice versa. The same is true of the Magician. We care about you two because we are part of you. We are not, however, part of your world, or part of each other's, technically.'

'That's confusing.'

'Because you do not see the Pattern as we do. But I can tell you that the protection you have woven around yourself is quite potent. You have infused my power into your own. Well done.'

My head is trying to understand what she has told me about the nature of gods, but I can't quite grasp it.

'Am I safe from him?' I ask. It's the only question I really want to wrestle with right now.

'What you consider safety and what he considers safety may not be the same thing. But he will be less inclined to have anything to do with you at all with these modifications you've made.'

I nod. Good enough, and probably as direct an answer as I'm going to get. I drift back down into full consciousness.

I wasn't sure how long I had been meditating, but I was feeling very tired. Apparently, tapping into Goddess energy and making use of it takes a lot out of a person. I crawled into bed, opting to figure out a traffic-stopping outfit in the morning.

I woke up ten minutes before my alarm was set to go off. Honestly, is there anything worse than that? Not enough time to doze back off, just enough to let you know you're up early. Ugh. But I resolved to put the time to good use. I jumped through the shower, dried my hair quickly with the blow-dryer, and parked myself in front of my open closet. Alex and I had been on several dates, and I'd already shown my A-game. I was going to have to figure out how to impress him yet again, this time without my magical enhancements. No glamour, just me.

That thought gave me a moment of clarity.

Just me.

I stopped rifling through my closet looking for the "perfect" ensemble. If Alex was going to like me, it was going to have to be without all the crazy effort to look my "best", whatever that meant. I reached in and pulled out a deep green sundress. It might be too cool out for a sundress...it was the first day of December, for goodness sake...but I wanted to wear something that made ME feel strong, something that I liked, not something I thought he might like. I threw the dress on and pulled on my Docs. I wound my hair into a messy, spiky bun and put a coat of mascara on my eye lashes. My lips got a quick coat of dark purple lip stain. No twenty-minute make-up jobs, no thirty minutes curling or straightening my hair. I grabbed a black leather jacket and surveyed my handiwork in the mirror. A grand total of thirty minutes to get ready, half of which was spent drying my hair. Yep, this was me. He would like me or he wouldn't, and at least this time it would be his choice.

We had a test in English, so we didn't get to talk much, but he did grin and give me an appreciative thumbs-up when I walked in. At the end of class, he asked me to meet him at his car and he'd drive to the coffee shop. He seemed unfazed by my new and improved protections, so I felt pretty confident he wasn't another accomplice to the Magician.

I got to his car before he did, and leaned on his trunk while I waited. I had to admit, standing out in the open like this made me a little nervous, so I imagined pulses of electricity crackling over my aura to try and energize the protection surrounding me. When he finally arrived at the car, he opened the passenger door for me and I slid into the seat, my stomach flipping and flopping, but more out of excitement than fear.

We stood in line and gave our orders to the barista, a jaded looking twenty-something, most likely a student at Flagler. Once our names were called, we took our coffees and sunk into the over-stuffed chairs that had been put in to make the corporate chain seem somehow less corporate.

"I'm glad you decided to give me another shot," he began.

I couldn't let him go down the apology road again. He had no idea that he had nothing to apologize for, and I couldn't explain to him why that was.

"Let's not focus on past events, okay? Let's just be in the present." I took a deep breath and sipped my blonde vanilla latte. Not Goth at all, but here I was, just being me, and I was not an edgy coffee drinker.

"Yeah, cool," he agreed. And then he asked about how I thought Gemma and I would do on Wicked, complained about leading rude tourists on ghost tours, talked about school. Just normal stuff. No great pronouncements about his feelings or my beauty. Just a nice, relaxed, friendly conversation. Not exactly the stuff of romance novels, but a good place to start if we had any chance to build anything real.

Once we finished our drinks, we sat and talked for another half an hour, and then rose to leave. As he let me back into the passenger seat, I felt a little electrical prickle on my arm. I looked for the source, expecting to see Quinn standing in a doorway somewhere, but didn't see anything out of the ordinary. Alex backed out of the parking spot and headed toward my house. I was pleased that he remembered the way without having to ask. He pulled up at the end of my front walk, the way he had done seven weeks earlier.

"This was really nice," I smiled, wondering what he would do next.

"Yeah, it really was." He seemed to be wondering, too.

So I leaned over and kissed him softly, and maybe a little bit lingeringly, on the cheek. As I pulled away, he turned toward me and brushed his lips against mine. We smiled at each other, blushing.

"See you tomorrow," I said, buzzing with adrenaline.

"Yeah, tomorrow," he replied, and I sort of liked that he wasn't eloquent or smooth about it. I got out of the car and trotted up the front walk. When I reached the screen door to the front porch, I looked back. He was still sitting there, watching me and grinning.

Good date. Very good date.

Chapter 31

The next few days passed by smoothly. Gemma seemed fine, and in fact, didn't seem to miss the ring at all. At least she never mentioned it.

Treigh and I were good, and Treigh and Michael were good, too. I more or less stayed away from the subject, and let Treigh give me updates when he wanted to. I never brought Michael up or asked about their relationship. Which apparently it had become. I was very happy for Treigh, even if there was still a little bit of tension between us on that particular subject.

I didn't sense any more little electrical *pings* on my magical alarm system, and I started to feel just a little bit safer than I had for weeks.

I felt like I was starting to get a handle on this magical abilities thing. According to what my aunt had told me, though, my grandmother had spent decades exploring the capabilities and limitations of her abilities, so the odds were that I had just scratched the surface. I decided to see if the stuff Aunt Kitty brought would bring any further enlightenment.

I unzipped the suitcase in order to inventory the contents of what Aunt Kitty had brought. In one pocket, I found a bag of crystals, a couple of books about meditation and herbal medicine, a black cloth with silver embroidery. In another pocket, I found a pamphlet about chakras and a chart about something called the Tree of Life. In the center section, I found the motherlode: several notebooks and cookbooks in my grandmother's handwriting, and a shoebox full of pictures.

I flipped through the journals and saw very little of interest at first glance. They appeared to be actual day-to-day diaries, mostly, filled with her reflections on daily activities. I would have to go through them in more detail, though, as there might be references to some of the things she'd learned about her abilities during the course of her trial-and-error experimentation.

I began sorting through the photographs, some of which seemed to go back to the fifties, while others were clearly taken within my lifetime. It was astonishing to me to see photos of my grandmother with long, straight hair and a headband, smiling awkwardly for an elementary school picture. Her face was unlined and youthful, but she still had those same intense dark eyes. I found a similar picture of me from preschool, with the same long, straight hair, but with eyes not quite as dark or as intense.

I found pictures of my mother and aunt at various ages, and a few rare shots with my grandfather, who died before I was born, in them. As I neared the bottom of the stack, I found a photo which made my blood run cold and set my hands shaking.

My mother was smiling and young, probably fresh out of college. She had that signature Alvarez hair up in a high ponytail, and her face was lit up with laughter. Her left arm was flung affectionately around the waist of a man who was obviously the object of her affection: a handsome man with thick, black hair and gray eyes. Dominic Quinn.

Trembling, I moved slowly across the hall to my mother's room.

"Mom?" I handed her the photo, afraid to say more.

She took the photo and looked at it, and her expression changed from curiosity to one of reverie and maybe a little sadness.

"Oh, I don't think I've ever seen this picture before. I didn't even know your grandmother had it." She gazed wistfully at the photo, transfixed and lost in thought. Then, as if suddenly remembering my presence, she looked up at me. She seemed unable to interpret the expression on my face, but she looked vaguely ashamed.

"This must have been quite a surprise for you to find," she said.

Fear, rage, confusion...my emotions spun through me so quickly that I almost couldn't feel anything at all.

"You could say that," I replied.

"I didn't know I had any pictures of him. We weren't really together all that long before he left me and moved back home to London."

Wait.

No.

"Are you saying that's my father?" I asked, panic trumping out all the other feelings.

"Yes, Lia, that's your dad, Dorian Blair. He..."

"Mom, that's Dominic Quinn. That's the man who kidnapped me!"

"What?"

"The man in this picture...my father, apparently...is the Magician."

The implications of this information were overwhelming. I wasn't sure where to begin or how to feel. My mother and I just stared at each other for a moment, trying to take in the many facets of this knowledge.

1. I now knew what my father looked like.
2. Not only had I met him several times in the past couple of months, but he had apparently sought me out as soon as I became the Moon.
3. My father's idea of dad-daughter bonding was a little stalking and kidnapping.

4. My father was a very powerful Arcana, and apparently had plans for me magically speaking.

And then, the questions:
1. What, exactly, did my father want from me, and why did he think kidnapping was the way to get it?
2. Did he know when he met my mother that we were the keepers of the Moon card?
3. And if the answer to #2 was yes, did he somehow influence my mother into a relationship?
4. Also, if #2 was a yes, why not just stay involved in my life instead of disappearing for 16 years and then showing up like this?
5. And, on a much more random level, if he was from London, why didn't he have an accent during any of the times I'd met him?

We called my aunt and told her the news, which alarmed her greatly.

"There's something much deeper going on here. The odds of this being coincidental are astronomical. The Arcana are scattered all over North America and Europe. Most of us have only met one or two others in our lives. There's no way this wasn't orchestrated. The question is, what does he hope to gain?"

My mother was on the edge of tears. Here was a man she had cared for, who had played her in potentially the worst of ways. He likely hadn't cared for her at all. And as if that weren't bad enough, he was posing danger to the child they shared, the child who had been the center of her life for nearly 17 years. "I don't know what Dorian's up to, but there's no way he's getting to Lia again." And then she let loose a string of profanity that was as impressive as it was rare for her. I understood. Rage was preferable to pain and fear as feelings went. My father had taught me that, too.

I felt a gentle tug at my mind. I wasn't sure how I knew, but I was certain that Selene had been waiting for me to make this discovery, and now she wanted to talk. I excused myself and left my mother on the phone with her sister.

Alone in my room, I took the card in my hand and sat on my floor like I had so many times recently.

I am in a canoe on the ocean. This time I'm sitting up, staring at the Goddess who had been waiting for me.

'You knew,' I accuse her.

She shrugs noncommittally. 'Of course I knew. I'm the Mistress of Secrets, I told you. All secrets belong to me, not just yours."

'So why didn't you just tell me?'

'I am the Keeper of Secrets, not the Revealer of Secrets. But now that you know, there is a great deal for us to talk about. You are the bloodline of two Arcana. That presents certain...complexities.'

Her logic makes sense, and I realize that I am not angry at her, but at him. It was his secret to share all along, and the fact that he hadn't not only robbed me of a father, which I could live with, but also placed my family in danger and emotionally wounded my mother.

'What complexities?' I ask.

'You have twice the magic in your blood. And you have both my abilities and the potential for his.'

This is something I had not considered. 'What does that mean, in a practical sense?'

She looks off to sea, but I can see that the conundrum intrigues her. 'You are very powerful, certainly, or you will be once you learn more. Your grandmother would greatly envy your position. She was always experimenting, trying to stretch her powers, but ultimately, her powers were limited to what I offered her. Yours do not have those same limits. You are not just the Moon's child, but potentially the Magician's as well.'

'What does that mean?' I lean forward, and the canoe rocks slightly. She turns to face me.

'You are the Moon, Lia, but you could be the Magician also.'

'At the same time?' This revelation is mind-blowing. I can't imagine what that would look like, or what it would mean. My life is already out of control.

'Perhaps. This is a new phenomenon. But you can be sure of this: he has a plan. The Magician is the embodiment of strength of will. He will not give up on whatever goal he has in mind. You might consider learning more about what you can do. Follow your grandmother's example in this. You must prepare."

'Prepare for what?'

'The Magician's next move. His endgame. There is one, you know, and your innocence and naiveté means nothing to him, except that he can use you more easily. Learn. Prepare. Be the strongest.'

And then she dissolves into the moonlight's reflection on the water.

I opened my eyes and tried to digest what she was saying. I was going to need help. And snacks. Lots of snacks.

Chapter 32

Among all my other problems was the fact that the regular, daily grind of school and teenaged drama didn't just disappear because I was dealing with the complications of having a two-headed magical lineage. I still had homework and tests. I still felt awkward about talking to Treigh about his relationship with Michael (which might seem minor, but when someone is your best friend, it's a big deal), I still had a budding *something* with Alex that I didn't know how to define.

On the bright side, Gemma and I knocked Mr. Adams' socks off with our *Wicked* performance, and she got highly praised (a very rare occurrence in any advanced drama class, I assure you) on her cutting, which left her glowing with pride. She also didn't seem too upset about her missing ring, so I felt pretty solid about what I'd done. I was still careful about what I said around her, though, just in case.

I spent a lot of time on the phone with Aunt Kitty, talking about what it meant to have two magical parents, but she said she'd never heard of it happening before, so we couldn't be totally sure of what the implications were. I spent about a half an hour each night working on my telekinesis and was getting pretty adept with anything less than ten pounds.

I read through my grandmother's journals, and found very little of value. Either she kept her magical notes somewhere else, or she didn't write them down. I did find one passage which alluded to her magical experiments, but I wasn't sure how useful it was.

April 14, 1987
  Progress is slow and incremental. I hate having limits, but I understand why it's necessary. Combinations equal complications, but oh, what an adventure that would be! There are those who would breed a reigning family who blend several cards together, but the danger outweighs the potential in my mind. I've seen what experiments from only one can do...combined power would be a great temptation, and could alter the Pattern altogether. Too risky. They aren't happy with my decision not to join them, but I think they'll leave me alone as long as I don't stand in their way. After all, I have my girls to think of, and one of them will be heir to my decisions.

So, my grandmother had been approached, just as my aunt had thought, and had refused this idea of combining magical lineages. I had to agree; that sounded like too much power for humans to wield.

On Friday night, Treigh came over for dinner, and I updated him on the week's discoveries. We had agreed not to discuss my abilities at school or over text or phone, since there was no way to be sure our communications were safe from the Magician's or the Tower's ears. After dinner, I talked Treigh into going with me to surprise Alex on the ghost tour he was leading.

We showed up to the tour office in the Colonial Quarter just a few minutes before departure and bought our tickets. Alex beamed when he saw us, then flipped into tour guide mode and off we went.

This time, though, I was ready. I had put on my mental "ghost glasses" and was astonished at the number of spirits wandering the streets of Old St. Augustine. Most of them were what the ghost books called "residuals". Not really ghosts exactly, more like trapped recordings, replaying past events and unaware of the humans around them. Funnily enough, of all the tourists in the group, there seemed to be one woman, maybe 50 years old, who seemed to be able to sense some of what I could see.

When we passed the many of the haunted homes on the tour, there was nothing there to see. Maybe some energy, but no ghosts. But when we passed by one alley in particular, things changed.

As we walked by, I was shocked to see two men struggling. At first, I thought it was two men from a nearby bar arguing, but then I realized that they had that translucent shimmer that set spirits apart from the living. Even so, I almost cried out out when one man stabbed the other.

At that same moment, the sensitive woman (that's what Aunt Kitty called normal humans who could perceive spirits) gasped and grabbed her husband's arm.

"What's up?" I heard him say softly. "Everything okay?"

She shook her head, eyes fixed on the spot where the residual spirits no doubt replayed the same murder over and over every night. "Someone died here. Stabbed," she whispered back, and clung to him until we'd moved past the area.

Interesting. I wished I could talk to her about what she'd seen.

When we approached the Old City Gate and the Huguenot Cemetery, I saw several spirits wandering around the grounds. A couple of them turned and regarded the group as we passed by. I looked for the little girl, and found her sitting in the crook of an oak tree. I made eye contact and nodded to her. She pointed again at the gate, and I nodded again.

When we stopped at the gate for Alex to narrate the next-to-last stop on the tour, I opened up my mouth without thinking. "Is the ghost of a little girl ever seen near here?"

Alex looked a little uncomfortable, but recovered quickly. "Not right here, exactly, but there's a little girl ghost who has been spotted several times in the cemetery over there. It's believed that she may be the spirit of a girl who died of yellow fever about 200 years ago. Her body was dumped here by the gate, but no one claimed her, so she was buried there."

Many of the guests oohed and aahed at his explanation, and the middle-aged woman stared at me intently. When our eyes met, she nodded, a silent understanding passing between us.

At the end of the tour, I gave Alex a hug and complimented his guide skills. I was rewarded with a kiss on the top of my head and a promise to text me sometime over the weekend. I couldn't help wondering if he'd remember to do it, now that it was his own idea. Treigh took me home with a promise to see me Monday, because he and Michael would be Christmas shopping and hanging out over the weekend.

Overall, it was a pretty good Friday night.

Chapter 33

Saturday was quiet. Alex did remember to text, but he was working all weekend, so getting together was out of the question. As a result, I got some much-needed binge-watching done and finished my homework.

Sunday morning, by tradition, was housecleaning morning. Mom went out to the grocery store, and made me promise not to leave the house until she got home. She didn't have to tell me twice! She had been gone maybe 40 minutes, and I was cleaning my room. As I carried the vacuum upstairs, I felt my phone buzz.

Lia, I'm stuck in the garage. Can you come help?
Yep, on my way.

Stuck in the garage? How does that even happen? I slipped my shoes on and headed out back to the detached garage where my mother kept her car. I tried pulling up on the rolling door, but it wouldn't budge. Stuck indeed.

I walked around to the side door and turned the knob. It opened easily.

"Mom?" I called into the dimness.

I heard a sound on the far side of the car, but I couldn't see her. My skin prickled fiercely, and I felt a new fear creep into my heart.

"Mom, are you okay?" She had to be okay...if something had happened to her... I stepped in and flipped the light switch. The fluorescent light blazed to life above me, and suddenly I was yanked inside by an unseen force. The door slammed shut behind me.

Across the garage stood the Magician, my father, Dorian Blair, with a sneer plastered on his face. Despite what he had put me through less than two weeks earlier, I had only one thought:

"Where's Mom?"

He inclined his head to the left. There she stood...my mother...my rock...holding a screwdriver to her own throat. She made a whimpering sound, but didn't speak. Her eyes were full of apologies. "Wouldn't want anything to happen to her, now would we?" He looked at her, and she pressed the screwdriver against her neck, denting the skin, but not breaking it.

"What is that, mind control? How could you do this to her?" I demanded of him. "Let her go!"

"Ah, my girl, so full of fire." Now evident in his voice was that English accent I had wondered about.

"You don't get to call me that. I'm not yours. Let. Her. Go. NOW."

He chuckled. "Ah, but you are mine. You know that now, don't you? My blood runs through you just as surely as hers does. Now, I don't want to hurt Maddy any more than you want to see her hurt. But you and I have unfinished business. That was awfully clever of you, getting rid of that talisman. But you've forced me into a more direct approach."

"If you harm one cell in her body, we won't have any business at all." My mind raced, searching for solutions. I had escaped him once, and I doubt he would underestimate me again. My first priority was my mother's safety; he was still unlikely to physically hurt me. But I wasn't too eager to take that chance either. "How are you even here right now? And what's with the accent?" I did want to know how he got past the wards, but I was also buying time to think, searching for solutions.

"Ah, yes, well, that's why we find ourselves in the garage. It seems your aunt only warded the house. Rather short-sighted, I'd say, but a boon from my point of view. As far as my accent is concerned," here he flipped into the American accent I'd heard earlier, "the simplest disguise is often the best one. Didn't want to tip you off to my identity too soon, after all."

"What is it you want?"

"Didn't we already have this conversation? There's a great deal of power to be had, and while one god's power is nice, why should I stop there when I can have more?"

"What makes you think that's even possible?" *Keep him talking, distract him, buy time...*

He smiled wickedly. "Won't it be fun finding out exactly WHAT is possible? I wouldn't be the only one to benefit, you know. You'd gain as well. Surely you can see the benefits." He was trying to use his abilities on me; I could feel it. I felt the violet swirls in my aura transform into outward-facing spikes. He winced.

"Well, well. It appears you're a quick study."

"Stay out of my head. And get out of hers."

He shook his head. "Think of it as insurance, my girl. If I can't control you one way, I'll control you another. You have no idea what greatness we could be destined for. You can't see it, but I can. Sometimes a father has to make the hard decisions for his children, wouldn't you agree?"

"You're not a father. You're a sperm donor." Something he said had resonated in the back of my mind. *...not the only one to benefit...greatness we could be destined for...* In one respect, he was my father: blood. Which in this case meant POWER. I had some of his power, I knew it. I just had to figure out how to use it. I took a deep breath.

Keeping my eyes locked on his, I went to the closet in my mind and stood in front of the boxes. I whipped the tops off of all the ones I had used before and armed myself with their items. Ghost-seeing glasses, intuition headband, influence binoculars, glamour lip gloss, and then I added the others I hadn't worked much with telekinetic gloves, beguiling fan... But that wasn't enough. I needed more than Selene's gifts to fight him. I started pulling the tops off of the boxes I couldn't read. A whip, a hat, a bindi dot, a magnifying glass on a chain...I adorned myself with all of them.

When I refocused my attention on the present, I realized he was looking impatient. "Well, what will it be? Leave with me, and I will release your mother's will. But don't forget that I can take control of her anytime I please. I'd hate for her to be driven to self-harm as a result of your stubbornness."

A wavering in the air behind him caught my attention, and my grandmother's ghost materialized, looking angrier than I'd ever seen her. She focused herself on him, but he could not see her, and she couldn't affect any of the physical environment.

He couldn't see her, but I could. And she knew things.

"What do I do?" I pleaded. My father thought I was talking to him, but she knew better.

"I should think that's obvious," he began. His hubris reared its ugly head. He assumed he had won. My mother started to cry silently.

But Grandma understood. She turned to me and a truly frightening smile spread across her face. She was suddenly beside me, and I could feel the energy field around me begin to surge. I drew more and more power from within me, and I could feel my grandmother taking possession of my left hand while I maintained control of my right. In my mind, I saw her plan. It was a reckless gamble, but it was the only plan I had other than giving in to the Magician's will. My energy pulsed all around me.

He could feel it, too. "I credit you for your intentions, my girl, but you don't have the experience to attend to your mother and me at the same time. If you try to do anything to me, she will stab herself. If you try to pull that screwdriver away from her throat, you'll be weak enough for me to control you. You're out of your league here. See reason. You only have one choice."

He was right about my experience but not about my grandmother's. I visualized a bolt of my white and violet energy being pulled back like an arrow on a bow. My grandmother guided the arrow away from me and angled it behind my mother, pointing at my father.

With one more deep breath, I let out a yell that carried all the strength my soul possessed. I heard the *twang* of the bow, and a wide beam of energy shot out, knocking my mother's hand away from her throat on its way to knock full-force into the man who would hurt us both. He slammed into the concrete wall, his head snapping back hard against the stone. His eyes rolled upward, and he crumpled to the ground, unconscious.

My grandmother appeared beside him, glared down at him, then faded.

The screwdriver clattered to the floor next to my mother, and she ran to me, sobbing. I hugged her fiercely, but then broke away, afraid to take my eyes off of the inert form of my father. We had to find a way to secure him until we could figure out what to do with him, and unfortunately, I didn't have syringes full of sedatives to keep him under control.

So we did what any logical, intelligent women would do. We bound him with zip ties (HA. PAYBACK.), blindfolded and gagged him, and tossed him in the trunk of my mother's car. Then we called my aunt and she called the Empress. They told us to meet them off Dixie Highway in the the Twelve-Mile Swamp.

It was an ambitious plan, but the only thing they could think of to do about him was some sort of binding spell. They weren't even sure it would work, but the only other option was for him to agree to behave himself, and it was clear he couldn't be trusted to keep his word.

We sped along Dixie Highway, our nerves severely frayed.

"What if he wakes up?" I asked nervously.

"He may already be awake," Mom replied. "There's no way to know. Lia, I'm so sorry. I…"

"Mom, you have nothing to apologize for. There's no way you could have prevented any of this."

She didn't respond, and I knew she was trying to find ways to blame herself for what my father had done. That was just one more reason to hate him.

We were maybe five minutes out from the place we'd agreed to meet when I spotted it. Roaring up behind us at alarming speed was a burgundy van. THE burgundy van. A realization sunk in. I wasn't sure why it hadn't occurred to me before.

He hadn't been alone when he grabbed me off the street. Of course not. That would have been reckless. And now his accomplice was coming to his rescue. And judging by the speed of that van, the accomplice WAS reckless.

"Mom, we've got a problem."

"Another one? Nope, no more problems. I'm full."

"Yeah, funny. But seriously, that van coming up behind us? That's the van Quinn…Blair…used when he grabbed me!"

"Oh, crap." Eloquent and accurate.

The van pulled up alongside and then passed us, and I couldn't make out the face of the driver in the quick glimpse that I got. Then the van whipped around to the right in front of us and slammed on its brakes, blocking the path in front of us. We hit our brakes as well, screeching to a stop, but not in time to avoid impact with the passenger side of the van. It wasn't a strong impact, but it was enough to jar us forward and activate the airbags.

I was momentarily stunned, but knew that I had to try and gather myself quickly. My mother grunted beside me, so I knew she was at least mostly alright. I fought the now-deflating airbag, knowing the driver wouldn't be taking his time in coming for me. I was partially right. When I got the white canvas sufficiently out of my face, I saw the driver walking purposefully around the front of the van, heading for our car. But it wasn't a he.

She was an imposing figure, to be sure. Close to six feet tall, if I had to guess, with rich ebony skin and long dreadlocks tied up on top of her head. I judged her to be a little bit older than I was, maybe early twenties. She was muscular, too, and I had no doubt it was those arms that had pinned me while my father had put a chloroform-soaked cloth over my nose and mouth a couple of weeks ago. I was wrestling with my seat belt, which didn't want to come free, but I was also afraid to take my eyes off of her.

"Well, sis, you've made a right mess of things," she remarked in a clipped accent that reminded me of a tougher version of his. "Looks like I'ma have to clean it up. But this ain't over, make no mistake. We'll meet again." She stopped walking and raised her hand Iron-Man style, all the while staring at me with her piercing gray eyes. There was a blinding flash of light, and when my vision cleared, I caught sight of her back as she went back around the van toward the driver's seat. I heard the door slam shut, and then she threw the engine into gear and drove away.

Somehow I knew that the trunk was going to be empty when we finally extracted ourselves from the car and were able to check it.

Gray eyes.

She had gray eyes.

Like his.

Oh, crap.

Chapter 34

December became the winter holidays, and it appeared that the Magician had run off, maybe back across the Atlantic, to lick his wounds. Everything was quiet, even the bi-weekly check-in from Claudia.

My mother had decided that a tree-trimming party was just the thing for me to celebrate three whole weeks without mortal danger.

I stood in front of my mirror, wearing a black tee under red-and-black plaid overalls. I had holly in my hair and blazing red lipstick. I was feeling pretty darn festive. A cool wind swirled around me, a brief greeting from Selene, and I trotted downstairs, prepared to bring on the merry.

Aunt Kitty showed up with her signature basket of baked goodies, this time an assortment of cookies and spiced cakes. We spread it all out next to a small punchbowl of eggnog and a few cans of Yoo-hoo. In the kitchen, my mother was mulling cider on the stove top.

"Everything going okay?" she asked.

"Couldn't be better," I responded honestly. "I mean, I'm still on-guard all the time, bordering on paranoid when it comes to new people, but I keep my personal alarm system powered up, and I'm taking it day-by-day."

"You're continuing to study your abilities?"

"Yeah, but not every day. Mostly I meditate, do little experiments kind of like Grandmother did. I've talked to Kai and Mary a couple of times, and they have good advice. But I sort of want a break from all of it other than what I need for safety, you know?" I set out the boxes of ornaments on the card table I'd set up earlier.

"I know that feeling better than you might think. I felt it so strongly, I gave up the card."

I thought about that for a minute. "I don't think I want to do that. My father is still out there, and it appears I have at least one other magical sibling. I believe them when they say they aren't done with me. But for now…"

I was interrupted by the doorbell chiming throughout the house. I grinned and skipped to the door. When I opened it, I was greeted by the smiling faces of Treigh, Michael, Gemma, Alex, and Trina. Alex snaked his arm around my waist and kissed my cheek, Gemma hugged me, and Trina handed me a box of gold-wrapped chocolates.

Treigh sniffed the air. "Oh, yeah. Aunt Kitty's been baking."

They all slid past me into the house.

For the moment, at least, life was perfect. And that was good enough for me.

Made in the USA
Monee, IL
29 December 2020